BEST
LESBIAN
EROTICA
2000

B E S T
LESBIAN
EROTICA
2 0 0 0

Tristan Taormino,
Series Editor

**Selected and
Introduced by**

Joan Nestle

CLEIS
PRESS

Published in the United States
Cleis Press Inc., P.O. Box 14684, San Francisco, California 94114.
Printed in the United States.
Cover design: Scott Idleman
Text design: Karen Huff
Cleis logo art: Juana Alicia
First Edition.
10 9 8 7 6 5 4 3 2 1

Foreword © 1999 by Tristan Taormino; Introduction © 1999 by Joan
Nestle; "A Struggle for Peace" © 1999 by M. N. Schoeman first
appeared in *The Mammoth Book of Lesbian Erotica* edited by Rose
Collis (Robinson, 2000); "By the Boots" © 1999 by Lauren Sanders is
an excerpt from her novel *Kamikaze Lust* (Akashic Books, 2000);
"Black Vinyl" © 1999 by M R Daniel first appeared in *Lip Service*
edited by Jess Wells (Alyson, 1999); A different version of "Cleo's
Back" © 1999 by Gwendolyn Bikis first appeared in *Hers 3* edited by
Terry Wolverton (Faber & Faber, 1999); "Denouement" © 1999 by
River Light first appeared in *Hot & Bothered 2* edited by Karen X.
Tulchinsky (Arsenal Pulp Press, 1999); "The Great Bravura" © 1995
by Jill Dearman is an excerpt from the forthcoming novel of the same
name and was originally performed as a play at the Westbeth Theater,
New York, June 1995; "A Real Life Superhero" © 1999 by Kate
Dominic first appeared in *Lip Service* edited by Jess Wells (Alyson,
1999); "Always" © 1999 by Cecilia Tan first appeared in *Herotica 6*
edited by Marcy Sheiner (Down There Press, 1999); "Fetish" © 1999
by Terry Wolverton is reprinted from her poetry collection *Mystery
Bruise* (Red Hen Press, 1999); "Asshole" © 1999 by Gerry Gomez
Pearlberg first appeared in *The Fish Tank*; "Shy Girl" © 1999 by
Elizabeth Stark is an excerpt from her novel *Shy Girl* (Farrar Straus
Giroux, 1999). "Descent to the Butch of the Realm" © 1987 by Judy
Grahn reprinted from *The Queen of Swords,* first published by
Beacon Press and now available at www.serpentina.com.

Acknowledgments

I would like to thank the following people for their contributions to the book:

Again and always to Frédérique Delacoste, Felice Newman, Don Weise, Karen Huff, Karyn DiCastri, and everyone at Cleis Press for kicking ass. To Taji Duntomb of FSG and Judy Grahn for help with permissions. To Scott Idleman for his inspired book covers.

To Joan Nestle for all her hard work (and Diane Otto for her part too!). To Heather Lewis, Jewelle Gomez, Jenifer Levin, Chrystos, and all the contributors of the previous collections for continuing to be part of the *Best Lesbian Erotica* family. Special thanks to the folks at bookstores, especially the independents, who continue to support, promote, and host events for the book. All my gratitude, devotion, and appreciation to Toni Amato, Jenna Behm, Teresa Cooper, Michelle Duff, Morgan Dunbar, Heather Findlay and everyone at *On Our Backs*, Gerry Gomez Pearlberg, Hannah Doress and Hanarchy Now Productions, Sarah Lashes, Ira Levine, Reggie Love and Jordan, Audrey Prins-Patt, Alicia Relles, Jill Muir Sukenick, the women of Toys in Babeland, Sir Turino and Fireball Productions, Winston Wilde and my mother for their ongoing support, encouragement, love, inspiration, and understanding. To Audrey and Sarah especially for taking care of me in San Francisco during production hell. To my assistant Anna for her endless hard work, support, dog wrangling, and housesitting.

To Red, for everything. I dedicate the erotic energy of this book to you.

Contents

Foreword
Tristan Taormino

You really should be reading this foreword after you read Joan Nestle's introduction. I know—it's out of order, flipped around, not the way it's supposed to be. You can stop now, skip ahead to the introduction, and come back to my foreword.

You see, where Joan leaves off, I begin. As Joan searched the scarcity of early erotica, she become one of the women who created the body of work that created me. I came out to *Coming to Power, Macho Sluts, A Restricted Country,* Pat Califia, Dorothy Allison, Susie Bright, Robbi Sommers, Artemis Oakgrove, *On Our Backs, Bad Attitude, Brat Attack* and dozens of other writers and 'zines. This growing genre of lesbian erotica informed my erotic aesthetic sensibilities, both personally and professionally. Still another generation of queer women is now coming out to *The Second Coming, Bushfire, Melting Point, Herotica, Best American Erotica, The Leatherdaddy and the Femme,* and the new *On Our Backs.* Plus they have a brand new medium offering brand new erotica—the Internet.

I had never met Joan face to face, yet she had been such an important figure in my life. After years of reading her work, we finally met in San Francisco at a celebration in tribute to her. Joan's friends and colleagues told stories of sitting around the big wooden table in her apartment, which was also the home of the Lesbian Herstory Archives for more than twenty years. I never had the chance to sit at that table, rich with memories and history. When I began researching my thesis on butch/femme sexuality in college, I called the Archives, but was disappointed to learn that they were closed temporarily. The Archives had found a new, permanent home in Brooklyn and had shut down in order make the move. So, when I first went looking for Joan and her Herstory, they were both at a juncture of growth and change, both moving into a new age.

To me, Joan Nestle has always been the Grand Dame of Femmes. Her writing had such an impact on my identity and my sexuality, spoke to me so deeply, that I considered her a role model, mentor, friend, sister, lover, mother even before we ever met. It was such an honor to work with her on this collection, which seems so appropriate to be the first collection of lesbian erotica of the new millennium. What I have learned from Joan is that erotic stories are part of our history—an important part, just as the erotic is an important part of our lives. Although they may be called "erotic fiction," these are the stories of the erotic lives that queer women live everyday, that we have lived, that we want to live. These are also stories of the ways queer women dream the erotic, the ways we create the erotic with words. Even the imagined tales are significant to our history as women who love and desire and fuck other women.

My job as the editor of this series is a gift for which I am deeply grateful. I have the privilege of reading so many wonderful stories each year. I wish I could share all the stories I've read, including the ones that don't make it into the anthology, because they move me, too. I get excited by writers whose submissions are rejected one year, but who submit again the next year. I love to see how their work has grown and changed. I respect their perseverance and courage. I feel like I know them through their stories, though again, we rarely meet face to face.

I am thrilled by the writers whose stories have appeared in the series. They are a group of fierce women who hone their craft, unafraid to continue writing sex. I believe these erotic pioneers are not one-hit wonders, but will continue to touch, inspire, seduce, and provoke us in the next century.

Tristan Taormino
New York, NY
October 1999

Introduction
Joan Nestle

I sit on the balcony of a flat in Melbourne, Australia, so far away from my New York home, reading the fifty stories Tristan has forwarded to me. But it is not only I that have traveled so far, so has lesbian erotic writing.

Because of my long association with the Lesbian Herstory Archives, I am cursed with the need to give context; even if I wanted to, I could not discuss works of the imagination without seeing the living shadows of the authors who came before, not because they demand a continuous history, but simply because they are part of the complex wonder of it all, the shifting politics of gender and sexuality that shape our visions of love and want.

My journey with lesbian erotica started when I discovered the "dirty book" corner in a local drug store in the mid-1950s. With covers made lurid only by suggestion, their themes were revealed by shadowy titles—*The Third Sex, Unnatural Sisters, The Dark Street, Whisper Their Love* (the latter written by the peace activist Valerie Taylor who recently died.) These books offered me my first taste of fem longing and butch rogueries on a printed page. For thirty-five cents I could walk on the wild side. I think of these small square books as steeped in yearning—and secrets. With few words but much tension, kisses were given and bodies taken. Specifics were few, but the hugeness of breaking taboos made up for the lack of graphic detail. For me, this was sex within sex, it seemed, since the books themselves were labeled "adult reading" and buying them was an act of public erotic announcement.

I am speaking here only of the specific erotic content in lesbian books that started to appear in the second half of the twentieth century. I had been reading heterosexual sex from the late 1940s on—writers like Mickey Spillaine and Henry Miller, even Anaïs Nin—but they were "literature," not the hot secrets of forbidden love. The lesbian paperbacks were for me the first knowledge that everyday sexual deviants had a cultural metaphor for their communal position. They were obscene, cheap, hidden small treasures. Years later, I interviewed the woman who wrote lesbian erotica under the name of Randy Salem, and she told me that she made a conscious choice to write books for this genre, that her lesbian paperbacks were the only vehicles she had for writing about the passion of her life. She would never tell me her real name because she was now a respectable writer of travel books.

The late 1950s saw the emergence of *The Ladder,* my next source of lesbian erotica. Almost every issue had a few short stories of almost mythic scenarios of lesbian erotic drama: young women, now adults, returning to the teachers they had lusted after, or bar-going narrators delicately rendering one-night stands or visitations to lovers lost to marriage. Again the specifics of a body moving on or in another body barely existed in these pages, but the sexual tension they depicted was a sensuous experience in itself. With the gay liberation and lesbian feminist movements of the early 1970s, the drugstore pulps disappeared and the shadowy depictions of what women did with one another began to be filled in.

As I write this, I am far removed from my own Archives, but two public erotic moments come to mind; the first is the orange dittoed front page of a short-lived lesbian feminist newsletter called *Echoes of Sappho* (1972) coming out of a collective in New York. On the cover of its first edition—and there were only two— was a line drawing of two full-bodied naked African American women, their bodies intertwined, their mouths locked in a head turning kiss. Not even the frail tracings of the ditto machine could obscure the sensuality of the image. The second is a scene from the novel *Sita,* written in 1976 by Kate Millett, a writer whose erotic power still startles me. Thanks to the wonder of a shared feminist culture that transcends national borders, I can quote from my Australian lover's copy of the same book. Speaking of the woman Millett so desperately desires, the narrator says "her flesh...seen as vividly with my eyes closed as open, touched as unerringly with my mind as with my hands, putting all my concentration of passion into the tips of my fingers, entering her knowing she wants me and has made room, made the way smooth and liquid." Plunged as we were then deep in the debates over what was the right kind of orgasm to have and the unacceptability of penetration as a lesbian sex act, these words were themselves a sexual moment for me. I learned that beneath the public discourse there were hotbeds of desire subverting the demand for a monolithic political stance.

The lesbian erotic was to have a rocky time during the next fifteen years. The "sex wars" of the 1980s took their toll, but always there were pockets of resistance; writers like Pat Califia, Dorothy Allison, Jewelle Gomez, and myself, among others. We continued to produce stories in which the lesbian body was touched by power, lust, seduction, and entry. Shoestring publications like *Bad Attitude* (out of print for some time now) and *On Our Backs* (the earlier version) were an essential link between the hard days and the present, giving over their pages to grainy black-and-white erotic photographs that broke new ground in sexual explicitness. They published stories whose content shifted the boundaries of what it was permissible to say about sex between women. Books like *Coming to Power* and organizations like Samois, the first American lesbian S/M support group, gave an erotic community a specifically American lesbian literary history.

With the second part of the 1990s came the erotic publishing deluge, yet today there are still new erotic discoveries to be made, new stories of desires, and old communities finding a new public voice. The stories in *Best Lesbian Erotica 2000* are freer, fiercer, and more touched by both gender-specific erotics and gender play than any I have read before.

I am honored that Tristan gave me this opportunity to read through the stories she had collected and, in a way, bring my own journey as a reader of lesbian erotica into a new era. In 1928, Radclyffe Hall created a character, Stephen, who wanted to give all of herself to the women she loved: "…Stephen must kiss her many times, for the hot blood of youth stirs quickly and the mystical sea became Angela's lips that so eagerly gave and took kisses." This eagerness was not well rewarded in the world; it has taken many years of many different kinds of courage to win for us, both writers and readers, the fullness of expression to be found in this anthology.

Joan Nestle
Melbourne
October 1999

Hedonism 1992

C. C. Carter

i'm, i'm thinkin, i'm thinkin bout, i'm thinkin bout missed
    opportunity
i'm thinkin bout missed opportunity with you

i'm thinkin bout
breakfast at ten
a table set for four
laced white on solid oak
your skin and wood contrast
to smothered antique ceramics
the smell of hot croissants
layered with dripping cheese
spiced butter, two kinds
cinnamon and plum
a bowl full of mixed fruits
melons, kiwis, and blueberries
a compote cream to glaze them in

i'm thinkin bout
how I want

to lie across laced linen
give myself to you
as a sacrificial offering
bless me
like you praise the food
part my legs
like you peel layered croissants
pour cream over my body
like you drench the fruit
taste honey dew
now all sweet and ripe
melt over me like cheddar
until I bubble
spread your loving across
my body
churning butter
two kinds,
your flavor and mine

but i'm thinkin
there's a table
set for four
so we're not alone
just me and you
and my thinkin
has to be enough for now

it's late evening
same table
we sit
eye to eye
lip to lip
talking
i'm thinkin bout

how I want to tell you
to love me
like you worship your dreds
start with the hair on my body
that is unpermed
part it into sections
take some strands
slip a thumb inside my bees wax
twist my wet emotions
around your index finger
until I'm molded into locks

but i'm thinkin
femme etiquette
doesn't allow for such honesty
what would you think
of me thinkin like this?
so i'm thinkin
this is another missed opportunity with you

i'm thinkin bout
against a kitchen counter
where you kiss me
I inhale your tongue
exchanging breaths
slowly in the beginning
until our lips make 1+1=1
the "umh" you moan
when they finally touch
how if I wasn't conditioned
at being a Miss Thang
I would tell you
to bend me over this counter
so we can begin doing

"that thang"
kiss the other lips
with the same "umh"
that you are breathing into these
stir with a finger, a spoon, a ladle
or whatever else you could find
cause the kitchen
is as good a place as any
to cook you up some shit

but i'm thinkin
the inn keepers get up at five
and it's four thirty
so breathing in kisses
has to be enough for now

i'm thinkin bout
the irony of the Garden Room
your room
where you unfasten
my chastity belt
claim it yours
I bite the apple
no seduction required
we recognize our nakedness
no shame admitted
we love each others bodies
the same is required
the granddaughter
of a Caribbean Indian
and the legacy
of a Dominican Servant
rewrite Genesis
In the beginning

there was Eva
created from red clay
and Eve
was taken from her breast
they were crowned
butch and femme
and given the queendom of goddess
but i'm thinkin
that's not what really happened
just what i'm thinkin
but given another opportunity
I won't be thinkin
you won't be guessin
cause we will be doin

A Struggle for Peace
M. N. Schoeman

May months in South Africa can be smoulderingly hot, even though the smooth winds and fiery colours of autumn are usually only a few days away. It was on a scorching day in May 1971 that South Africa commemorated its tenth year as an independent republic. That day at school we did not attend classes. Instead, everyone marched down to the sport stadium to join neighbouring schools for the celebration ceremonies. We waved miniature flags in the orange, white, and blue colours of the new republic, and a rosette of the same colours was pinned to my grey school uniform. It looked like a flattened rose. The flag and rosette became proud possessions that I treasured in a shoebox for years.

The school's principal, Mr. Van der Merwe, made a speech in rapid, enthusiastic bursts of sentences, telling us in his coarse voice about our ancestors' battles for autonomy and the subsequent freedom from British Imperialists. In the relentless heat I became aware of the slow dawning of nausea and the pain of a headache moving to other parts of my body. We, the children of this country, had the proud legacy of freedom that rested in our hands, and we had to guard it against foreign and dark forces that might claim this God-given right from us, we heard. I was twelve years old and believed what I was told, although the seriousness of the occasion left me with a diffuse feeling of anxiety and confusion, intermingled—of course—with my swelling nausea.

Much later in my life I learned about another event that took place during May 1961. A few days before the declaration of the new republic a nonviolent national strike led by Nelson Mandela and supported by millions of oppressed people in South Africa took to the streets. This historical strike challenged the creation of an exclusively white man's republic on African soil and the supremacy of white rule. Africans were called on to refuse to cooperate with the new republic. The Union Defence Force left its barracks in full strength and violently suppressed the strike. More than ten thousand Africans were arrested, and any further meetings were banned. After this event the freedom struggle mobilised underground.

Anyway, that day at the sport stadium we stood at attention as the parade of awkward military vehicles rolled past, followed by the stomping of heavy army boots and fed-up sunburnt faces of young men behind the shiny display of their R1 machine guns. Then we sang patriotic songs. Though my head was swirling by the time the thousands of young voices carried the last notes—a long-winded "aaaa" at the end of South Africa—high into infinity, I thought that the songs were the most beautiful I had ever heard.

When I decided to write a story about us, my love, it was this incident that flooded my mind and refused to leave. I am not exactly sure why, but I can speculate up to a point that would put Freud to shame. Perhaps it was the first amorphous beginning of my collective identity as a citizen of a country of which I had to be proud of without ever knowing or questioning why. At the risk of sounding inept, I can also insinuate that on that specific day I made my first connection between the peaceful sham that the apartheid regime made me believe in and the undercurrent of pain and violence that ran well concealed and parallel to most South African's lives. I still cannot grasp the full symbolism, but I do recall that my headache became worse, settling intensely behind my eyes as if someone was pouring lead into my skull. I tried to swallow the thick sweet smell, but eventually it was so unbearable that I emptied my stomach over my black school shoes. Let it be sufficient then to say that, for some reason or another, I could not write our story without relating it to the incident of the shoebox with the little flag and rosette and the feeling of lead in my head before I threw up.

When I met you roundabout 1982, you already had a sturdy reputation in underground circles as a political activist and freedom fighter. It was also known that you were a lesbian and that your lover was killed in a township skirmish with the South African Defense Force, although her death was never reported by any news agency. My role as sympathetic bystander to the freedom struggle was clear and simple. At that stage, restrictions were imposed on people who were suspected of being involved in the struggle or having connections with underground cells of banned political parties. House arrests became frequent, persecutions were spreading, and people disappeared either behind bars or in shallow graves in desolate areas and were never heard of again. Even today some bodies have not been found. Freedom fighters retaliated with acts of sabotage. Some left the borders of the regime to be trained in supportive foreign countries as guerilla fighters. There were times that you would need a safe place to stay over and lay low before moving on, and that was where I came in. Whenever you called, I was to give you shelter—no questions asked.

Your first call came, quite coincidentally, on my birthday. Half past one in the morning the telephone rang. When you arrived, I offered you some champagne, which you declined with a tired flicker of your eyes. A conversation of polite questions and answers followed. Then you made a few telephone calls. Even today I remember how I immediately noticed the casual and generous movements of your hands. Yes, your hands definitely exuded the temperament of an exceptional dancer. I was sure that you could move like shimmering satin billowing in a gentle, warm wind, with your hands framing the curving movements of your body. Once I caught you staring at me from across the table, unabashedly holding my eyes for the few seconds that it took me to look away and empty my champagne glass down my throat.

As I later passed your bedroom I heard you shuffling, then you clicked off the light and sighed. For a moment I stood in the dark, pretending to hear you breathe. Perhaps it had only been my imagination, but I was sure that I could hear your breath slowly filling the apartment. I immediately felt closer to you, as if I possessed some private knowledge about your life that was usually only reserved for sharing during intimate moments.

After that first sojourn you continued entering my life like a wave freeing itself from the deepest indigo of the sea, bringing to shore all kinds of secrets and debris. And at the appropriate time you swiftly and quietly retreated, leaving nothing but a glittering trace that soon disappeared in the sand, until the next wave. Often you only stayed for a night and you left boxes of leaflets smelling of printers' ink behind for safe keeping, which other comrades would collect just as mysteriously as you had left them.

Every time I remembered something different about you. It started with your dancer's hands and the click of a light switch followed by a sigh. But soon my head was filled by the way in

9

which you held a tumbler moments before you sipped, or your shoes tainted by rain while travelling on remote roads between tropical green villages. I also recalled the way in which you frowned when trying to elude any emotional reflections in your eyes, the way that the bed and cushion slightly preserved the shape of your body, your fingers teasing a candle flame. Ah yes, of course, your hands, there was so much passion in the way that you moved your hands.

You were continuously on the move and sometimes disappeared for months on end. Often you arrived exhausted at my apartment with fragrances of foreign countries and desolate places surrounding you and persistently inhabiting your body, even after a hot bath. Through you I inhaled the yellow desert sand and copper sunsets that nested beneath your skin, the vapor of pine needles after a thunderstorm, the herbs and leather from outlandish craft markets, and *souks* entangled in your hair. Once I caught the crude iron stench of dried blood mixed with the scent of bones and burning hair—it must have shown on my face, and for a moment I thought that you were going to say something.

It was probably a mixture of similar images that was continuously clogging your dreams, eventually immersing your mind and spilling over into nightmares. Night after night I woke up to your terrified screams. I would go to you, gently wake you, and stay with you until you were asleep again.

One night I heard you open the back door to the small balcony and close it again. You were probably afraid of having another nightmare. From my bedroom window I watched you sitting with your back against the wall. You shoved your hands deep into your jeans' pockets. I could see your breathing deepening until your body became uncomfortable with its own yearning. Then your one hand moved to your jeans' zipper, teasing and stroking, skillfully disappearing deeper into the front of your pants. I saw your fingers kneading yourself in a gentle and kind way under the heavy material of your jeans, and I could hardly breathe. Then you looked up at the skies. Silver stars pricked through the purple and black hues of the night. You became impatient; I could see agitated lines forming around your mouth and a vein rising across your forehead. You started moving your hand violently, sucking your lips, licking, gasping, and softly moaning, but apparently without any release. I went back to bed and waited for you, but you never came. You left early the following morning. I heard the key turning in the lock and once again thought about the raw and painful country we were living in.

After a long absence the doorbell rang one morning at three o'clock. You appeared tired and frail at my doorstep; your turbulent eyes imitating the swaying movements of grass in a fervid wind. I noticed that your hair was sun bleached and you smelled like grey smoke and disinfectant. That night you did not wait for the nightmares to unfold. You simply got into my bed as if it was the natural thing to do. I felt no surprise. Rather, despite the daily violence ripping through the country, I felt a strange peacefulness while holding you. Your body relaxed in my arms, and you smiled in your sleep.

The following morning you told me in a thick and sleepy voice about a woman who was doused in petrol and set alight in the township. Violence breeds violence, you said, and people were turning against each other. Apparently the woman was suspected of being a traitor. I could feel your breath on my cheek while you were talking, your words against my face. I wanted to cry. You got up and ran a bath.

Afterward you came into the bedroom with a towel wrapped around your body. Your shoulders were bony and sharp. Then you dropped your towel and sat on my face. Your eyes were closed as you moved yourself into my mouth, your fingers strangled in my hair. I opened you up with my tongue, licking and prodding until my face was covered with your warm moisture. The strong muscles of your buttocks rested like a half moon in my hands. Then time accelerated. Moons and millenniums flashed by, exploded and revived themselves again under a new firmament where the breeze carried the rich fragrance of musk and jasmine through my head.

"That is why I need to love you now," you said as you got up.

A week later a bomb went off in a restaurant in a well-off white area. A boy lost his sight, and a pregnant woman aborted under a table while waiting for the ambulance. You disappeared for over six months. When I saw you again, you seemed older. Folds of aging lines around your mouth made your voice seem sluggish, and sometimes you got caught up in your own words. You also smoked more than you used to. I helped to bathe you and noticed that your hands were chapped and hardened. Your fingers seemed scarred and spongy, your fingertips hard and unconscious.

Then you sat down, took my hand and told me that your flight to London departed at 20h30. I had to take you to the airport. A national state of emergency was just declared and the regime's security forces were closing in on you. I still remember the hollow scream with which your airplane lifted its stump nose and swallowed its wheels. Fragments of the wing and tail lights flashed farther and farther and then faded into the night. It was cloudy, I noticed, the stars were far apart from each other and vague, the moon a pale cold glimmer.

"Remember that I will always love you," you said at the airport as I was overcome with sorrow. "So many people have been forced to choose between this country and their loved ones, so many people...." Before I could think of anything to say, you were gone.

So I decided to write this story.

In April 1994 Nelson Rolihlahla Mandela was elected president of South Africa. It was the first general election in South

African history where all citizens were allowed to vote. I am sure that you voted on a grey and rainy morning in London. Most likely your hands were so cold that you could hardly hold a pencil and an icy wind pierced your eyes so that it almost seemed as if you were crying. Through mutual friends I heard that you visited South Africa twice after the elections, and that you were granted political amnesty. You never contacted me. Perhaps you could not bear the familiarity that my body would hold, the memories that would be evoked every time that we made love. Even though we shared a deep found peace in my apartment, we were always aware of the struggle raging outside the windows. We both knew that you would never be able to separate your memories of peace from the violent images of the struggle. We had to let all memories go.

But, my love, African summers still swell with a heat that wakes me up early in the mornings and warms my body with yellow rays. At night I sleep next to a woman who is kind and soft spoken and knows me well enough not to ask certain questions. And sometimes, when the phone rings at an ungodly hour, I still think that it might be you, smelling of sun dried wheat and burnished copper.

I still need my time alone. And during these times I am an expert in pleasing my own body. Then I recall your face, imagine the way that you closed your eyes as your body waited expectantly for my tongue to open you up, the way your back arched as you moaned for more, and the sensitive way in which your hands danced through my body. But most of all, I remember the peaceful feeling that followed as you fell asleep in my arms. And I can still recall with uncanny detail how vulnerable you used to look early in the morning.

Taking Rita Hayworth in My Mouth

Joan Nestle

I sit on the edge of a couch in a dark room, the dark is the dark of night. This nearly empty apartment on the edge of the Village is lit only by the street lights of Soho and the red and green lights of late night traffic. Muffled sounds of a summer city night float into the room. I am a person waiting for something, waiting in near darkness, sitting on the edge of my seat. I am a customer awaiting the appearance of a dream I had ordered. She is in the other room, getting ready to make an entrance. It is a rare thing in life to be able to call into being the haunting mysteries that have followed one since childhood. If I tell you I am almost sixty when this night dawns, this night of apparitions, will it make it harder to hear what follows? An aging woman waiting on the edge of her seat for the dream only another woman can give her?

I smell her perfume before I see her. She comes out of the darkness, and I turn my gaze from the direction of the windows to take her in, her steady even progress towards me. Her red hair falls down around her shoulders, her face is marked by the redness of her lips, the hard blue gray brightness of her eyes; she has the slightly worn look of a woman who has seen it all. A small smile plays around the edges of her large mouth. Her broad shoulders push the darkness open.

I hear nothing now but the sound of her approach. She stands before me for a minute, a tall, broad woman in a black blouse opened at the throat so her breasts swell above me, a short leopard-printed skirt rides high on her thighs, all done to my order. "Is this what you wanted ?" she says, half amused, confident that this is exactly what I wanted. I cannot take my eyes off her face, off the world of work and experience she is radiating in the darkness. I see again, as I did as a child, my mother dressed for work and, at the same time, dressed for her lovers. My mother in that erotic blend of self-support and desire on the prowl, her costume, the black dress, the small hat with its veil of stars, the nylons with their seams down the back of her legs. I watched her dress, saw her arms raise before the mirror. I saw that mix of pain and pleasure that came to my mother, her beauty, her leaving.

I cannot drop my eyes from my dream's face. I do not want to. She sits in the chair we have placed right in front of me a few inches from the edge of the couch. Still smiling, she raises one leg and tucks her toes under the sofa's pillow. Her skirt is now a band around her lap, and she sits, waiting for me to drop my eyes. She grows larger in the darkness, in her solid angular position, waiting for me to do what I must, what I have waited all these years to do. I am hardly breathing; I have lost all sense of what sex I am. The dark night has become illuminated by the power of myth, the power of legend. "Go ahead," she encourages. My breath escapes me now, and I lower my head, taking my eyes from her large, strong face with its worldly, cool welcome, to what she is exposing to my view. It is only a small distance to travel, but I am terrified of the journey.

Right in front of me now, I see a second face, its red lips flaring in a nest of hair, drops of liquid caught in its strands, its own perfume opening up to me, right in front of me, the naked center of a woman. I raise my eyes once again to the public face, and I reel with the contrast. I cannot keep the two faces in the same place, on the same body. It is as if I am being allowed to see below the surface of all the days, all the mothers. I almost plead with her, don't let me go under, again but she says nothing, just watches. I feel the pull of her other face and give in to its ancient world. I let go of all pretense and gaze totally at the sex right before my eyes, smell it, hunger for it. And then, I fall to my knees, onto the pillow we have arranged in just the right place to catch my weight as I fall to my knees before this gleaming mask that is as real as hair and bone and flesh can be. I push my face into the one between her legs, my mouth as wide as a whale's, my tongue pulling all of this dream into me, I swallow, I hunger, I drink, I eat. She allows it all, giving herself to my relentless hunger, to this beggar on her knees. My tongue swirls, finding hidden passage ways, pushing at the confines of her wet, red walls. I am nothing but this exploration, kept from me by so many years, by so many laws. Above, I feel tremors and know that in some other place, the country has shifted. Somewhere on what remains of the surface, I know she is coming. I have sucked pleasure into her, but that is part of the more common world, the one I have known for all the past years. Where I am now is somewhere else, somewhere beyond gender, in the labyrinth of myth and legend, where mothers are falling stars and shame sprouts wings.

Becoming Stone
Sandra Lee Golvin

Summer is becoming. Gone to Africa says A. Now you on the blue couch becoming my fist. My arm becoming the cradle. Your hair becoming the yellow dream.

I did dream you another summer. I was trying to decide about my life. I was believing in the *I* of decision making. I was believing in the *I* of dreaming. Now that *I* does not know so much and would say you dreamed me or perhaps the dream dreamed us both. An old lady's corpse was being kissed. In the kissing she became you, the fairy tale princess. Someday my prince(ss) will becoming. I will becoming her. Or him. We had not yet met, my *I* and yours. Not then. Not that summer.

You were wearing chocolate panties. Even now, with my fist inside, the wet silk wraps my wrist at the place where it wants cutting open. You let me be the one who knows. I so wanted that. I have a chocolate dick, the one A never liked because it looked too real. You don't mind though. You're such a girl. Until you, being the girl was *my* job.

When you first approached I had no way to understand. You, all midwest blond, the wife and mother, legs long as prairie sky. Can you hear the longing for what I thought could never be mine? Me, the frog, my lipstick androgyny a cover for what only you saw living in stone.

You would chip away my protection bit by bit until I knelt naked before you in an attitude of wanting. I did not make your job easy any more than the stone yields to the chisel with the first blow. No, persistence was required, and more than that, desire. Inexorably you made me, a me whom I did not know was there. Is the figure the creation of the artist or is it hidden there in rock, only waiting to be revealed? Am I now what you imagined, or was I always so?

It's not only the change in clothes, the end of dresses and wide-brimmed hats. My hips have narrowed, my jaw grown more square, suddenly I know how to let my gaze linger on the pretty girl as if I might presume to know her. And my friends, those few who remain, do not recognize me. All of this I want to say you wrought. Lady of alchemy, Aphrodite of dreams.

Another one last night, another not able to reach you. You were in a Presbyterian hospital by the sea. You had given birth to our daughter. Things are breaking all around me. Things made of glass like the nautilus you brought me from Paris after you already knew you were done with me. (That week with your mother rendered me an impossibility.) Still months later I dream of you and my hand awakens hot, curled in on itself, bereft of you.

Jealous of my own fist. It knows something I never will. Your wet heat imprinted in traces at the grooves that mark the knuckles. My palm forever empty of the sweet, flat place at the base of your spine. My thighs that held the curve of your ass, lonely. I never held a woman that way before. Don't you see?

I was your mother, your boylover, and you my midwife, my child.

There was A, for many years my man. I'd been faithful to her. You had your husband and two sons, your woman lovers on the side (you'd brought them out.) For nine months I refused to be one of them. You always got what you wanted, on your terms. This time you wanted a real dyke. I needed terms of my own.

Then A went to Africa.

When the sculptor works with stone, a long time passes where nothing shows. There is a circling and a tapping, and it is all an act of faith. Then comes a moment, seemingly out of nowhere, in which what has been only surface and raw edges suddenly becomes the thing that was always there. The soul in the stone unfolds.

I don't want to tell this story. Once it is written it is over. I can't bear that. When the phone rings I still imagine it might be you. When it is silent I wonder why you do not call. How ridiculous I am.

The moment.

You didn't come to class, and we exchanged angry messages. I remember I called you chickenshit. You gave it right back. Your temper opened up the place in me where violence fuels my sex. It felt good, the lust and the killing rage. Made it possible for me to say I humble myself and demand your presence at the same time. You liked that and came to find me at the beach. As I told you to do. In the parking lot I didn't say hello, just pulled your head down to mine and gave you the kiss you'd been wanting. What I wanted was to fuck you there in public. I didn't. I made you demonstrate your desire though, all the way back to my house, and a man on a bicycle rode by calling "Lovers, yoo-hoo, lovers" like an enchanted bird.

I made you wait on the blue couch while I searched for the poem. The one by Judy Grahn where Ereshkegal Butch Queen of the Underworld dares Inanna Queen of Beauty to face her secret want. This is you, I said, Queen of Beauty. And you were, too, so lovely in the shock of what you had provoked in me. I grabbed your hair, that blond mane, tight and read to you. Do you remember the words?

> *Strange to everyone but me that*
> *you would leave the great green rangy*
> *heaven of the american dream,*
> *your husband and your beloved children,*
> *the convenient machines,*
> *the lucky lawn and the possible*
> *picture window—to come down here below.*
> *You left your ladyhood, your queenship, risking*
> *everything, even a custody suit,*
> *even your sanity, even your life. It is*
> *this that tells me you have a warrior*
> *living inside you. It is for this*
> *I could adore you.*

My fist is remembering the rough of your hair.

You cried as I forced your face down into my lap. Being a dyke isn't fun and games, baby. It's serious business. It's warrior business. Like the poem says. I think you complained then, that I was being hard on you. You should thank me for that, I shook you, thank me for caring enough not to play your little secret on the side. For caring enough to try to bring you down here, to my world. To where you want to be. You cried some more. And then you thanked me. You did.

You were the most beautiful to me then, all your perfect passing prettiness stripped away by real grief.

Was that when you bared your belly, so that I could witness the site of your devastation? Not only the scars of childbirth, but the ravages of bulimia, the muscles destroyed by years of laxatives and vomit. I thought of napalm, dead places too poisoned for anything to live, and I believed I understood something about the price of your fortune.

You were a connoisseur, bred for private jets and crystal. I was proud you'd picked me. Cocky. At one point—not that first night, but soon—I put Mick Jagger on and danced for you to "Gimme Shelter." *We all need someone we can cream on,* he sang. Baby, you squirmed with so much delight I thought I was king of the world. You had the power to put me there. And to take me down. You were the Queen of Beauty, after all.

I wouldn't let you touch me. I don't know how I knew to do that.

Not much happened that first night. You remembered your boys whom you'd dumped at a neighbor's for a minute, not knowing I had other plans. I didn't like it, you leaving in the middle of a scene. You begged for a return engagement the next night, and I said I'd think about it. In the morning you called, and I told you what to wear. A dress with a full skirt. No underwear. A more interesting bra. You confessed you'd thrown out all your sexy bras and bought plain ones because you thought that's what lesbians like. Since you were trying to please me I forgave you. But I was clear. I wanted you in lace.

So cool and yet out of my mind. What was happening to me? My hands, my hands, my hands do all the remembering.

I put on my man's suit. You swooned at the door. Trousers, you whispered, eyeing me in a way no girl ever had before. I said we're going out in public. Your assignment is to let everyone know you are with me. That you're mine. We went to the Pleasure Chest. We looked at dildos and porn. I said I need to know what you like. You fumbled, dropped your keys, acted silly. Then I took you to an upscale industry panel on gay parenting. The kind of thing I hate. But I endured it because I wanted you to see there were people like you with children and money. I wanted you to be able to imagine a life with me.

I think that was the night I danced for you. Yes, I'm sure of it now. You got on your knees in front of me, undid my slacks. It was a mistake to let you touch me. I knew it right away but didn't know how to stop. You went home to your husband, and I raged all night, feverish to find my way back to that place of power I'd let slip away under the stroke of your fingers.

At 6:00 A.M. I telephoned, woke you. I knew he'd be gone already. Come to me now, I demanded. I'm not through with you. Of course you couldn't comply, couldn't leave your boys. What can I do for you, you asked. I said I need you to touch yourself. As if you were me. Now. And you did. Are you touching yourself? Yes, yes I am. Are you thinking of me? Yes, yes I am. Does it feel good. Oh yes. Do you want me to fuck you? Yes. Say it. Yes. Please fuck me. Now say this: I'm a dyke. I'm a dyke. I've always been a dyke. I've always been a dyke. I love women. I love women. I want to be fucked by women. I want to be fucked by women. I want to be fucked by you. I want to be fucked by you.

That afternoon you told me you'd decided. No more lies. You wouldn't come to me again until you told him. It was not what I expected. I didn't believe you. That you would risk everything. *Even a custody suit, even your sanity, even your life.* To come to me. To come to yourself. But you had already made the plan to speak with him that night. I was in awe.

Walking the long stretch of beach miles beyond home I thought only of you and your courage. How I could hold you while you did this warrior thing you could only do alone. For three days and three nights I hadn't taken in food or been able to sleep. Running on some other source, my body feeding on a part of itself I no longer needed. The detritus of my own passing. A fire burned. What becoming was happening to me? Then I remembered the poem, the invocation between us. How for three days and three nights Inanna hung on the peg of the underworld stripped to nothing. And when they stole into Hell to find the Queen of Beauty, they found Ereshkegal writhing on the ground beside her, out of her mind. Giving birth to Inanna.

Yes, I am the Butch of the Realm, the Lady
of the great Below. It is hard for me
to let you go.
When next you say "you bitch"—"wild cherry"—
and "it just happens"—
you will think of me
as she who bore you to your new and lawful
place of rising,
took the time and effort
just to get you there
so you could moan Inanna
you could cry
and everyone you ever were
could die.

You told him you were a lover of women. He said that's okay, just tell me the truth. I slept then.

We had one more night before A returned from Africa.

You were waiting for me when I got home. I had on trousers. You wore a red dress. Tight so I could know you had nothing underneath. You had made me dinner. Up against the kitchen counter, I wrapped my hands strong around your rib cage. You said, You make me feel so female. You said, You're my man. I think I died then. In that moment. Everything I'd ever pretended to be. Gone. With you in my hands.

I must have taken you on my lap then, on the blue couch, the sweet of you all over me, and I think I called you Baby, Baby. You must have moaned or I did and then my hand went looking for you. I remember my hand and the weight of you and my face in your hair. Jesus how you opened to me. Let me reach up into the wound, curl inside and fill your empty places. Did I do it? Did I ease the rawness for a moment? Is it sacrilege to try to speak of this? To describe the unnameable? Something eased in me, a coming home, a landing. Into a hot pink hyperactive stillness.

Who is screaming? My hand has not forgiven me for leaving. If I'd believed I could not return I would never have left. But I thought it was only the beginning, and that night I wanted you to have it all. So I strapped on the chocolate dick, lay you down on the carpet among the pillows and knelt over your belly.

I traced the folds and pocks of that tender place with my fingers, a sureness in my hands that meant something about arriving into a knowing that was mine and more than mine— a birthright, an ancient lineage. I guess I was praying for a healing when I saw them. Judy Grahn and Pat Parker and other butch elders there in the room. I didn't say anything at the time because I didn't know if I was going crazy. You had taken me so far from all I'd been, I could easily have been out of my mind. They gathered around us to watch. And then I knew they were there to welcome me into a secret circle. Into the same sacred holy office they'd held for me two decades before in Berkeley, when I was trying to find a way into my life and their poetry was all I had to go by. I've never had a vision before, actually seen people not in the flesh. Even now talking about it I know it sounds like fiction. But those poet butches were there with us, and they were telling me what I needed to know. That I had descended to the underworld and now had to learn to live there. That it was not at all clear between you and me who had taken who down. That this was not only your initiation, baby, but mine. That they would watch over me on the long rock road ahead.

That was the moment, really. You know the rest. How I left A to wait for you, how school ended, how you said you needed to not see me while you went through the process of divorce. I didn't tell you how stupid I felt that last time you came by. Me in my new trousers I'd bought with you in mind. You asked me about them, as if you knew I was trying to look sexy for you. As if you knew how I needed you to find my way home. I knew better than to let you kiss me on your way out the door, but I couldn't stop myself. If only I'd really done it, gotten on my knees and pleaded, in the attitude of the beggar you'd revealed in me. Chipped away, bit by bit, with your wild beauty.

Stone is a living thing. Only more slow moving than most. There are processes. Once in a great while eruptions come, fire, ice. It is in these moments that the stone comes to know itself as stone. Its limitations. Its capacity. Its longing.

Makeover
Jill Nagle

Thursday

Clarity knew this was the moment to ask her.

Shane's cunt ringed Clarity's knuckles like a tight jar. Clarity's eyes lingered on her contracting stomach muscles, her small fists curling around clumps of bedding. "More..." she begged like a deprived child, between gasps, "...harder!"

Clarity's hand slowed inside Shane, and she found the younger woman's eyes. Shane's whole body trembled to be slammed insanely, but Clarity slowed, like a sea anemone, to the tiniest tickle inside her.. Shane's lower lip disappeared under her teeth several times, and she almost whispered, "fuck me," but she knew it would make her lover slow down even more. Still, she wanted Clarity to see how much she wanted her, how obedient she could be, stifling her desire even as it shot through her slight body, jolting her from side to side.

Shane's head relaxed as Clarity gripped the back of her neck.

"Do you trust me?" Clarity demanded.

"Yes," Shane gasped in a small voice.

"Will you do anything I say?"

"Yes!"

"Say it all for me."

"I'll do anything you say."

"Tell me again."

"I'll do anything you say!"

"Anything."

"Anything."

"You trust me that much."

"I trust you that much."

"Tell me the whole thing."

"I'll do anything you say. I trust you that much."

"Yes…you…do."

Clarity took her charge in her arms and stroked the length of her body, which began pulsing in waves. Clarity's own desire leapt inside her like a flooding river dammed. She longed to twine her body with Shane's and fuck until morning, but tonight was Thursday: Shane had to get up in the morning, and she wanted Shane's body positively taut with sexual tension for tomorrow's scene, which could, after all, go on for hours and hours.

She swept her hands slowly outward from Shane's convulsing vulva, up her torso, around her breasts, down her arms, under her ass, over her thighs, and down to the tips of her toes. When Shane's body quieted a bit, Clarity covered Shane's mouth with her own and kissed her deeply, feeling her own passion rear again. Shane mewed like a hungry kitten, and for a few seconds, Clarity thought her whole plan would be shot straight to hell, and it would be her own damned fault. Maturity, a voice inside her began to lecture, is the ability to postpone immediate gratification for a greater future end. Who the hell was that? She leaned over her whimpering lover and circled her ear with her lips while she dug all ten fingernails into her torso.

Shane heard a low voice say, "Tomorrow after work, go straight to Janny's house. Everything will be taken care of from there. Don't touch yourself until then."

Shane began to make crying noises and pulled Clarity toward her. Clarity's resolve wore thin, and she moved toward Shane, grabbing her roughly. They rolled over and over, heads swimming in the rising ecstasy. I can't stand not to make love to her, Clarity thought. Then, she pulled away, back in role. Shane was behaving very badly, she thought. Shaking off the dizziness, Clarity pinned the recalcitrant Shane to the bed, made a fist around her chin, and said in a stern voice, "Maturity…is the ability to postpone immediate gratification for a greater future end."

"Rrrmmmpfff!" Shane protested.

"There are times when you will be tempted to go for the shortcut…the cheap thrill…to cut a deal. Sometimes that's wise. However, I'm here to tell you," Clarity forced Shane's legs open, pressed her squirming body down and hissed into her ear, "This is not one of those times. Do you understand?" Shane looked up at Clarity so sweetly that the older woman was caught off guard for a moment. In that tiny sliver of time, Shane's lips brushed Clarity's ever so gently, and Clarity's body waved over Shane's so that she almost relaxed her full-body grip. But not quite. Her hand lifted and stung Shane's cheek so quickly it made Shane gasp, "Yes! Yes I under-stand…Sir." Clarity smiled, stroking Shane's throbbing cheek.

Friday

Clarity wasn't sure how she would pull this part off. But she had to admit, she got very turned on looking at herself in chaps, leather vest, and leather cap. It didn't take much for her fem look and demeanor to shift to masculine. She had fine bone structure; she couldn't hide that, but the goatee lent more of a yang edge to her face and transformed her expressions. Or perhaps it was the surprising fierceness and resolve that moved from deep inside her; she shuddered at the menacing eyes that returned her glance in the mirror.

Janny was a gem to agree to help with this. When Shane arrived at Janny's house after work, she had already drawn a bubble bath for her. Clarity had disappeared into Janny's back room, as prearranged, with a video monitor to view the whole scene, and overheard Shane's gurgles and moans as she relaxed into perfectly scented warmth.

"What have you got up your sleeve, anyway?" Shane had squealed to Janny who lounged in the living room, arranging the unsuspecting Shane's costume. Janny said nothing. Shane murmured to herself under the bubbles, knowing full well, as with most of Clarity's schemes, she would find out only once it was too late.

"Make sure to wash and condition your hair!" Janny called in to the soaking baby-dyke in the bathtub.

"Whyeee?" Shane whined, her voice echoing with that enclosed-in-a-small-porcelain-space ring.

"Don't make me have to call Clarity!" Only silence, then, from the bathroom.

Shane emerged in a pink bathrobe with her hair up in a blue towel and sat on the couch facing Janny. Her face glowed, and Janny thought she looked even younger than her twenty-two years. Slightly disturbed, Janny felt a warm flush in her own groin. She quickly began arranging her cosmetics. Shane looked at the coffee table, the makeup mirror, and Janny's impressive array of feminine trappings.

"What's all this crap?" Shane asked, brow furrowing, "I didn't think—"

"Don't turn around," came Clarity's menacing voice from the other room. "No one told you to think."

Shane's face assumed a meek posture, and she looked at Janny and whispered, "All right, I'm ready." Janny dipped a triangular sponge into the bowl of water she had carefully poured, then unscrewed the lid of a dark blue shallow tray. She swiped the sponge over the pancake a few times, then turned to Shane and said, "C'mere."

With small, jerky strokes, Janny applied the beige pigment to Shane's face, creating a smooth canvas for the shadows and illusions she was about to create. Janny had been a real-life makeup artist some years back and had confessed to Clarity her long-standing fantasy of feminizing the boyishly beautiful Shane. Shane felt Janny's hands tremble slightly at her cheek.

Shane was used to trembling women. Her understated, yet extremely confident and focused manner threw for a curve most young women who'd ever given sex with another woman more than a moment's passing thought. She'd take young women to places they'd never been, show them passion that stunned their wide eyes. She loved sharing pleasure rides. She was so comfortable driving that it was hard to imagine handing over the keys to anyone else, especially when they were so obviously less experienced. So, up until she met Clarity, she had stuck with what worked, had her pick of Boston's finest, and hadn't realized that she had gotten so bored.

"Close your eyes." Shane did so. Janny swiped pancake over the young woman's pristine eyelids, laughing inwardly at the redundancy of the camouflage, since Shane's skin was so dewy and perfect, with no wrinkles or other blemishes to mask. Removing a dark brown pencil from her tackle box, she drew a series of lines along Shane's brow, emphasizing her natural arch, then used a brush to blend in the lines.

"Look at me." said Janny. Shane's dark eyes obediently peered back at her through a thin mask of foundation, set off by the dark arches of brows. She looked rather ghostly and strangely feminine at the same time. Janny dragged a large, soft brush across a small, mauve mound and gently traced the young woman's cheekbone several times on each side of her face. The addition of blush rendered Shane's face a close approximation of a teen magazine model. Even her expression seemed to grow more submissive and eager to please with each additional layer of color.

Janny took a tiny brush loaded with dark charcoal-colored powder and painted shadows atop and outside Shane's almond eyes, emphasizing their bedroomy, come-hither quality. She filled in the rest with a soft gold powder, erasing the lines of demarcation with her expert blending skills. With a black pencil, she lined the delicate skin where Shane's dark lashes curled up from her eyes, then told Shane to look at the ceiling while she lined the lower lid. Finally, Janny applied two coats of shiny dark paste to Shane's lashes and fluffed them with a small brush. Janny's heart was beating at twice its normal rate. She sat back, flushed, and stared at her handiwork.

Clarity's pulse, too, accelerated at this transformation. Shane looked like a commercially attractive young woman, a striking contrast to her usual urban-fashion-victim-butch-boy look.

The makeup artist picked up a large, clean, soft brush and dusted the beauty's face with powder along her forehead, nose, cheeks, and chin. All that remained now were her naked lips. With a small, stiff brush, she lined Shane's small, tender mouth with a deep burgundy shade, then twirled up the tip of a matching lipstick and slowly drew it across Shane's lips, blotting them with a tissue. Finally, she painted on clear gloss.

Shane, now another animal entirely, peered out at Janny from behind slightly parted, shiny crimson lips, kohl-rimmed eyes, and accentuated cheekbones.

Watching from the back room, Clarity couldn't take her eyes off Shane's. She had trouble recognizing the glamorous creature as the bratty, boyish dyke that thrashed around at the end of her arm less than twenty-four hours before.

Janny slowly removed the towel from Shane's hair, untangling her dark curls. She took a large, round brush with natural bristles and yanked gobs of her own blond hair out of the brush, twisting them around her index finger. Shane's brow crinkled. Janny tossed the hairballs into the waste can under the coffee table. She picked up a long, gray narrow can, shook it several times, and sprayed a puff of white foam into her palm, the foam continuing to grow. Shane looked at her quizzically.

"It's mousse," Janny announced tersely. "It provides both hold and conditioning, so you don't end up with an afro."

Shane's face looked like one big question mark, but both women knew she dare not ask anything. The corners of Janny's mouth began to quiver as she suppressed a smile, which became a chuckle and finally burst out into an unfettered guffaw.

"Fuck you," Shane whispered.

"Oh my. Getting bold, are we, little girl?" Janny countered. Shane turned crimson under her makeup.

"Sit down in front of the couch!" Shane obliged.

Janny distributed the conditioning mousse throughout Shane's hair. She picked up a blow dryer and slowly began twirling strands of Shane's curly hair around the large brush, warming them dry with the heat of her tool. When she finished with each one, they fell in silky, gentle curves onto Shane's face, across her head, over her ear, and on the nape of her neck. Normally, Shane slicked her wiry curls back or stuffed them under a cap. She treated her hair as an extraneity to be managed, hidden, controlled; never as a secondary sex symbol, and certainly not as an ornate frame to compliment and highlight her beautiful face.

Now, Shane swept her own hands easily through the soft mane, and her tresses fell gently around her now finely accentuated features. Shane raised a manicured eyebrow toward Janny, with uncharacteristic feminine seductiveness.

"How do I look?" she asked.

Watching on the video monitor, Clarity scarcely recognized her lover. Even in her masturbatory imaginings of this scenario, she had not envisioned such a dramatic transformation. And it wasn't over yet. The butterflies in her stomach turned into almost pain. She put her hands over her solar plexus and felt small contractions. How could she want to possess one being so much? Sometimes she became afraid she might be over somebody's, some doctor's, edge. Her mind stopped working, thoughts stopped flowing, and instead, only desire occupied her body: raw, crackling, blinding, unadulterated, desire.

"Go hang up the bathrobe and come back in here," Janny said. All three women waited for Janny to say "naked," but it wasn't necessary to say it.

Shane returned to the quiet room. Janny and Clarity both breathed long and slow. Shane was a page out of *Penthouse,* a sweet teen bunny, a stripper before the show. Even the way she walked already had a feminine sway. Her dark nipples formed hard points against the open air, and her creamy body formed a vortex of light against which the rest of the room fell into shadows.

"Put those on—slowly." Janny pointed to a pile of burgundy lace topped by a pair of patent leather stilettos. Shane fumbled for a few moments with the feminine goods, then slowly picked out the crimson silk stockings and pulled them up each leg. She pulled on the lacy thong that spliced her ass cheeks and wrapped around her waist.

"What's this?" Shane wrinkled her brow, picking up a tangle of lace, ribbon, and metal.

"We'll do that last. First, the bra!" Janny commanded.

Shane picked up the article of intimate apparel with her index and thumb and held it in front of her, inspecting it. She glanced sideways at Janny, a skeptical look on her face. Janny nodded, closing her eyes. Shane slipped her arms through the straps and struggled for a few moments with the contraption. Janny walked over and, sticking her hand between fabric and flesh, adjusted Shane's handful-sized breasts for optimal cleavage exposure. The black cherry fabric cupped her mounds into two scoops of vanilla ice cream perched on her chest.

Janny then wrapped Shane's waist in the matching garter belt and summarily attached the stockings and adjusted the fasteners. In another moment, Shane's feet were being guided into the extremely high, black patent leather shoes, which made her moan and squeak a bit. Janny then placed Shane's hand on the wall for balance and blindfolded her. Shane began to giggle.

Clarity walked out from behind her vantage point, took Shane's face in her hand and hissed, "Shut up," into her ear. Shane's body straightened and came to attention. Clarity wrapped the helpless Shane in a long overcoat and led her slowly out to the car, but not before squeezing Janny's hand and looking directly into her eyes.

"You're amazing," she told her.

"Shane's amazing," Janny replied. Clarity looked at Shane, back at Janny, and shook her head, with a shit-eating grin like a fisherman with The Big One.

"I guess I'm gonna have my hands full tonight!" Clarity said.

Me too, Janny thought; but she only smiled and slammed her buddy on the back.

"You go, Clare!" Janny whispered after her as they strode out.

The two women drove home in silence. Clarity had to remove the blindfold, if only for the visual effect of the two women together in the truck. Clarity, with her goatee, leather hat, vest, and chaps, in the driver's seat next to the newly rendered fem beauty queen. Shane and Clarity alternately stole glances at one another. It was all Clarity could do not to drive the truck off the side of the road, throw Shane in the back, and fuck her like a crazed demon. She almost swerved out of her lane a couple of times. Shane showed the faintest smile.

Once home, Clarity positioned herself on the couch and instructed Shane to parade back and forth in front of her. Shane walked slowly, deliberately, and quite gracefully, as if she were a top runway model giving a free show to a beloved fan.

Clarity kept running her eyes along Shane's newly visible lines from her ass, down her legs, to her calves and heels, the ankle-heel shape echoing the waist-ass curves.

A perfect sphere is one of only five Platonic solids, universal shapes we are hardwired to see and create. A woman's body constantly evokes the tension of unfinished orbs, and lingerie teases the mind by promising to complete the circles. So Clarity's eyes traveled, again and again, never satisfied. Breast curves. Ass cheeks. Calves. Heels. Up and down, back and forth, again and again, in hypnotic bliss. She swore she felt her dick swell.

Her mood, however, surprised her. She had envisioned a scene humiliating Shane, the boy, by dressing her/him as a girl. But Clarity was in no mood to humiliate. Instead, she felt worshipful. She was lying down, Shane towering over her. Shane was not a bad boy in drag, but a goddess of extraordinary proportions and power.

Clarity felt her body moving across the floor on her hands and knees to Shane's feet. She lifted Shane's foot and ran her lips across the smooth leather and around her ankle. She made her way up Shane's leg, silently savoring each curve. With trembling fingers, she slowly stroked Shane's ass and pussy again and again, just for herself, just to touch the body that loomed ethereal before her, to make it flesh under her fingers. Shane's knees began to buckle, her breathing to labor.

Without taking off her chaps, Clarity stood and liberated her throbbing cock from its denim prison, the button fly holding it in place. She pressed her member between the sex goddess's legs, yearning to plunge deep inside. Shane dropped to her knees and began to suck her master's dick. Clarity ran her hands through Shane's hair, stopping occasionally to pull and squeeze Shane farther onto her.

Finally, she pulled her up, lifted her in her arms, and carried her into the bedroom where he was on top of her in no time flat. He rolled the crisscrossing lace off her body in a single, masterful motion and jammed his cock into her wet pussy. Again and again, the sound of hard leather slapped against tender skin. Taking the goddess that humbled him, possessing the source of his awe, his dick throbbing from the pressure on his clit, the woman underneath him screamed and he drove his dick into her harder and harder. Clarity sunk into Shane's depths as into the depth of his own driving, maddening desire as Shane came, bucking and howling like a banshee. She jacked her man's dick until he came, too; his wetness soaking her stomach.

This part, no one knew but God. Just as Clarity and Shane exploded, one after the other, Janny, too, came rushing into third place with goblets of girl jism, all over her hairbrush handle.

She would take days to put away all her cosmetics.

Unknown Territory
Helen Bradley

Why the hell am I here?

I feel embarrassed and severely out of my depth.

I'm surrounded by things that I can't identify and, well, I'm not so sure I ever want to know what half of them do. There's rubber and chrome enough to give a hard-on to the most jaded of petrol heads, and the smell of leather is prickling my nostrils uncomfortably. I look to the door. Perhaps I can duck out and she won't see me.

"Don't even think about it!" she hisses, stopping me dead in my tracks. "This was *your* idea, so face it!"

"Perhaps it wasn't such a good idea." I hear an unpleasant whine in my voice. PJ's right, it was my idea, and I thought it would be so easy. Now I'm beating myself for being naive and all I can think of is making a quick exit before I totally screw up. Her teasing will come later, and I'll just have to cope with it when it does but, right now, I want out of here.

My salvation arrives, not in the shape of the door handle in my hand and a blast of hot summer air in my face, but the understanding smile of a woman who has appeared like a fairy godmother at my side. Although, I have to be honest, fairy godmother is a term I'm using loosely here. She's actually five foot nothing of raw butch energy, number one hair cut, and tattoos on every part of her body that's showing—and that's a fair proportion of it. But when she smiles, and right now she's aiming one in my direction at point-blank range, it reaches all the way to her eyes and carves deep dimples in her cheeks. God, how she must hate them! Her entire butch persona is ruined by a cute little smile that any nun would die for. It makes me want to get down on my knees and confess my every sin.

I resist the temptation to spill my guts entirely but explain enough for her to send me another smile and direct me to the far end of the store. As I pass PJ, I grab her arm and introduce her as the body in question. In no time she and I have PJ fitted with a harness and a blindingly pink cock. It's funny how she's got hold of the script and is playing her part to perfection. She's asking me all the questions and looking PJ over to get her size without even meeting her eye. She tells PJ to go and try it on in a voice that has all the authority I'll can only dream of having. And PJ, like the soft-hearted butch that she is, is behaving to perfection.

When my purchase is organized, like a light switch, she flicks her attention to PJ. All of a sudden I'm the body and PJ's getting all the smiles. From where I stand I can see PJ is lapping up the attention like a fawning puppy. I aim a kick at her shins to tell her to stop flirting and concentrate on me. But together they conspire to ignore me and continue their in-depth discussion of PJ's purchase.

Minutes later PJ and I leave the store, side by side, but unable to meet each other's eyes. We've taken a step into unknown territory, and after ten years together, all of a sudden the clear path we've been traveling has petered out. There's a dirt track ahead, but it's overgrown and almost invisible in the distance. Neither of us knows where we're headed, but we both know that this path we're taking is the only option we have left for joint travel.

When we get home, we're still avoiding looking at each other. I make a bee line to one of the cats and pick her up for a cuddle. Although she's fighting me, I hold tight. I need something else to focus on, anything but having to face PJ and the implications of what we are doing.

"We have to talk about this, Cate." Her voice is croaky. This is costing her dearly too, I realize. I'm overcome with guilt. It is my idea, and she has given it her best, and I've left her with all the work.

I apologize. I meet her eyes. I see a deep love in them, and I am touched to my core. This is our problem. In my head I understand I carry only half the responsibility, but my heart is weighed down under the full burden of guilt. I've been playing a scene of alternately lashing out and clamming up for weeks now. I'm an emotional wreck, but through it all PJ has only ever looked at me like this. Her love for me shines naked and raw in her eyes. I owe her.

PJ hands me the parcel she bought at the store. I play the game, I know what's in it, but I open it like I don't. My future, our future, is in my hands. This is her message to me, and I must listen to what she is saying and honor this. The book feels heavy in my hands, like it contains the weight of all the knowledge that I lack. My thumb rubs its cover, as if its learning could be absorbed this way. PJ talks to me, her voice is low pitched, slow, and deliberate. She would like to try things differently she says. She couldn't find exactly what she wanted, but the basics are there; it's not only how but where she says.

I try to ignore that my lover is telling me she doesn't like the way we do it and wants it differently. I want to be angry, to lash out, but a combination of exhaustion and a prickly sensation in the back of my neck stops me. I investigate my neck, I feel sure the fine down is standing erect. There is a thickness developing in my stomach. I look down. My present to PJ is on the floor beside me. It's wrapped in plain brown paper and tied with string. No one uses string these days, I think to myself. I finger the rough hessian, it prickles my fingers.

I open the book PJ has given me. The pictures jump off the page. It is compelling; I can't not look. The paper is matte, inexpensive, and the drawings are simple. I read some of the words. This is a book that has been created for lovers. Half a paragraph and I am absorbed. I flick forward, more pictures, simple explanations. What PJ will feel, how it will be for me. This book is written for us, at least the physical us. I give voice to a wish that the emotional should be so easy to document and pleasure.

"We have to try, Cate." PJ's voice is still determined. Her large hand squeezes mine gently. Suddenly aware that I have spoken, I look up and meet her eye. The eyes of my lover and my friend are asking me to find her still worthy of loving. I smile, slowly, almost hesitantly at first, then it bursts forth, stretching my face, all my energy is focused in the effort. My eyes brim with unshed tears.

I push PJ's parcel towards her.

"Open it," I demand.

She's a better actor than me. She pokes at the parcel, lifting it, weighing it in her broad, butch hands, making wide-of-the-mark guesses. We are laughing like we used to, and PJ is pulling wildly at the paper. Free from its wrapping, PJ makes much of the harness, inspecting the clasps, holding it up and exclaiming that the size looks perfect. Pink, she says, what a wonderful pink cock she will wear.

Suddenly, her voice drops a full octave. In a flash, the humor is gone. She is almost whispering, a deep throaty sound that pierces me to my core. She tells me what she would do to me with her cock as she fucks me with her words. PJ has never spoken to me like this before, it's like a phoenix is rising from her ashes. The harness in her hand has unleashed something inside her, something raw and exciting. She is at once so new and yet strangely familiar. The room is charged with electricity. Sparks shoot between us as she tells me what a sweet cunt I have and what her pink cock will look like buried in it. Her words stir something deep within me. I feel a yearning for her that I haven't felt for way too long. I want to reach out to her, to take her to me, but something stops me. This is her scene, she is in charge here. I am a passenger, not the driver, and there is no map for where we are headed.

But I need her to know that I want her. I want her now, and I want her right here on the floor, surrounded by brown paper and string and new promises. She sits still, opposite me, cross legged, thick thighs pressed open, inviting. Her words continue, unabated, long and slow. I am wet for her, the seam of my trousers is damp. I hear myself groan. I sound like an animal in pain. I feel the gnawing hunger of my need. In a second she has responded to my cry. She is touching me, her hand gentle on my cheek. She tips my chin with her finger, makes me meet her eyes. There is a question there, and I answer it without hesitation. Yes, my eyes answer her, unashamed. Yes I want you, and yes right here, now. Please, I beg. I need her to know how hungry I am for her.

She folds me into her arms. I am pressed hard into her soft marshmallow breasts, my arms reach round her, and I hold her tight against me. She is kissing the top of my head, and her hand is heavy on my neck. She brings my face up to hers, but before our lips meet, she stops, like someone has pressed her pause button. I hear her take a ragged breath, and I feel a shudder run like an earthquake through her body. It's like the last vestiges of politeness have been shaken out of her, and she lets herself loose on me. Everything that has been pent up in her for so long explodes and suddenly she is all over me and her urgency is carrying me along with her like a powerful wave.

Her lips and teeth rake my face. Her tongue ravages my mouth, whipping deep inside me. She bites my neck, and I am in agony for wanting her. My back is arched and my hips are pressing into hers. She forces her thigh between my legs and jams it into me, holding me to her as I ride her muscular limb. The dam inside me breaks and a flood of wetness spurts from me. She murmurs her appreciation as it seeps onto her leg. She tells me I want her cock inside me. I agree.

Pushing back from me, she picks up the harness, fingering the soft leather. She asks the question again. I have rejected her as a lover so often that I have exhausted her confidence. For once I am not faking my need as I tear roughly at the buttons of her fly. I would undo them with my teeth if my mouth were not jammed into hers as I try to make her understand that the urgency I am feeling for her is real. I press her jeans and shorts down off her arse. As she raises off her knees I catch sight of her thick bush, and one hand homes in on her, pushing hard into her. She pulls me away and hands me the harness. We work together to strap her in, my hands reaching deep between her fleshy thighs and brushing past her moist cunt as I work. When we are finished, I lean back to admire our handiwork.

I have never seen her like this. The dark leather contrasts strongly with her white skin as it puckers around the clasps. The sweet butch is gone; she oozes power and hot sex. Desire rips through me, threatening to overwhelm me. I take her cock in one hand and tell her what I want her to do to me as I demonstrate with my finger in her mouth. She bites it, hungry for me as I am for her. The pain I feel is a welcome relief from the burning between my legs. Her hands roughly pull my shirt out of my trousers and over my head. I hear a seam rip, the fragile threads give way under her strong hands. I want her to deal with me as roughly as she has with my shirt. I want her to take me with no care for the damage she might do. I am stronger than mere cloth; I know that, and I want to prove it to myself and to her.

Her hands are on my breasts, kneading them like heavy dough. Her rough skin is raspy against my nipples, and I press into her, wanting more, groaning my longing. She pinches my nipples hard and pain shoots through me, arcing in my crotch. I want something between my legs—I grab her hand to jam it down there to assuage the burning, but she is stronger than me. She will not satisfy me that way; the only pleasure I will have is her cock between my legs. She is being nasty. You asked for it, she insists. This is the way I will take you, she spits at me. She is a mean, hard, butch, and I am soaking wet. I both hate and want her dominance at the same time. My body is dripping; I am crying my longing as if, in the face of death, I am begging for my life. There are no niceties between us anymore; she is rough with me, her words and her actions are masterful, she will accept no interference from me she says. She will take me as she wants, I have no part in orchestrating our sex, she will fuck my body as she wants to. Has she made herself clear? she asks. Before I can answer, if I could form any sound that wasn't a deep urgent moan, the buttons of my fly are torn apart and she thrusts her hand in under my panties between my legs. I lose all control, closing my legs tight on her hand and sitting hard on her. All rational thought is focused on my cunt and extracting pleasure from her hand.

Too soon, she pulls it away from me before I have done much more than heighten my pleasure. Her hand not being there is more erotic than having it there. I press my thighs together to exorcise the pain that threatens to engulf me. She pulls my trousers and panties down to my knees, removing the precious seam that has pleasured me as she will not. She tells me to stand, and she helps me out of my boots and clothes. I am naked; she is fully clothed, her pink cock bouncing wildly as she helps me undress. I would laugh at the vision if I didn't want it jammed inside me so badly.

She turns me round; my back is to her. It is too much for me, my knees will not support me anymore, and I sink, moaning, to the ground. I know now how she will take me, and I am unprepared for this. As in the shop, I am amazed at my naïveté. I have learned more about us today than I have in all the time we have been together. And what I have learned is that I have never really known her and I have never known myself. My cunt is throbbing with a need to be filled by her. My hands hit the floor, she pushes past me to get a pillow from the couch and place it next to me. I understand I will need protection from the rough fabric of the carpet. I understand what she is about to do to me, and I take the pillow and rest my arms on it. I press my arse high and back towards her. I need her inside me, and my invitation is clear. I feel her hands on my hips. She is pulling herself up onto her knees against me; I sense her hand on the tip of her cock as she uses it to push apart my swollen sex, seeking out my seeping cunt. She is murmuring to me, telling me what she is doing, how she is finding my body, how beautiful and wet I am. She is my eyes, I can't see what she is doing, but she is sketching the outline of a picture for me with her words, and my other senses are filling in the detail. I feel the tip of her cock against my hole, my aching agony to be filled drives me farther back onto her so it is hard for me to know who is pressing into whom. I take the full length of her in one plunge. I cry out as her cock invades deep into me, pressing aside delicate tissue, stretching me, filling me deliciously full. I sit back against her, trying to breathe. Her hands reach under me and cup my breasts. I feel her T-shirt tickle my arse cheeks and the fabric of her jeans rub my inner calves as I mold myself into her.

Gently she pulls back out, easing the hard rubber from me. I mourn the loss and beg for her to return. She does. Faster this time, she pushes in hard and then eases out just far enough to leave me empty and crying for her return, but not so far to relieve the pressure. She is hard and fast, and I can take all she is giving me and I scream for more. I demand she fill me and beg for her to take me with all her power. One hand leaves my breast to reappear between my legs. She grabs my clit between her thick fingers, and the pressure on me builds to fever pitch as, with one last deep plunge of her cock inside me, I explode in her hands. My body is racked with contractions that slam down onto the harsh rod inside me, increasing my pleasure. I come with a strength I have never felt. Pulse follows dying pulse until there is no more; my strength is replete, and I collapse backwards into her soft arms. I want to laugh and cry with joy, and all I can do is to sob, deep diaphragm-spasming sobs.

She holds me tight, supporting my weight as she has supported me for so long. Nurturing my needs, always there, always patiently picking up the pieces of our love and caringly cellotaping them together when they threaten to fall apart. She slips herself out of me and gently lifts me up and turns me around to face her. She pushes a stray lock of hair from my eyes and kisses each eyelid in turn. She whispers sweetly, holding me firm against her solid body. My sobbing dies down. My arms, which have been hanging uselessly by my side, find a new energy and reach up to touch her.

They move over her fleshy shoulders, caressing her. Holding her close with one hand, I trace the outline of her breast squashed between our sweaty bodies. Desire rises within me again. The edge has gone from my hunger, and now I am ready to slowly sample her. I will taste each mouthful of her at my leisure. I whisper my love for her and my intentions for her body. She laughs a deep guttural laugh. It makes her body shake like jelly. It is a laugh of pure delight in being alive and in love again. It is a laugh I last heard too long ago to remember. Tears prick my eyes as I give passing thought to the precious months we have wasted for want of telling each other of our needs. I tell her again of my love, of my pleasure in her large body. I tell her what I am doing to her as my lips reach down to seek out a flat wide nipple to suck. Her hands stop me, bringing my face to meet hers. The look she gives me is intensely wicked, as if she alone has noticed something funny. I shoot her a questioning look. I don't understand what she has found so amusing. I tell her so. She leans down and whispers in my ear. Like little girls, we break into hoots of laughter.

She struggles unevenly to her feet and heaves her jeans up over her hips. We walk together to the bedroom to finish what we have started. I will speak to her later about her choice of location. She is wimping out and so soon. But I will leave off reminding her until I have taken her to the point of exhaustion and beyond and she has responded in kind. I will get my chance to tease. All in good time. And I sense we have time on our side. Again.

By the Boots
Lauren Sanders

So evening came, and morning came; it was the first day and then the second before we left my apartment. We walked the wet streets as if we were inside of a bubble, one of those scenes you shake and the snowflakes fall. It wasn't snowing yet, but the air was heavy, the sky a mist of gray guncotton.

We bought coffee in paper cups and continued on, going nowhere. Shade stopped in front of a vendor hawking hats, modeling a few as I sipped my coffee through a crack in the plastic lid. She chose a black knit cap, the kind worn by urban thugs on television. "Are you planning on turning over a candy store?" I asked. She smiled, said the hat made her feel tough. But she was more of a sap than I was. When we passed the multiplex just as the feel-good movie of the season was about to begin, she begged me to go inside.

"Come on, Rachel," she cocked her upper lip at me. "Ever make out in the movies?"

I didn't have to answer. I'd always been urbane about movie going, arriving early to be coke-and-popcorned by the first preview and barring all communication once the lights went out.

On occasion, I'd even shushed a peanut-gallery commentator or two. But there I sat kissing in the back row like a clumsy adolescent, though not my adolescence for I'd never even kissed a boy until I was eighteen years old, and I never would have imagined that all the boys I'd kissed since then would be obliterated by one woman in a dark movie theater.

We were feeling good, so much so that we skipped out before the movie ended—yet another filmgoer's faux pas— and ran back to my apartment, forgetting that we'd originally come out for food and toilet paper.

Home again, as if we'd never left the bed, I was overwhelmed by my craving for Shade, my longing to bind her hands and feet so she couldn't leave. Yet, whenever I tried to express these feelings without sounding like the mildly neurotic, too-needy, intimacy-shy adult I was, my language retreated to the vapid patterns of pornolinguistics.

"I'm waiting for this to blow up," I said, moving my leg beneath her until I felt her on my knee.

"What?"

"This you and me against the world thing."

"Don't say that."

"It can't last."

"Yes it can," she said, and despite the barrage of phone messages we ignored, I believed her. I would have believed anything she told me with her body on mine, her fingers slipping inside me, and her teeth biting my nipples a little bit hard, which I discovered I liked. Though I couldn't come, I felt closer than ever, beyond it even, the way the graze of a finger can, in the right circumstances, be more intense than a grasp. Still, there was the dark-continent part of me that believed our relationship would not be fully consummated until I had an orgasm.

Day four, alone in the shower, I gave in and masturbated. Though it wasn't the climax I'd wished for, I came in about two seconds. It was insidious, a litmus test that left me feeling physiologically defective. A sexual misfit. Not like Shade who could come when I fucked her, but only if I used two fingers at about a forty-five degree angle so the base of my hand hit her clit and, even then, only after she'd gotten off once already some other way. This kind of specificity amazed me. Clearly, Shade's was a sexual history spawned by trial and error, along with a few creative lovers all of whom I'd become insanely jealous of; jealous because they'd been with her, but also because of the things they'd done together. None of the men I'd been with even liked being on their backs.

In all fairness I couldn't blame them entirely. I never said what I wanted, what I liked, and through my frustrated silence I'd grown contemptuous of their easy orgasms. I'd lorded my frigidity over them as if it were a sacred cow. But it ruined me sexually. "I understand now," Shade said. It was day six, and I'd finally confessed that I was indeed troubled by my not coming.

"What?"

"The other night, at the benefit. There's just no letting go for you, is there?"

"I guess not," I looked up from the couch where I'd been clipping my toenails. She was sitting at the counter in my bathrobe, drinking a glass of orange juice and not reading a magazine.

"It's all inside," she pointed to her temple. "That's the real sex organ, the rest is just friction."

I pursed my lips, returned to my clipping.

"No, really. We'll figure it out."

Let her hope, but I knew better. People who came easily never understood this, how it felt to be perpetually on-the-verge, revved-up, and good-to-go, but then you're going and going and going and suddenly everything shuts down like someone flicked a switch in your head. Whatever you do next is inconsequential, you've passed the point of no return. Bottomed out. Sometimes when I hit bottom, I became so dejected and angry I couldn't speak for hours. Other times, I could pretend I'd actually come, feeling sated enough by wet sheets and a lover's arms. With Shade it was mostly the latter.

She took the nail clipper from my hands and sat down next to me. "There's something I want to ask, don't be mad, but..." She giggled so I knew it wasn't serious. "In your closet, I saw these...these boots."

"They're the real thing, straight from the dungeons of Mistress Wanda Lynne." I explained about the mishap on the set, yet in the telling it seemed as if the entire day had been lived by someone else.

At Shade's request, I took out the boots, and together we inspected them. "They're sort of scary," she said.

"I don't think so."

"Put them on." She smiled, and within seconds was helping me into the thigh-highs I'd inherited from the pissed-off dominatrix, inherited because that idiot porn star Robbie Rod had cajoled me into trying them on when he must have known it was bad karma to wear a dominatrix's boots without asking. That day I'd been devastated, but balancing around my apartment for Shade I wished I'd thanked him.

"Take off your underwear," Shade said, and I did, the sun making waves through my dirty blinds, and it was naughty and illicit, as if we were slumming in a dive bar in the middle of the afternoon. But if in these shoes with Robbie Rod I'd felt like a cheap whore, with Shade I was a woman, or I'd accepted some idea of femininity that had always felt like an act with men. I liked being sexy, I liked her watching me being sexy.

We danced naked, and I was suddenly tall. She put me in her lace bra and spun me around. "There, now you look like a porn star."

"I have way too much pubic hair."

"Let's get rid of it."

"You serious?"

She nodded, cheeks dimpling foolishly, but I knew she was indeed serious. She said she'd always wanted to shave a woman and, at that moment, she could have said she wanted to have a threesome with a goat, and my response would have been, "Let's find a petting zoo."

An occasional advocate of the clipped bikini line, I had the necessary accoutrements. Scissors. Shaving cream. Disposable razors. Vitamin E capsules and aloe vera lotion. Shade draped a towel over the toilet seat and sat me down, spreading my patent leather legs. She picked up the scissors and my thighs caved inward. I had this fear of sharp objects near my pussy, especially when they were in somebody else's hands.

"It's okay," she said. She kissed the top of my clit and stroked me with her fingers; already I wanted to scream. I leaned my head back, felt the pull of my pubes, the cold metal of the scissors and, then, a tense snip. My eyes shut to the clip of the shears, the hum of Shade's voice.

When I next looked down, my pubes were tightly buzzed; sort of prepubescent, sort of in-the-Navy, yet caught between these shiny leather lampposts. I almost liked my own body. Shade smiled and filled her palm with shaving cream as my heart beat wildly.

She started shaving from the top. The back of my neck tingled, and I had to bite my tongue to keep from whimpering. I could feel my legs shaking the closer she came to my vagina. "Trust me," she said, two fingers spreading my lower lips so she could get in further with the razor. "I was always really good at shaving the balloon. It was my favorite booth at the town fair. I won prizes."

"You're such a little suburban girl."

"I never said anything different. Everyone just assumes I'm from Brooklyn or wherever. From the hood, as it were."

"I'm more from the hood than you are."

"Exactly, but it's like that's the past I should have."

"You can have mine if you want."

"That's very kind of you...can you move your left leg up a bit? There, that's it." My right leg slanted against the sink like a contortionist's so Shade could get underneath. I was flooded with visions of losing my balance and sacrificing my clit to a disposable Bic. No coming, ever. Not even the hope of it. I shivered, felt the muscles in my stomach contract.

"Relax," Shade said, as if she'd read my mind. She softened the scrape of her razor, stopping every so often to stroke me with her fingertips. I felt them so intensely, the opposite of relaxing.

She pulled back, tapped the razor against her chin. "I'm wondering, maybe we should leave the hair on top."

"You're the stylist."

"Here." She tilted a hand-held mirror toward me.

"Ugh, it looks like a mustache."

"Our customers are mad for it, we call it the Charlie Chaplin."

The little black hairs sneered above my cunt. Bald, I could handle, but these few molded strands reeked of a slow, uncomfortable death. "More like Adolph Hitler," I said. "I hate it. Get it off."

She grabbed my chin in her free hand, kissed me, then returned gallantly to her shaving. When she finished she rubbed me clean with a warm washcloth, and I felt pampered, cared for in a way I'd never experienced.

White fluorescents streaming, she dropped to her knees in front of my bald vagina. She licked me slowly, so tenderly it hurt more than the pull of her razor. She pushed my legs farther apart, fingered me. On her knees, she was licking me and fucking me, and I could feel it this time, feel it for real. I was thinking please, please, please...but I lost it again, was soon ambushed by those familiar frustrations. There was just no letting go. I lifted Shade's head. "You're all wet," she panted. I started sobbing.

We fell down on the cold bathroom floor, Shade's arms mainlining relief as I wailed maniacally. I said I was sorry for not coming, and she said it was okay, it didn't matter. "I was almost there, I swear it," I hiccuped, and she held me, for hours it seemed. I'd never cried in front of a lover before, never cried so deeply with anyone before. Such emotion frightened me, felt more foreign than my shaved vagina.

I longed only to comfort her back, be good to her, but my own feelings were so overwhelming they left me mute and immobile. Ultimately, I was afraid I'd failed her and would always fail her because I couldn't give her what she wanted. I couldn't give her everything.

Darkness eclipsed my studio, offering a night-and-day contrast to the two of us in this light-bright bathroom.

"I'm starving," Shade said.

"I know, but I can't move."

Gently, she lifted me, put her arms around my waist and hugged me. "Sorry I ruined your fantasy," I said.

"You didn't ruin shit."

"It's not what you wanted; it should have been sexy."

"It is, Rachel," she whispered, her breath mingling with my ear lobe. "It really is."

I don't know whether I believed her or not, but the words felt right. As did her body on mine, stumbling from the bathroom and collapsing back into bed.

The Touch of Reality

Jeannie Sullivan

Devon turned her key in the lock and pushed open the front door. Bending at the waist, she gave her freshly cut hair another quick tousle to shake the last of the loose clippings free, then straightened and glanced down at her shoulders. She brushed a few chestnut strands from her chambray shirt and scooted excitedly into the tiled entryway.

Tossing her keys onto the antique secretary, she recalled the time she had wanted to dye her hair black, but Timothy, her hairdresser, had gasped, clapped his hands to his cheeks, and squealed, "What? With your fair complexion and those hazel eyes?" Then he had tsked. She had taken that as a no.

Timothy also disapproved of her current style, it being much shorter than she had worn before coming to work for Lena, but now she kept it that way for no other reason than to feel Lena's fingers run through it each time she had it trimmed. Timothy would just have to understand. She rubbed the belly of the ivory Buddha that sat on the cherry wood desk for luck, then hurried into the living room to find Lena.

The beauty of the woman's home still struck Devon as poignantly as it had the first day she had seen it. Two years ago, when the employment agency had sent her over as an applicant for the position of personal assistant to Lena Parker, attorney at law, Devon had been stunned by the blind woman's surroundings. Passing the marble statue of Venus in the corner of the dining room, Devon remembered the day Lena had purchased the art piece. Devon had watched, mesmerized, as her lovely boss had explored every inch of the five-foot figure with her hands. It was the first time, but far from the last, that she had wondered what Lena's touch would feel like on her own skin.

Quickening her pace, Devon shot a glance into the empty kitchen. "Lena?" she called down the hall toward the office.

No answer.

She headed for the stairs. Taking the wide, plushly carpeted steps two at a time, she released a soft giggle. She could hardly wait to show Lena her haircut.

The door to the master suite on the second floor stood half open.

Peeking into the room, Devon raised her fist to knock, then froze. Her breath caught.

Lena stood naked beside the king-sized brass bed, the length of her sable hair pulled up into a loose bun, her olive skin glistening with the moist residue of a recent bath. Balanced on one foot, the other resting on the edge of the mattress, she bent forward massaging her calf and shin. A bottle of lotion sat in front of her on the bed, and a large bath sheet laid in a heap on the floor. Her full breasts rose and fell as her torso moved with the rhythm of her hands.

Devon stared. She knew she should look away, back out of the room, and forget she had ever seen this gorgeous sight. But her gaze refused to shift, her feet to move, her mind to relinquish this prized image. A tiny pulse throbbed between her legs. Surrendering her conscience, she let her hand drop to her side.

Lena picked up the bottle and squeezed more of the creamy liquid into her palm. Placing the container carefully back onto the bed, she rubbed her hands together, spreading the lotion over both, then paused for the briefest of moments. When she resumed her task, her strokes seemed more deliberate, slower. One hand caressed her inner thigh while the other followed the curve of her shapely hip. She straightened and drew her fingers close to the small patch of dark curls nestled on her bare flesh.

Devon swallowed a small gasp.

"Did you get your hair cut?" Lena's voice was quiet, but it startled Devon with the force of a scream.

Her jaw went slack. Her mouth gaped open. Her cheeks flamed with embarrassment and shame.

"I know you're there," Lena said, her elbows resting on her raised thigh. "I know you've been there—watching."

"I—I'm sorry. I didn't mean—" Devon faltered. There was nothing she could say that would vindicate her.

Stepping back, Lena bent and retrieved the towel from the floor. She wrapped it around her body and tucked in the end to hold it in place. "So, did you get your hair cut?"

Still flustered, Devon shifted her weight from one foot to the other. She tried to recapture the excitement from a moment earlier, but it eluded her, dancing and twirling just out of her reach. It seemed to be holding back until she somehow managed to make things right, explain to Lena how she could care for and respect her so much and still commit such a violation of her privacy. "Yes, I got it cut." There was no explanation, no excuse.

"Can I see?" Lena reached out and wiggled her fingers, beckoning Devon to her. She did not appear angry or even perturbed.

Confused, Devon crossed to where Lena stood.

As if with vision of their own, Lena's hands slipped behind Devon's head and began a gentle exploration of the hairstyle. Her fingers twined through the cut, her palms caressed Devon's scalp, her thumbs brushed Devon's temples.

Was it Devon's imagination, or was the process taking longer than usual?

Lena's movements seemed slow, excruciatingly so. Her moss green eyes narrowed almost imperceptibly, the way they did sometimes when her thoughts were on something other than what she was doing. The warmth of her breath fanned Devon's cheek.

Turning her head ever so slightly, Devon tried to escape the tingling on her flesh. Her eyes fell on Lena's bare shoulders. The edge of the towel followed the swell of the brunette's scantily covered breasts. Devon squeezed her eyes shut, but the earlier image of their beauty burned in her mind. A soft moan threatened to betray her. She held her breath.

"What's the matter?" Lena whispered. "You feel hot. Tense."

A tremor of desire surged through Devon. She had to get control. Grabbing Lena's hands, she pulled them away from her and retreated a pace. She opened her eyes.

A slight smile played at the corners of Lena's lips. "Is something wrong?"

Devon cleared her throat. "Lena, I'm sorry I was watching you. I never should've—"

"It's not the first time," Lena interrupted.

"What?"

"I've felt you before, watching me."

"No, I promise—"

"Not in here," Lena corrected, "but when I'm working or eating."

Devon blinked. She had no defense. What she wouldn't have given many a time to be the Braille letters beneath this woman's fingertips or the spoonful of ice cream that disappeared between her warm, supple lips.

"It never bothered me," Lena continued. "In fact, I enjoy it. But now, you've seen me naked."

Devon's shame returned, flooding her body. "I—"

"Shhh." Lena cupped Devon's face between her hands. "It seems only fair that I should get to see you." She trailed her fingers down Devon's cheeks, across her jaw, and over the contour of her throat to the top button of her shirt. She opened it.

Devon's heartbeat quickened. Heat rose in her body.

With practiced ease, Lena dispensed with the rest of the buttons and tugged the shirttail free from the waistband of Devon's jeans. Her countenance revealed no sign of anything she might be feeling as she pushed the garment off Devon's shoulders and let it fall to the floor. Her hands continued a dilatory trek down Devon's back then made the return trip up. After a quick traversal of the back of Devon's bra, they followed the edge of the thin fabric around to the front clasp.

"Your skin's so soft," Lena said, her tone breathy. "I knew it would be."

The words caught Devon by surprise. Had Lena thought of this before—wondered about Devon as Devon had about her?

Lena unfastened the hook and freed Devon's breasts.

The undergarment joined the shirt at their feet.

Devon felt her nipples begin to harden at the mere thought of Lena's impending perusal.

Lena paused. "Finish for me." She brushed her thumb across Devon's lips.

They trembled.

"I want to see you all at once." A wistful expression sculpted Lena's features.

An ache of anticipation twisted through Devon. Lena had to know what she was doing to her, or at least Devon prayed she did. Hastening out of the rest of her clothing, she remembered the many times she had dreamt of a moment like this when Lena might see her as something other than a cook, or a driver, or even just a friend, when she might turn to Devon as a possible lover.

Devon had slowly fallen in love with Lena over a matter of months, and by the time she had realized what was happening, it was too late. She had tried to put aside her feelings and date off and on, but soon she found herself declining dinner invitations and potential new beginnings to spend quiet evenings in the company of this woman she had grown to cherish.

Lena entertained only professionally—clients or, occasionally, partners from her law firm. Devon was usually present as an employee, but she was always treated with respect and fondness. Only once in those months had Lena invited anyone into her personal life as more than a friend. An ex-lover had come to visit for the weekend and spent the night in Lena's bed.

Devon had lain in the darkness of her own room down the hall and yearned for the chance that this woman had been granted. Sounds of pleasure from behind closed doors had haunted her dreams. In the morning, she made the couple breakfast, then escaped her torment by spending the day at the mall, away from them.

Now, standing naked in Lena's bedroom, Devon's longing overcame her. Taking Lena's hands, she placed them at her shoulders, holding them gently as they began a meticulous exploration of her fevered form. Closing her eyes, she waited, anticipated, ached.

Lena traced Devon's collar bone, then trailed her fingertips down the swell of Devon's breasts. She circled the nipples, missing them by a shadow, then caressed the underside of the fleshy mounds. She cupped them, squeezed them, glided a palm across each, lingering just long enough to coax Devon's nipples to stiff peaks.

Devon gasped and arched into Lena's hands.

She moved away, denying Devon any satisfaction.

Devon released a moan of frustration.

"Did you enjoy looking at me as much as I'm enjoying looking at you?" Lena asked. Her voice tantalized.

The image of Lena, fresh from her bath, rushed back into Devon's mind. "Mmm, I did," she whispered.

"Then look again."

Devon opened her eyes just in time to catch the unveiling of Lena's body. This time, it was a full view, nothing hidden, nothing obscured.

A lustful smirk shaped Lena's lips. She stood straight and tall, her breasts flushed pink like a rose newly opened, her nipples taut and engorged like ripened buds eager to bloom. The slight pout of her tummy ebbed gracefully into the bow of her hips and descended downward beneath her soft curls.

Need seized Devon's senses, the need to touch and be touched, to feel and be felt. It pelted through her veins. It pooled in the hot folds between her thighs. "Oh, God," she said with a rush of breath. "I want to make love to you so bad."

Lena smiled. "Not yet." She stepped close to Devon. "We're still just looking." Her nipples feathered across Devon's skin.

Devon gazed down to where their bodies almost met. An agonized laugh battled with a guttural moan in her throat. "I never knew you were such a tease." She fought to keep from crushing Lena against her.

Lena chuckled. "You have a lot to learn." Her hands found Devon's sides and ran down her torso over her hips. She traced a path around Devon's buttocks and examined every centimeter, stroking, kneading. She leaned into Devon.

Devon released a loud groan.

Shifting slightly, Lena continued her examination of Devon's backside with one hand and slid the other around to slip between their bodies. She skimmed her nails across the tender flesh of Devon's abdomen, then lightly raked them through the lush crop of hair that covered her mound. She sighed, her breath hot on Devon's neck.

Devon's legs trembled.

Lena eased her fingers between them. She tickled the curls that veiled Devon's outer lips. She reached deeper, the heel of her hand pressing on Devon's still hidden clitoris.

Devon gasped and grabbed Lena's shoulders for balance.

Lena nuzzled her neck. She trailed the tip of her tongue over the hollow of Devon's throat. Her fingers found Devon's center.

Devon stiffened and cried out. The torment engulfed her.

Pursing her lips, Lena sucked in a long breath. "You're so wet," she whispered. "So beautiful." She dragged her fingers up the length of Devon's slit, opening her labia completely. Her lingering touch prodded and teased Devon's already throbbing clit.

Devon's knees buckled. She clung to Lena.

Their mouths met. Lena snaked her tongue between Devon's lips. Her kiss was everything Devon had imagined, soft, full, sensuous—hot with desire.

Clutching Lena in her arms, Devon spun them around, closer to the bed.

Lena squealed but seemed to trust that Devon would hold her tight, keep her secure. She wrapped her arms around Devon's neck and surrendered to the embrace.

They dropped onto the mattress, Lena on top. Devon combed her fingers through Lena's dark hair, loosening it from its bun. It fell down around her face, cascading across Devon's skin. Their bodies pressed together, breast to breast, belly to belly, thigh to thigh. Their mouths captured one another. They kissed long and deep.

It wasn't enough. Devon needed more. She squirmed, trying to make more direct contact by parting her legs and lifting her hips.

Tearing her mouth from Devon's, Lena raised up on her arms. She pushed backward, dragging her body down Devon's. Her hips dropped into the vee of Devon's open thighs. Her own legs straddled one of Devon's. She groaned as she snuggled in for a tighter fit.

Devon went wild. She ground her cunt against Lena. Her hips bucked and jerked.

Lena's fingers found one of Devon's tumid nipples and closed around it. She rolled it, fondled it. She lowered her head and covered the other with her mouth. Her breath enflamed the sensitized nub, but her lips eluded it.

Devon whimpered. Squeezing her eyes shut, she arched her back, forcing her breast higher, hard against Lena's mouth.

Lena tightened her lips. She sucked it in deep. Her hand never wavered from its exquisite torture of its own prize. She thrust her hips, spread her legs wide. Her cunt opened, hot and wet, over Devon's thigh. All control she had apparently been hanging onto vanished in a movement.

They rocked against each other.

Devon's orgasm grew close, too close. She wanted to savor this moment, make it last as long as she could. There were so many things she had imagined doing to Lena that she now wanted more than ever. With every bit of effort she could manage, she steadied her hips, gripped Lena's shoulders to raise her from Devon's breasts.

Lena fought her. She ground her pelvis down harder, sucked with more fervor.

Devon groaned. "Stop," she pleaded. "Please. I want to taste you."

Lena slowed as if pondering the thought, then lifted her head from Devon's chest. Her fingers still toyed with a nipple.

Her hips still rotated ever so slightly. "But this feels so good." Her words came in pants.

Devon stroked her back, cupped her buttocks and squeezed them while they still pumped lightly. "I promise I'll make it feel better."

Lena smiled, a slow, lascivious smile. "Better than this? You sound awfully sure of yourself."

A soft laugh slipped from between Devon's lips. "Let me show you."

Lena hesitated. "Well, I've liked what I've seen so far." Lifting herself from Devon's thigh, she groaned and eased down beside her.

Following closely, Devon raised up on an elbow and coaxed Lena onto her back. She gazed down at her.

Lena's body was tense, glistening with a fine layer of sweat. The hip that had nestled so snugly between Devon's legs shimmered with Devon's thick cream while Devon's thigh was wet with Lena.

A part of Devon wanted to just stay there and study the sight, memorize every detail. But she had made a promise. Intent on keeping it, she scooted to the edge of the bed. Kneeling between Lena's feet, she reached up and stroked the flat of her stomach.

Lena sighed and opened her legs wider. Her scent filled Devon's senses.

She inhaled the piquant fragrance, brushing her cheek against Lena's inner thigh. She kissed the sensitive flesh. She moved upward, closer and closer.

Lena shivered. Her breathing turned shallow.

Devon parted Lena's labia wider with the tips of her fingers. She admired the glistening, dark pink folds. Her own pussy quivered. Inching closer, she licked Lena's creamy slit from one end to the other in one full, long stroke.

Lena gasped and moved against Devon's mouth.

Devon licked her again, then trailed the tip of her tongue in circles around Lena's clit, around and around, careful not to make full contact, yet. Lena tasted so good—sweet, yet slightly salty. Devon savored every succulent drop. She pressed her lips around Lena's clit. She massaged it with their softness.

Lena's moans strengthened. She gripped the back of Devon's head, pushing her face deeper into her.

Devon licked harder, faster—all over the hot flesh of Lena's lips, down the shaft of her clit, up under the hood. She flicked the tip of her tongue across Lena's opening.

Lena let out a loud groan. "Yes, there. Right there." She panted. "I want you inside me."

Devon eased her tongue in, just the tip at first. She imagined what Lena's tongue would feel like, remembered how her fingers had felt. Devon's body ached, but she focused on Lena's pleasure. She dove deep into her new lover's pussy, shoving her tongue in all the way.

Lena's juices covered Devon's face. She clenched at Devon's hair.

Easing her mouth away for an instant, Devon slid a finger inside. She thrust into Lena's opening while she licked, she teased, she sucked the tender flesh of her hardened clit.

Lena's moans grew to cries. She thrashed from side to side.

Devon moved her finger in and out, in and out. Then another. She licked Lena's lips and clit, her whole body screaming for the same attention, yearning for her own release. Her own groans were muffled by her lover's pussy. She moved her mouth faster, sweeping her tongue across Lena's clit, dipping back into her hole, then returning to the throbbing, swollen nub.

Lena's hips pumped frantically. With a sudden scream of release, she came. Her cunt gripped Devon's fingers. Her clit pulsated in Devon's mouth.

Devon sucked it gently through a series of spasms. She felt Lena's body jerk and quiver, heard her cries of pleasure. She brought her lover down slowly, completely, through the very last shudder.

"Oh, my God," Lena said, her tone tempered with fulfillment. "That was incredible." Reaching down, she found Devon's hands and interlaced their fingers. Pulling gently, she coaxed Devon from her knees and onto the bed. Together, they moved up onto the pillows and nestled into each other's arms. They lay quietly in peaceful silence.

"Are you warm enough?" Devon asked, finally. She gazed into Lena's relaxed features.

"Mm...hm," Lena answered with a sigh. She snuggled closer. "I'm perfect."

Devon considered her, studied every detail of her face, her hair, her body pressing closely to Devon's. The absolute purity of Lena's words washed over her. "Yes, you are." Had she merely thought it or actually said it?

Lena smiled. "I think you might be biased."

"Mm. Maybe so." Devon traced Lena's lips with a light caress. She found it difficult to believe this was really happening.

Lena sucked Devon's fingertip into her mouth. Her teeth grazed it. Her tongue circled it. She closed her eyes and began to make love to it.

Devon watched, wondering what thoughts mingled in Lena's mind. Did she know what this moment meant to Devon? Had she figured out just how much Devon loved her? They had talked about many things, but never about that.

But Devon knew Lena. She knew her well. She knew this woman did not take just anyone into her bed. Making love to her was a gift she had given to only a chosen few, and now she had chosen Devon.

"Do you know how I feel about you?" Devon whispered. She withdrew her finger from between Lena's lips and followed the rise of her cheek to her ear. She thumbed the lobe.

Inhaling a deep breath, Lena lolled her head onto the pillow. "Yes. You show me every day in the way you take of things around here—the way you take care of me."

Disappointment rushed in. Devon didn't want appreciation for a job well done; she didn't care about Lena's recognition of her as a good employee. She wanted Lena to know that she desired nothing more than to spend the rest of her life meeting every one of Lena's needs. She swallowed her lament. "Well, Ms. Parker." She feigned a humorous tone. "Have you forgotten that you pay me for that?"

Lena remained serious. "That's not what I mean. I could pay anybody to drive me around or assist with the house and the gardeners, to cook for me and shop or just be here, in general, when I need help with something. But not just anybody would have my coffee waiting for me every morning when I come downstairs the way you do with just the right amount of creamer in it. Not just anybody would make sure that everything around here is in its exact spot in the house so I can find it even when I'm here alone. They wouldn't buy me E. L. Fudge cookies, even though I'm dieting, and bring them out only on those nights I can't sleep because I'm worried about a case."

Amazed, Devon listened. She couldn't believe Lena had noticed all those things.

"And I know for a fact," Lena continued, "that they wouldn't cut their hair shorter and shorter—" reaching up, she combed her long fingers through Devon's trimmed waves, "and shorter, just to let me touch them more intimately every five weeks."

"Oh, God." Devon flushed with embarrassment. "You even know about that?"

"I do," Lena answered, her voice reassuring.

Devon relaxed a little. "Well, Little Miss Know-It-All, since you're so smart, do you know I do all those things—" She hesitated. Was she really going to say it? She slipped her hand behind Lena's neck. "Do you know I do them because I love you?"

Tears darkened Lena's green eyes. "I do." She swallowed. "What I'm afraid of is that *you* don't know that *I* love *you.*"

Stunned, Devon searched for a response. She found none. This was her dream—her one true fantasy. Whether it started with sex or lust or watching Lena try to get a word in edgewise when talking to her mother on the phone, every fantasy she'd ever had ended this way. This was the pinnacle. Nothing followed.

"Are you there?" Worry etched Lena's expression.

"Yeah." Devon's answer was barely audible. "I just—I can't believe—maybe you need to pinch me."

A soft laugh drifted from Lena's throat. "Why don't I kiss you instead?" Taking Devon's face in her hands, she covered Devon's mouth with her own. Her lips were soft, her breath warm. Her tongue probed more tenderly now than it had before.

Devon's desire still smoldered, unsated. It took only seconds to re-ignite into full flame. Her kiss intensified. She still tasted Lena on her lips; it aggravated her need.

Gently, but firmly, Lena urged Devon onto her back. She took a nipple into her mouth. She no longer teased, no longer taunted, her obvious intention was to satisfy. She sucked fervently with a promise of compensation for her earlier torment. She fondled Devon's other breast, caressed her skin.

Embracing Lena, Devon dragged in a ragged breath and held it. She squeezed her thighs together and lifted her hips. Her clitoris throbbed under the pressure. She surrendered to a groan.

"Tell me what you want," Lena murmured against Devon's flesh. "This is just for you. I want to please you." Her words came in shallow pants.

The thought seized Devon like an iron lung. This woman—this beautiful, incredible woman—who Devon never truly believed she could ever have, wanted to give her pleasure.

Devon reveled in the sensations caused by Lena's mouth. The memory of Lena on top of her flashed in her mind. She recalled the images of past fantasies, envisioned Lena's examination of the statue of Venus, her delicate touch as her hands skimmed the pages of a book. "Your fingers." Devon's passion enflamed. "I want your fingers."

Without hesitation, Lena obliged. She reached between Devon's thighs.

Tightening her buttocks, Devon arched upward. She spread her legs wide, desperate for her lover's contact.

Lena stroked Devon's hair like she would pet a cat, then curled her hand down around Devon's mound. Her fingertips swirled through Devon's juices, grazed her hot folds.

Devon cried out. She tightened her grip and crushed Lena to her.

Lena nibbled the nipple. She tongued it. She sucked it. Her fingers found their way around Devon's slit, working together to tickle, to probe, stimulate.

Devon knew they searched for all her secrets. She gave them up freely.

Suddenly, Lena pressed her thumb to Devon's swollen clit.

Devon groaned and squirmed against it.

Kneading the hard nub, Lena eased two fingers into Devon, just barely at first, then a little deeper.

Devon's cunt clamped down hard, reaching, trying to pull them in.

Lena pushed them in farther, then eased them back out to the opening. In again, then out. She picked up a gentle rhythm, sinking deeper with each stroke. Little by little, she quickened the pace.

Reaching above her head, Devon grabbed the brass bars of the headboard. She thrust her hips with every lunge of Lena's hand. She ground her clit into Lena's thumb. Her orgasm built, then, with a sudden surge, peaked. She screamed with pleasure and release—long-awaited, much needed release. Tears burned her eyes. Every fantasy she had ever created about Lena flooded her mind, then washed away.

Today was reality.

Seed

Dia Naevé

Late afternoon light seeps in through the window and streaks shadows across her face. Neither of us has spoken.

Hours pass. Her breath reaches out and is finally upon me, around me. A hot wind stirs in her eyes. It storms impulsively, rushing and rattling the window shades shut. I fall back, landing hard on a pile of blankets and pillows. Her fingertip traces me from parted wet lips to pointed toes and back again, seeking something. She stops at my hips, hesitates, feels the shape and temperature of my curves. I close my eyes and my clothes are gone. I am shivering but not cold. Her hands glide firmly beneath my hips and lift them up, bringing fresh water to her parched mouth. I feel her face on my stomach, brushing side to side. Her tongue trails down to my thighs and drinks the stream of juice that has trickled out from me. Her tongue circles inward and rubs, a finger pushing beneath it, easing my tense muscles open. Her face pushes into me more, her mouth opens wide, and her teeth sink into me. Pain aches pleasingly over my skin, and I hear her swallow once, then twice. She reaches two more fingers inside me and pulls something out.

Over the rim of tight, dark curls I see her eyes smiling at her magic. Her slick fingers carry the thing up and slip it into my mouth where I catch it with my tongue and roll it around. It's a strawberry. She laughs. Her three fingers become four and then a whole hand reaching inside me. I think my muscles might tear, but I want more and she is up to her forearm in me now, her muscle flexing and relaxing as she pushes in and pulls out, a tattooed firefighter helmet dancing on the bulge. Blackness clouds my vision, but I don't faint because I don't want to miss this. Her hands bring the fruit of my body to my mouth and she fills me with berries—strawberries, raspberries, blackberries and cherries—until I blossom and consume her, my hips swelling in waves. I can't see past the rumbling curves now, but I feel her swimming inside me, hanging on. Juice washes the room red, washes the daylight away.

We lie at the foot of the bed, sheets and blankets around us like so much jetsam. I look into her eyes and wonder if she was there with me. She pulls a toothpick from behind the ridge of her ear and pushes a strawberry seed out from between her teeth and smiles.

Home from the Sea

Sacchi Green

The fog began to lift as the carrier rounded the Marin Headlands. Slowly, seductively, the Golden Gate emerged and San Francisco Bay spread her golden thighs to let us in.

Point Bonita thrust out like a rocky clit, but all my awareness was fixed on a spot around the curve of Point Diablo. "I'll wait there all afternoon," Romy had written, "and the next day too. Please come, Sage."

Romy had never said please to me. Well, maybe in erotic extremity; some of our games were pretty inventive for neophytes. But I was the one who had begged, fourteen years ago; and she had gone ahead and married my cousin Damian anyway, obsessed by some damned Earth-Mother-fertility-goddess fantasy. I hadn't seen her since.

I knew she was running a craft gallery in Oregon now. I send birthday presents to her daughter Phoebe every year and get nice notes back; she's about as close to posterity as I'm likely to have, and I don't regret her existence at all, but damnit, there were other ways! I'd heard through the family grapevine when Romy and Damian split up after a couple of years, and hoped for a while that she might get in touch. Nothing for years. I'd be damned if I'd beg her for anything ever again.

Sometimes, when I woke from a dream too soon, with the taste of her in my mouth and the feel of her small tight breasts against mine, I knew I was damned anyway.

But now she begged me to come.

Everyone else lucky enough to be off-duty was on the city side of the aircraft carrier. I looked toward Marin, searching with binoculars for the glint of other lenses searching for me. We used to imagine we were being watched through telescopes from the Presidio or passing ships; maybe we were. We put on a fine show.

But it was too early for her to be there. And when we did meet, we'd probably be strangers. Did her memory have the psychedelic intensity of mine? Not just of our trysts in that secret refuge on the headlands, though my body gave my mind a hard time getting past those. We had been just eighteen, in waitress hell in Sausalito, our first adventure away from our families' Mendocino commune. But we had been together since birth, Sage and Rosemary, toddlers waving at the TV cameras in Haight-Ashbury, poster babies for the Summer of Love. What had driven us so far apart?

The ship passed under the Golden Gate Bridge and I forced myself not to look back. San Francisco emerged from the lifting fog and caught the sun like a hoard of gold and crystals spilling down the hillsides and heaping on the flats. I scarcely noticed.

I was shaking in a way that had nothing to do with the cool morning breeze. A Chief Petty Officer can't be observed shaking; a CPO can't press against the rail and let memory and anticipation get her wet between the thighs. To get a grip, I reviewed the Bay's underwater topography all the way to the Alameda Naval Air Station, not just the familiar patterns from the sonar screen but the rocks and silt and sand that were as real to me as any landscape. The Station was being closed down at the end of the month as the peacetime Navy retrenched, and this was the last time a carrier would pass this way. I tried to focus all my nostalgia nodes on that, without success. The closing was probably what had impelled Romy to make contact at last.

On shore, I pushed through the throng of families. It was noon before I had picked up a rental car and was zipping across the Bay Bridge. I stopped in the Marina district to pick up some wine and fruit, as though planning a seduction, and wondered how I would bear it if she weren't planning the same thing.

It was past one thirty when I reached the Marin side of the Golden Gate. Joggers and tourists were thick along the walkways; any bird watcher training binoculars on the right spot would be able to see Romy—if she were there. In a while they might be able to see a whole lot more. Being visible and out of reach had always turned us on; not that we needed anything but each other for that.

I parked at the trailhead to Kirby Cove. One of the three cars there had to be hers; I hoped the owners of the others were well out of the way, maybe getting off on the old WWII gun emplacements uphill.

Half a mile down the trail I realized that scuba diving and jogging on deck don't prepare the legs for steep slopes. The weather was unusually warm, and I was sweating from both exertion and anticipation. I wondered whether I could still manage the tortuous off-trail route when I came to it, or even find it after all these years.

I found it all too easily. Others had climbed here over the last few years; I couldn't tell whether anyone had passed today.

My heart, along with various other pulse points, was pounding when at last I approached the thicket of stunted black oak. A single ancient bay tree, no more than shrub size in this harsh location, leaned out into space. It hadn't occurred to me to wonder whether it would still be there. I gripped a familiar branch, felt for the old footholds where the hill dropped sharply away, and swung myself over to the hidden ledge.

She was there, sitting on a blanket at the base of a sheltering outcropping of rock. The blanket was a good sign; so was the pack with the wine bottle sticking out. So was the fact that she was naked, unless she was just taking advantage of a rare chance to sunbathe. She must have heard me coming, although she just kept gazing out over the water. The wind was moderate, and the breakers beating against the rocks far below were about as leisurely as they get.

"Well, I'm here," I said, knowing it sounded too abrupt. I was having trouble saying anything at all. She was so close, and so distant, and so damned beautiful. Her tawny, sunlit hair hung in a long braid down her back, just as I remembered; mine was dark and cropped short, tinged now with silver at the temples.

She turned toward me at last with an odd sort of challenge in her green eyes. "It's nice that you could make it," she said formally, and I knew she remembered the bitterness of our parting. So much distance between us, so many years, so many aching dreams...

"Of course I made it." My throat was tight, and the rest of my body tightened as I looked at hers. She was, and wasn't, the vision and curse of my dreams. Motherhood and life had filled out her body, rounded her breasts and hips; I was shaken by how much I liked her this way.

She looked me over slowly, thoroughly. I wondered how much I had changed. "Somehow I was envisioning you in uniform," she said at last.

"For that, you should have met me at the ship."

"I almost did, but…'Don't ask, don't tell.' Isn't that the deal these days?"

"Did you think I'd jump you at the dock?" I tried for cool amusement, but she had zinged a nerve, the one that ached when I stood alone in a melee of clinching couples. I might have jumped her at that, and the Navy be damned.

"No, I was afraid I'd jump you and screw up your military career."

My career? She made it sound as though I'd left her, instead of the other way around. But she still wanted me, or wanted me again, and right at this moment nothing else mattered.

"Hey, if a uniform is what it takes to turn you on, I could go back for one."

"Maybe later." Her face lit with that tantalizing grin I knew too well. "Those cut-offs will do just fine for now. Damn, Sage, I've been dreaming of those long legs for so many years I thought I must be imagining them, but they're even finer than I remembered."

Those long legs moved me closer without any conscious command. She tilted back her head to look up at me, stroked me from ankle to thigh, and an exquisite pang ran from her touch up into my cunt. My knees started to buckle.

"Wait, Sage, don't sit down, let me…like this…" She rose to her knees, gripped my hips and pushed me against a high boulder. She pressed her mouth into my inner thigh and worked up and down and up again, nuzzling my crotch too briefly and moving on with lips, tongue, a hint of teeth, her full breasts brushing my knees. My breath came so hard and fast that it sounded like a rising storm in my ears, but the sky was clear and far above I could see a hawk lazily riding a thermal current higher and higher, gaining altitude for a final launch out over the straits.

Romy's teasing was pushing me higher and higher, too. I slid my fingers into her thick, vibrant hair and pulled her head toward where I needed it most. She dug her teeth into the thick denim seam at my crotch and tugged and bit, driving me wild, until I was so wet I knew she could taste me through the cloth.

"Come on girl, come on, you can do better than that, come on...." I let go to fumble with my zipper.

She leaned her head way back, her eyes glinting with laughter. "I always used to be afraid you'd turn into a mermaid someday. You know, back when we were kids in Mendocino and you'd dive into water too cold for any mere human." She slid her hands up my thighs into my tight shorts and stroked me with her thumbs, sliding them back and forth along my crotch, not quite reaching my aching clit, not quite probing into my cunt. The zipper resisted my frantic efforts.

"I was right that the ocean would take you," she went on, "but at least you're still human. I wouldn't know how to get between a mermaid's legs."

"I'll bet you'd manage," I muttered as she worked a little farther in. I gave up on the zipper and used my hands to brace myself against the rock, thrusting my pelvis forward into the maddening pressure of her fingers.

Then her grip shifted, moving around to the rear, and she cupped me behind, and murmured against my mound, "Your ass is still mine!"

"So do something with it!" I yanked again at the zipper, and the stitching tore loose and freed me. My shorts and her hands slid down together. I kicked off pants and shoes and pulled off the T-shirt that was my only other clothing.

"I'll do anything you want me to." Her voice was seductive as she rose to stand before me, her full, round breasts nearly touching mine, but I caught a flicker of uncertainty, even apprehension. I moved back a small step, puzzled by the trace of tension in her body. Didn't she want me, after all? Did she somehow feel she owed me? Had I changed too much?

Then I knew, and pulled her close, hard. "What's the matter, Romy, you think you're too much woman now for me to handle?" I stroked my hands down over her back and filled them with her rounded ass. "You think just because you could do a Marilyn impersonation I can't properly appreciate every...single...inch...of...gorgeous...flesh?" I punctuated my husky words with open-mouthed kisses on her lips, the silky hollow of her neck, the top of a swelling breast. I eased back a little to set her thrusting nipples free, brushed them for long, exquisite moments with my own, then bent in response to her wordless plea and worked her over with a demanding mouth.

Her taste, her scent, was still the same, her feel the same, but even more so. Her response was beyond anything in my dreams. I licked and sucked her nipples, gently and then harder and harder as she moaned and thrust and pulled my head closer against her silk-skinned abundance, all the while writhing against my thigh pressed between her legs, her crotch getting me as wet there as I was in my own cunt.

"Sage, please, I can't wait, I meant to do you first but I can't stand it, I need it, please, get inside me, please, don't stop, bite me, hard, but damnit get inside me get inside...."

My clit and cunt were pounding. I wasn't sure which was more urgent, my need to fuck or get fucked. But her begging turned me on as much as her touch, and I hadn't gone from queer hippie commune kid to Navy CPO without iron self-discipline.

I slid my hand between her thighs, teased her clit as I sucked and bit one engorged breast and then the other, and resisted her frantic attempts to push my hand farther into her slippery heat. Finally, as her curses mixed with high-pitched sobs and she tried to squeeze her hand past mine I gave in, gave her two fingers, then three, deep, deep; and then, as she opened to my probing, I slid down her body until my mouth was devouring her sweet-salt tang and her clenching cunt was devouring my whole pumping hand.

We tumbled together onto the blanket. Her raw cries lanced through me, and as they finally subsided my own need drove me harder and my own voice rose in wordless, gasping pleas. Romy scarcely took time to draw a full breath before she leaned between my legs, spread me open, and with insistent strokes and deep-thrust tongue blew me all the way into the stratosphere. The shock wave should have blown that circling hawk down the coast as far as Monterey.

A full moon was rising over the Golden Gate and the enchanted city by the time we made our way, sore but not quite yet exhausted, up the steep slope. What had to be said had been said:

"Damnit, Romy, you didn't have to marry him, just fuck him a few times, maybe not even that, there are other ways to get pregnant—"

"Sure, now, maybe even then, but I was just a kid, what did I know? He was my only way to get some of you into my child. And you were going to leave anyway, no matter what you said, the sea was going to take you, and the Navy was your best chance—"

"But you said—"

"And you said—"

We stood together at the overlook, reluctant to pull apart long enough to drive our cars back over the bridge. The wine and food, almost untouched, we would share at a bed-and-breakfast on Divisadero where anyone with Navy connections who saw us would be unlikely to advertise the fact. I had two weeks leave before heading back to Honolulu for six months, six more years of service before qualifying for a pension; we would manage, we'd do whatever it took.

There were a dozen cars of moon watchers parked at the overlook now. I didn't give a damn. I pulled Romy close and kissed her hard and felt a pull as deep as any ocean current. She drew me as compellingly as the moon draws the tides. I might never know her depths as thoroughly as I know the sea's; sonar technology can't probe the soul. But she was my center, the irresistible force that would always bring me safely home.

The object of these lofty thoughts slipped a hand into my zipperless shorts. "Is your ass as bruised as mine?" she whispered. "Maybe it's time to experiment on a real bed."

Her touch set me off again, but the prospect of a bed seemed worth a few minutes apart. I opened her car door and shoved her in, almost forgetting to let go of her before the door slammed shut. She grinned and gunned the motor. I sprinted for my car and followed that irresistible force across the moon-bright Golden Gate.

Thermal Stress
María Helena Dolan

I'm an ass woman. I can't help it; that's just the way I'm wired. Oh, of course I love the way women look and feel and taste and smell and sound. But I really love the way women sway. Uh-hmm.

And a woman who knows how to work it…whew! A thoroughly religious feeling just comes all over me. When I see a positively heart-stopping ass, it makes me want to get right down on my knees and…say the rosary! Oh yeah!

Especially when they make it sway, honey. Swaying on the street, swaying in the breeze, swaying on the dance floor, swaying like it has a mind of its own, if you please. Any one of those moves can knock me down and roll me over; but you know I'll be right back up for more.

And, truth be told, I should say that I especially love the way *she* sways, my sweet, sweet thing. Uh-hmm.

I must declare, she has got to be the finest work of womankind on the Goddess's green Earth, built with the roundest, sweetest, firmest, ripest, shakinest, succulentist mounds imaginable. I swear, grown women start to weep, and even faint dead away, when they see that garden of delights crossing their paths. Woo.

Now, this kind of thing is a gift you've got to be born with. You can't fake it, you can't acquire it, you can't learn it. There can't be any doubt that my woman started out from toddlerhood with handfuls of the stuff. Hell, when she was just a teen queen, trying to figure out which way to go—you know, whether it'd be boys or girls or both—she already knew that a pair of tight jeans exhibited her best and most stirring calling card.

Oh yeah. And being a southern gal, she liked to strut—even before she knew how to work it. Some innate pool of female knowledge bubbled up to the surface long enough to let her know that punctuating her arrivals and departures with that undiagrammable but definitely declarative sentence was precisely the way to proceed.

Some things just come instinctively to the naturally gifted. It ain't as if anyone put her up to it. In fact, all kinds of folks tried to get her to change her ways.

Shoot, for years, the neighbors could hear her mama hollering out the window, "Come on in here, girl, before you shake yourself all to pieces!"

But thank God that didn't succeed. 'Cuz now I am the happy beneficiary of all that bounty. It's a glory so sweet that sometimes it just about makes my teeth ache....

Just watching her walk is a thrilling, fulfilling thing. But actually making love to her...I can hardly stand it! Sometimes, it just comes upon me, like a veritable force of nature.

Take the other night, for instance. We were lying in bed, just reading. It was late, and I was dog-boned weary from work and meetings and the daily runnings around. The most I could muster was a chaste little peck, which I'd already administered on her Oil-of-Olayed forehead.

She has a lamp on her side of the bed, and I have one on mine; she held a book, and so did I. Mine was a murder mystery with a dyke dick, and hers was poetry.

So we were content, just laying there together, heads on respective pillows, arms barely touching, bodies relaxed and ready for sleep. Calm, comfortable, homey.

But then, she rolls over to her side of the bed, propping her head with one arm as she continues reading, and her butt is all of a sudden touching my hip. A tornado siren wouldn't have shocked my nerves as much as just registering her firm but oh-so-soft flesh against my suddenly awakened body.

I can't help myself; it's just the way I'm wired.

So I naturally have to roll over too, putting my arms around her and pressing my starting-to-get-bothered-about-it pussy against her butt. She smiles, turning her head toward me for a moment. And then, she keeps on reading!

Well, I'm afraid that my now-discarded *novelus interruptus* won't hold my attention any longer. Not with all this soft warmth blending with my own. "Turn over, baby," I croon. She rotates her head over her shoulder and gives me a pointed "have you lost your mind?" look.

By now, I'm working one hand around to her dark triangle in front. Pressing down, the way she likes, I give her that low, lazy voice: "Ooh baby, you know I just want one little lick. Just one lick, and I can die happy."

"Yeah," she rejoinders. "As if one was ever enough for you."

"Ah now baby, it ain't as if you don't receive some benefit, too."

"I'm reading," she says, not quite dismissively.

"Not any more," I point out. "In fact, I think your butt is having some thoughts of her own."

It's undeniably true; just that small circular pressure at the origin of her clit has got her hips moving in circles, and little explosions set off quivers in various other parts.

"Mmm, baby, I can feel your heat. I want to give you some lovin.'"

She doesn't reply; but her hips grind a little faster and a little harder, as I kiss her neck from her ear down to her shoulder.

With one hand working her mound, the other comes around to pleasure the nearest breast; once that preliminary negotiation is established, I part her thighs with my leg. And that lets me feel her slick wetness already beginning to collect there, like some kind of thermal spring, as the temperature rises dramatically.

"Ooh, honey, you better lay on your belly. There's something I've just got to give you."

In an evil voice, she asks, "Jewelry?"

"Uh, huh. Pearls of great price." And then I stop what my hands and leg are doing—which she hates.

"Oh, all right," she grumbles and lays belly down. Which puts her butt right where I can reach it.

At first, I simply have to lean back and admire this natural wonder. I marvel that I can't even span all the way across it with both hands stretched out, like a piano player searching for the last, best chord. But even that attempt sends shudders through her and me.

Kneeling now, I run my hands up and down her mounds, sometimes kneading and sometimes just drawing my fingertips lightly across her puckering skin. Keeping it going, I reposition myself over her and then drag my breasts across her back, just barely touching her skin with them. Slowly, ever so achingly slowly, I trail my now-hardened nipples down her ass to the tops of her thighs. Ah, her hips are really grinding now.

Inspired, I take my right tit in my hand and stuff it up into her crack, so she can feel my flesh all up and down her. Her heat rises higher, and her hips move more furiously, sucking my tit into her.

She protests heartily when I pull out of her, but she quiets as I begin to once more rub my breasts up her back. Reaching her hairline, I stop and hover over her. Then, starting at her neck, this time with my lips, I kiss downward, slow, with deliberate torpor; velvet mating with satin to form a wondrous combination. This delicious mating takes so long because I simply have to cover every inch along her perspiring spine.

As I finally claim the territory of her left cheek with sovereign kisses, I cheat with an unexpected infiltration and cross over to her coccyx with my indefatigably exploratory mouth. That bony tail remnant twitches mightily as I part her mounds with my hands and kiss inside the crack.

Her smell is so sweet and so like her that I can't imagine ever wanting to stop. With my reverential tongue tip, I begin my search of her quivering ring, that delicate, puckered peach pit. I work my assertive tip of tongue flesh against those folds, dispatching trills of sensation which expand into undulating surges of excitement as they spiral through her. She moans out her pleasure into the mattress as I work her more and more feverishly, her asshole clutching and shaking.

But I can't resist the pull of her pussy any longer. My mouth races down to her near-gaping hole, and I lick the outer walls in a circular motion.

Fixing to boil, she blurts out, "Give it to me, honey. Put it in me. I need it now. Tongue-fuck me!" she calls out in an imperious plea.

And I do, thrusting my face against her, my nose seeping into her ass, my tongue charging in and out with a great heat, a ferocity usually seen in people desperately trying to save treasured objects from furiously burning buildings.

She screams, and I keep at it. I can't breath, but it doesn't matter. I just keep moving my head against her, my hands on her hips, pulling her butt up towards my face with fast, hard strokes. I just keep fucking her with my tongue, as her fingers fly to her now-frantic clit.

When she's just about to come, I somehow pry my head up and out of her. She screams in terrible frustration, but she knows what's coming next. And so, still breathing in the savor of her wetness laying atop my upper lip, I slip the first finger of each hand into her unbelievably hot and seeping pussy, thus simultaneously following both her upward thrust and her downward path. I slide in and out with shuddering ease, letting her really feel the penetration as I move against her wet walls, which begin to lengthen and deepen and open wider. Getting it from two angles at the same time drives her harder and hotter still.

As she thrashes, I withdraw one hand and allow the other hand's forefinger to remain in order to meet up inside the palace walls with the rest of her sister digits. I then ease the withdrawn hand's slickly coated finger into her waiting asshole. Her proprietary folds surround me, hold onto me, demand me. I fuck her ass with gentle force, steady and targeted and continual between her yielding tightness. And I haven't neglected the right hand, which keeps fucking her other, slippery hole, just up to the end of the fingers, which I wiggle against her inner wall at the end of each thrust.

She begins to come as I push first with one hand, then the other, alternating strokes so she and I can both really feel the fiery, thin wall between them. Screaming and clenching, she tightens both of her realms against both of my hands.

"Oh yeah, baby. Give it up. Give it to me," I chant over and over again with mantralike intensity, fucking her for all I'm worth.

And wonder of wonders, she does! She flat out gives it up, wailing and rocking with the force of her orgasms, clenching me tighter and tighter as her limbs thrash and then collapse.

She has me right where she wants me. And I couldn't be happier, with my fingers still inside her, as I bend down to kiss her ass one more time, feeling the radiating heat flush my awestruck face.

"Mmmmphh," she half sighs as I gently withdraw from her still-holding-tight districts. "You know what you do to me is a sin and a crime," she chides in a voice which reverberates low and nastylike, accompanied by that slow and slight smile.

Holding my expatriate fingers against my nose and inhaling deeply, I reply, "Well, it certainly is in most of these contiguous southern states. But not, apparently, in your sovereign territories."

Used to me and my ways, she smiles again, touches my face, and reaches up for a last little kiss. Then, she curls against me, her ass snuggling up to my pulsating pussy. Ah, there she is again, her ass abutting me as it had over an hour ago.

After a moment of luscious silence, I ask, "Isn't this how we got started in the first place?"

"No. Actually honey, I think it was when you said something about giving me jewelry."

At that, we have to laugh.

These southern gals—they sure know how to work it.

Drowning

Alex Wilder

Have you ever felt like you were going to explode if you couldn't hold someone that very second? That's how I felt tonight. There was a sense of incredible urgency surrounding me. In my head, in my heart. A panic. I felt like I was at the bottom of a swimming pool, in the deep end, looking up at the surface with all that watery space above me. Airless space.

I wanted her to feel even a glimpse of being known and understood. I wanted to give her that. Just that. Right then. But I couldn't. I couldn't follow her breathing as she drifted into sleep. I couldn't touch her face with my fingertips or put my head on her chest and witness her heartbeat. I couldn't hold her through this night.

Her name is April. Her absence did not ring true to a single cell in my body. I had to get out of town.

The thick brush filtered the light from the street lamps. I breathed in the damp, sweetened air and, in an instant, remembered, like water exerting forces in all directions, the last time I smelled her.

Cautiously moving forward, I spotted a clearing bordered by dense bushes and trees. Despite my isolation in this foreign place at this foreign hour, I was not the least bit apprehensive or nervous. Just aching. I never would have found myself in this situation back home. April was everywhere and nowhere, and since I couldn't get her off my mind, I had to pursue the only other option available to my senses. I had to drown her vividness in someone else's flesh.

Coming outside is like making love to the sky. Taking the cool night air into my passages and seeing the never-ending, vast clarity of the sky when my head falls back...it is unearthly. Add the anonymity of these gardens and the flow of a female body, and I hardly even need to be touched.

She said she would be here at two A.M. I did not know this city or this place, but I would know her hands in the dark. Back at the bar, her hands fell to her knees as she laughed. They had the most exquisite strength—soft but not timid. I wanted them all over me.

When April and I touched, I was reminded of an entire life inside my body, a life that my mind knows nothing about. Thinking was irrelevant.

It was my pulse, my heat, my blood and my fluids that mattered. The tangible, earthly components of me. The things that go unchanged.

I was fascinated by this woman's hands, and I think she figured out my desire quickly because the next thing I knew she was pressing a note into my hand, saying to find her here in these gardens at two A.M. We split up at the club at twelve forty-five A.M. We had not exchanged a word.

Waiting was the hottest kind of restraint. It created tension between my legs—a collage of fleeting visuals from watching her in the club and physical memories of April. I tried to fight those, but they only made me wetter.

The energy of this place was mystifying. I heard an occasional nearby rustle and could make out a couple of silhouettes moving together slowly, rhythmically. It was the kind of place that I could not imagine even existing in the daylight. The temperature of the air seemed to change as I neared the opening to the clearing. It was like a cave with lush types of sweet-smelling, thick bushes and trees for walls. Growing more and more used to my night eyes, I could see a white bench in the middle of the clearing. I approached it slowly and stood behind it, listening. In what seemed like almost an instant, I felt hands grasp the curve of my waist—her hands. My insides liquefied. She was just what I had hoped. She was confident. She possessed the kind of sexual power that could make you forget. I did not want my heart softened; I just wanted to be taken over for a while.

Reading my body language with precision, she pressed herself against me and slowly dropped her hands over my hips to my ass, holding me there and then lifting my flesh slightly. I tensed briefly until I felt her lips against the back of my neck. My eyes closed, and a moan released itself as she moistened my neck with her lips and tongue tip.

Imagining the intimacy of her mouth, I desperately wanted to turn around and face her, but I was enjoying this too much to move. I just wanted her to control my senses. I did not need to see her face. I knew she possessed beauty; I remembered from the bar. Seeing her would only remind me that she wasn't April. I didn't need any help remembering that. I just needed to come.

She ran her fantastic hands around to my front and up to my breasts, pressing her hips against me with more force. My goddess, how I love it from behind. I'm not sure how she knew, but she did. She toyed with my nipples, stroking their tips with her fingers, then squeezing them harder until I gave up another moan, tilting my head back. It was apparent how much this excited her. My clit was throbbing as she continued to massage my breasts. I opened my eyes to the crisp, dark beauty of the star-filled sky. Oh, that sky. It was as if pleasure could go on forever. I wondered what April was dreaming about, what position she was sleeping in at that moment.

My panties grew more and more saturated. I wanted this stranger to fuck April out of me, at least for tonight. My entire body felt like the soles of bare feet on scorching blacktop. She reached between my legs from behind, and I fell forward, grabbing the back of the bench in front of me. Instantaneously, this position opened my insides up. I could feel her tense behind me, trying to control her aggression, but not too much. She was skilled. She kicked my feet farther apart and pressed my head down firmly with her left hand. I felt uncontrollably desperate. I needed her inside me that instant. I needed the scents of the wet grass and sex to merge and fill my lungs when I came. I needed to know there was nothing above me but that sky.

She reached under my dress, tore down my panties, and, without a moment's hesitation, slid two of those beautiful fingers deep inside of me. I came almost immediately, as a thousand thoughts and images flooded my mind. I saw April's face—her perfectly gorgeous and expressive face. The crickets seemed louder, my breathing faster, her grip stronger. My insides molded around her fingers, throbbing and clinging to this intense and anticipated pleasure. She loosened her hold but stayed inside, absorbing my pulse for a minute. The air was so rich now that I closed my eyes and imagined becoming part of the atmosphere.

She pulled out slowly and gently. I gathered myself but did not turn to face her. My senses were still recovering. I stood still, wondering if she was waiting for me to speak, wondering if she was going to leave first. After a couple of silent minutes, I started to turn but she stopped me. With one hand on my shoulder, she touched my hair gently with the other. She leaned towards me and spoke softly in my ear. "Go back to her," she said, and I listened to the rustle of her footsteps until I could hear nothing more than my own heart.

Dodi's Ode
Robin Bernstein

Party photograph

Me: the Bat Mitzvah girl; white polyester dress with pastel pink and purple trim, homemade barrettes braided through with pink and purple ribbons. You: guest at the dais; brown blazer and wool skirt, cream-colored silk blouse. We hold identical Shirley Temples, but the one in your hand seems sophisticated, like a daiquiri. You are fourteen, but you look like a Wall Street secretary. The one the boss wants to fuck.

It is 1984, and I have loved you continuously for ten years. I have loved you since the first moment I saw you, when some aperture in me tensed, adjusted, and then clicked shut. Your face was recorded inside me, Dodi, as if the coils of my intestines had turned to film. The most gorgeous four-year-old in preschool.

Kindergarten photograph

Me: a gummy tub with home-cut hair and a sweaty green turtleneck. You: fresh and breezy in a red-checked blouse, bobbed hair curling against your cheekbones. Your eyes are dark, enormous; they dominate your face like a cat's. Like me, you are a white Jewish girl, but your skin is perpetually tan; your teeth, contrasting with your dark lips, glint white as Dynamints.

I have watched your body change, Dodi. Always mesmerized by your shaded skin, I have witnessed its evolution in microscopic detail. When you stretch your spine, I see newly formed muscles ridging the skin of your stomach. I notice the oil that now collects on your nose and chin, the hairs on your legs that thicken and darken.

"It's so smooth," you say with wonder, stroking your shin, which your mother has finally allowed you to wax. "Touch it," you say, and the world telescopes in on my hand, your knee, your smooth, tan calf. I neither think nor breathe. You are womanly, a year older—as you constantly remind me. I hide my pus-white legs and their scraggly hairs beneath Jordache jeans (my mother's recent concession); my breasts are little pads of fat. Your breasts have thickened and become meaty; the tiny hairs on them stand up as if reaching toward me. I close my eyes, and I can see your breasts so clearly, Dodi: round and firm as softballs, light sweat in that mysterious crack between them, where I long to burrow. My hand on your shin.

"Freshie!" you taunt, waving your hand in my face. You are in the eighth grade; you embrace your God-given right to torture seventh graders like me. You gleefully describe the mutant teachers I will encounter: Mr. Green, who sprays spit on the first three rows of his science classes; Mrs. Stein, who dyes white streaks into her hair and hikes up her miniskirts for the boys; and Mr. Fishbein, who told his English class that he was a homo. I am not sure whether to believe you. You tell many lies, especially ones you know will frighten me. If you step on a subway grate, it might collapse beneath your feet. Never watch TV during a thunderstorm; you could get electrocuted. The dumpster behind the junior high is infested with rats the size of cats.

Diagram

You dictate my sexual timetable. Seventh graders should pet, you say. That sounds to me like something you'd do with a dog. You show me a book that says it's normal. You tell me a boy will stick his tongue in my mouth. This, too, is normal, you say, showing me the page in your manual. I stare at labeled diagrams of vaginas, line drawings of naked girls in graduating stages of puberty.

I watch your hips grow round and broad; you use them to slam doors closed and to nudge me out of a chair you want to sit in. I watch skinny hairs grow under your arms, which are becoming muscled and strong. You wrestle me to the floor and pin my arms over my head; your breasts, sheathed only by a thin T-shirt, swing inches above my face. "Whatcha gonna do now, freshie?" you tease. I struggle to free myself. You push my arms perpendicular to my body, as if I am being crucified. Legs folded, you kneel on me, one waxed shin pinning each of my arms. Your hips grind against my mashed-potato breasts; your crotch wiggles inches from my chin. You smell different than you did in kindergarten.

I try rocking from side to side, but I cannot tip you off me. I try bucking, kicking my legs into the air. You laugh and work your knees deeper into my arm sockets. You lick your hand and wave it near my cheek. I screw my mouth and eyes closed, trying to avoid your wet palm, which you wipe anyway against my forehead and ear.

We play dolls in your basement rumpus room; together, we propel leggy plastic surrogates through tempestuous romances. Twice, you lock me in the basement and do not release me until I cry. Sometimes you fling your body flat on top of mine, pin my ankles with your feet and my arms with your hands. You prop yourself up, face a foot above mine, and allow a long thread of spit to dangle out of your mouth. You swing the spit near my nose and lips, threatening as I struggle against you.

We do this every day for two years.

A dream

We are in your basement playroom, standing on the orange shag carpet near the box that holds your Barbies. Your arms are around me. We are kissing. Your lips are against mine, and it feels so good, Dodi.

Soon after the dream, I pick a fight with you, and we break up. I next see you three years later, at the beach. You wear a bikini; from the neck down, you look exactly like Veronica Lodge, only tan. A thin gold chain circles your ankle; I know you think, correctly, that this is sexy. Your skin gleams with suntan lotion. Your arm curls around the waist of a pimply boy with a crew cut and a large tattoo of an eagle. You tell me he is a Marine. I think his tattoo is a cliché; couldn't you find someone with a little imagination? I hate Marines forever after.

The year is 2001. I am twenty-nine to your thirty. For ten years, I have wondered about your pimply boyfriend: did you pet, did he stick his tongue in your mouth? Or was he just for show, Dodi? For ten years I have searched for your cat eyes and sleek curves in women's bars, dyke marches, AIDS rallies.

A fantasy

I walk into the professional women's piano bar on the Upper East Side, aware that I am underdressed in my jeans and green turtleneck. As my pupils stretch wide in the darkness, I count the Wall Street dykes leaning over whiskey sours, whispering corporate secrets into each other's ears. Then, I see you. In the far corner, you are tall, muscles crafted by a machine you probably own. You wear a brown skirt and a wool blazer. The top three buttons of your cream-colored silk blouse are undone; your breasts are brown and firm and tempting beneath the gleaming cloth. One of your hands holds a daiquiri; the other curls around a woman's waist. She is smaller than you, with tight blond curls, a short skirt, and seamed stockings. You hold her hip protectively, possessively. I imagine your hands wriggling up her skirt; imagine you pinning her down and licking her breasts, your sharp teeth glinting white as Dynamints. I want to flirt with her, just so you will punch me.

Do you see me? Did you ever see me? I stare across the room, begging your eyes to meet mine. For an instant, they do, and you put your drink down. But your face remains unchanged, a stone. You turn from me and part your lips against your Barbie-girl's neck.

Barbie's eyes half close, her plum lips half smile, and she pushes you away with her hand while she nudges her hips closer to you. You nuzzle your lips against her ear, whispering. And upon your word, Barbie stands. Now I see that she's small, with a short waist and compact breasts. Her eyes contain no questions, only devotion to you. You put your hand on the small of her back and propel her out of the bar. As you glide past me, you do not turn your head, do not acknowledge me. But I smell your command—*follow me.*

Now we are in the drizzly night. Your arm is around your Barbie-girl, but I sense you sensing me ten feet behind you. I know every hair on your body, Dodi. You turn down a dark street and enter a posh apartment building. The doorman opens the door for you, and I despair at the way you nod to him, as you did not to me. The door closes behind you, and I am alone on the street, rain trickling down my turtleneck. I will follow you, Dodi, as the hairs on your neck have reached out to me.

From the gutter, I look up and see you in a lit window, three floors above. Framed in the glow, you hand Barbie another drink, which she accepts, looking into your cat eyes. Dodi, I am cold in the street; I am alone when I want to be with you. I close my eyes, squeeze my wet fists, and breathe in sharply. I demand your closeness. And suddenly, I am lifted by an invisible hand. As smoothly as a girl transfers her doll from the carpet to the second floor of a dollhouse, I have glided to the fire escape outside your window. This iron scaffold, this cold, lit window, are mine to create. I know every hair on your body, Dodi.

Barbie sits on your couch; you hold a glass of red wine to her lips. She drinks obediently, as you want her to. I press my cheek against the flat glass of the window, imagining the curved glass between your warm hands. When Barbie drains the liquid, you refill it, and again pour it slowly into her mouth.

She has finished three glasses now, and you draw back. You say a word I cannot hear, and she stands for you, teetering slightly. She is as open to your inspection as a diagram on a page. Her legs are parted slightly; I imagine you imagining her moist pussy touching the warm air in the apartment. You take a step back and probe her with your eyes. I know you are contemplating the task before you: how will you conquer her this time? Will you grind your cunt against her chest and chin? Pin her down and hiss lies until she sobs with fear? Your face is stone. My breath fogs the glass. You could see me if you looked, but you do not need to look. You know I am here, rain cutting gullies in my home-cut hair. It was your hand that lifted me to this place.

And the wine is your hand inside her, coaxing warm compliance through her veins. You stand before her and slowly unbutton her blouse. Her eyes, half closed, slide to the window, and for a moment I imagine she sees me. But you do not want her to see me, Dodi, so her eyes unfocus, her mouth slides open, and she gasps as you reach inside her blouse. You reach for what you want, as casually as you once plucked a candy bar from my hand. Now you want her breasts in your hands, so you peel her blouse back to her shoulders.

Her bra is lacy, red; a delicate rosebud peeks from beneath the left strap. Your lovers still have clichéd tattoos, Dodi. I take smug satisfaction in this knowledge. You take her breasts in your hands, kneading them, squeezing her nipples. You look not at your hands but at her face, a landscape shaped by the pleasure and pain you control with your fingers. You pinch her; she winces. You stroke her; she melts deeper into your hands, where you pinch her again. The wine flows through her veins; she could not stop you, even if it occurred to her to try.

You remove her blouse, and she offers no resistance. I imagine the apartment's warm air swirling against her naked skin. You tease her, bite her shoulders, pinch her arms. She hangs her head and cries a little, but you do not cease your work. Now you grasp her waist from behind and whisper a command in her ear. She unzips her skirt, which falls to the floor as tears fall down her face. You whisper comforting words in her ear as you reach over—never loosening your grip on her waist—and remove the skirt from her ankles. Like a dazed colt, she steps each leg out of the skirt.

Your smile is hard as you contemplate her now. Her red panties match her bra; I imagine her wet pussy pressing against the cloth. As I suspected, her seamed stockings attach to red garters. You do not wait; still grasping her firmly from behind, you shove your hand against her mound. She gasps and rubs herself against your hand, trying to ride it. But you keep your hand high, crunching her pubic hair through the silk.

Suddenly, you spin her, throw her on the floor. You are on top of her now, licking her ferociously. You do not tease her with your tongue's sensitive tip; rather, you swipe the flat of your tongue over every inch of her exposed skin. You do not care if your tongue gives her pleasure. You are licking her because you choose to do so, because she is yours to mark and consume. I watch your rough tongue run equally over the reddened skin you pinched and the pale, newly exposed skin of her upper thighs. I watch you work your tongue beneath the straps of her bra and garters; then you chew them, stretching them out and releasing them to snap against her.

You are breathing hard with your exertion; I see sweat on your upper lip and imagine the moisture in your dark armpits. You are still fully dressed, and I know you will remain that way. But it doesn't matter, Dodi. I can imagine every inch of your skin with every muscle beneath it and every hair upon it. When your breasts, sheathed only by your thin blouse, swing inches above Barbie's face, I imagine them from the inside, nipples rubbing against your bra.

Now you're ripping off her garters, stripping her stockings, bra, and panties from her body. She's naked for you now, on all fours, moaning with anticipation. Again, you use one arm to grip her securely from behind. Without preliminaries, you drive your other fist into her cunt. You concentrate savagely as you pump her over and over. She screams like a siren; if I press my wet ear against the cold window, I can hear her faintly. She bucks against your fist, shuddering again and again. Finally, you are done, and you slide out your hand. You flip your gasping Barbie-girl on her back, where she collapses, slick and exhausted. Then, slowly, you undo one button from the middle of your blouse. You insert your right hand, wet from Barbie's cunt, into your own shirt. Slowly, you draw your nipple through the gap between the buttons. You bring this nipple to her lips, and allow her to kiss it—once. I am locked outside, sobbing in the rain.

The truth

Last week, my mother bumped into your mother at the post office. The news has reached me: you are married, pregnant, and have converted to Catholicism.

Dodi, do you pin your husband down, stretch his arms perpendicular in a mock crucifixion? Do you kneel on his shoulder sockets, rub your belly against his chest? Does he burrow in the miraculous crack between your breasts? Could he close his eyes and imagine every hair on your perfect skin? Does he buck beneath you, you beneath him? *Or is he just for show?*

Self-centered as a teenager, I imagine your marriage as one final meanness, another lie concocted to scare and thrill me.

Cleo's Back
Gwendolyn Bikis

When finally me and Sister Marla arrive at the outside prison parking lot, it is exactly twelve twenty-three; and we pull up to a booth and offer proof of who we are to a man whose elbows and arms—it's all I catch a look at before I look away—have the pink cooked look of an old dry piece of smoked ham meat.

"Drive in through the gate," he twangs, "and to the left, to the back of Module C."

I feel the air around me thin out as we drive through, and I gulp for breath: I am inside a prison. Marla hadn't said that I would have to come this far inside.

Marla sees me wipe my sweaty palms on my skirt and says, "We are not inside, Tammy. We just on the grounds around the outbuildings. They can't be kidnapping you out here."

"Ha, ha, ha," I say. She's making fun of my so-called softness once again.

We've driven 'round the back of Module C, an L-shaped building made of something looking like cement, painted in the moldy gray of old worn-out, packed-down street dirt. We park beside an opening in the wire fence that's surrounding us.

Marla turns the car off. "Wait here," she orders and opens up her door. As though I'm gonna move an inch out of this car. I know she's only giving orders 'cause real soon she's gonna have to take some—and taking orders disagrees with her digestion.

I give her Cleo's clothes, folded in a red-and-purple pile, and she gets out. I watch her as she walks in through the gate and stops to talk to a white guard who opens up the metal door into the building. Marla walks in, and the door slaps closed behind her.

I climb around the front seat to the back, where me and Cleo could sit together in some privacy—and, if she wanted to, Cleo could stretch out them long legs of hers.

I wait. And wait. And wait. Not wanting to look at the dashboard clock to see if I've been waiting long as it is feeling like—because it feels like half an hour. What if Cleo isn't—

But then the door opens, and Marla steps out, but then it's Cleo, coming out now with a shopping bag and duffel in her hands. And she's wearing her new clothes the way I wished for her to wear them: the red tank over top of the purple T-shirt, all tucked into her purple pedal pushers. Against the building's wall, the colors seem to pulse. And she's got her high-top Converse on. It is the sight of her old lucky shoes that breaks me up—I've missed those shoes so much; the happy sorrow fills my throat.

I step out the car, leaving the back seat open so she'll come back here. I offer to take her bag, to hide my face. "I got it, baby sis," she says.

Marla smiles at me, tightly, and walks back to the trunk, and Cleo sneaks a pat on the back of my neck. I bite my lips.

"Looking good, Cleo," I manage. How can she be looking this good, coming out of there? She's got the same sweet barber shop smell, the same strong body, her same old swagger.

It seems she's heard my thoughts, 'cause she looks at me, then stops to pose and pull an arm muscle. "Good Black is hard to crack," she says and grins.

We get into the car—me and Cleo in the back together, where we roll our windows down. Wisely, Marla doesn't say a word, although I think I catch a grunt or two.

"I like your hairstyle," I offer, admiring the tight sparkly curls that make her hair look sudsy soft.

She runs her hand across the top of her head as though it is her halo I've done complimented. "Thanks, baby sis," she smiles at me, "It's callt an S-curl. My girl Rita done it for me. It's the newest style in perms."

I feel my shoulders rise: who is "my girl Rita"? I am getting ready to ask just this, when Marla interrupts: "Well I've got news for you, Cool Cleo," she says, "Out here, that is one *an*cient-ass style."

"Hmm," Cleo says, so unimpressed. "Who cares? I *define* the style."

Marla frowns down toward the road in front of her. "Cleo needs to be paying more attention to what is *in* her head than what is *on* it," she says.

At the gate, we stop again, and Cleo rolls her window up and hums while the guard asks us to open up our trunk, like we've done sprung someone.

"SSShhiit," Marla hisses and climbs out to open it.

Cleo hums and looks out the window.

"Y'all have a pleasant evening," he says as Marla climbs back in the car.

"I wonder do they think they're serious when they say that?" Marla says as we drive through to freedom. Cleo rolls her window down again. She noisily lets go her breath. "I'm out of here like last year, " she says as she grins and flashes her front-tooth gap at me. I press my thighs together to control the sudden pulse between them.

Marla turns onto the road that leads to open country. "Have you been working on your math?" she asks Cleo.

"I'm up to trignomics in the book, but who's go' check it for me?"

"I'll get a tutor at the Girls' Club, and I want Tammy to be helping you with your reading and your writing."

Well, Lord knows I would love to help her with her reading and writing, but who could guarantee that's all that it would be, just studies? Certainly I can't.

"Now," Marla instructs, "I want you to stop for a minute and breathe deep and feel how good this feels—feel it when you get to thinking how it might be easier to be inside."

Cleo sucks her teeth. "Inside ain't easy." She looks out the window at the tree line. "Inside done made me hard."

"Let's get up off the truth now, Cleo. Inside done made you soft. You got a lot of proving of yourself to do to me."

Cleo tsks her teeth and jerks her legs back and forth.

I suddenly remember the giant box of Good 'n' Plenty I bought. I bring it out to sweeten up the moment, shaking it in rhythm like the Choo-Choo Charlie TV commercial, and I smile at her.

'Member those first kisses that you gave me, I am asking with my smile, 'member their taste of sweet black licorice? What I mean to be my meaning, without Marla getting in the middle, is that I want those Cleo kisses back. "Got some candy for you, Cleo," I say and open up the box to pour some in her hand.

Cleo grins down at her palm full of pink-and-white sweet pellets and puts them in her mouth—all of them at once—and chews. "Mmmm," she says and grins; and she is looking at my thighs. "I likes good 'n' juicy candy too," she whispers in my ear while Marla's too intent on checking her rear blind spot and changing lanes to notice us too closely. "You got you some of that?" Cleo asks me softly in my ear, "Got you good ' n' juicy?"

I love-slap her and shake my earrings. My nose is stinging with my held-in tears—I have missed her nastiness so much.

But then Marla, you know she has a sense when something that she disapproves of is taking place, even when she hasn't seen it, so she has to say, "You and Tammy can have your little visits on the weekends." As though she is Cleo's rightful, righteous mother. "I am laying down the conditions right now," she continues.

"Who are you, our mama?" I ask. My mama's passed away, and Marla hasn't filled her place, even if Marla was the one who raised me.

"Who you anyway, my po?" Cleo flares.

"I am your play-aunt," Marla answers, "and I've set you up with an officer that I personally know, and between us we are going to know what you are up to every woke or sleeping moment. You can't afford to blow this one now, Cleo."

I know I'm supposedly a part of this big plan…but me, all I want is just to slather warmed-up cocoa butter all over her back, her arms, the ropey training-school scars across her neck and shoulders; I want to kiss her throat. I want Marla to forget, just for a minute, about the worrisome little details of this parole plan. What Cleo needs, more than a vocation, a parole officer, a raise in reading scores, is love.

I want my sister to plug in her Isley Brothers so we can cruise back down to Charlotte inside some kind of happy groove, so I can smile at Cleo and dream of loving her all the whole way down. I want Marla to forget, just for a single second, that her loved ones could be snatched from her at any minute. I want her to forget that fear just long enough to *enjoy* her loved one's presence. Cleo's really back.

Marla's driveway's soft and squishy in the afternoon heat, and my sandals sink into it as I step out the car with Cleo's shopping bag in my hand. It is really *heavy*, and I look to see what is in it—math books and a big, thick dictionary.

"That bag too heavy for you, baby?" She's leaning over me. She's so close I feel her body heat, I feel my arm hairs rise as though a warm and furry breeze has blown across them, I feel my gaze go soft. I want her heat, her weight, on me; I want her thigh between mine. Thank goodness Marla's run up ahead of us to open up her door, because my breath has suddenly become very hard for me to catch, and an uncaught breath is very hard to hide.

Cleo takes the bag from me, and for a precious minute, her hand is holding mine. My first time touching her again is like touching thirst to water—for just a second.

Marla's finally noticed us. "Cleo!" she calls, from just inside the house, and Cleo steps away. I breathe, deep from my stomach, and straighten up my skirt and follow her.

In the living room, Marla points Cleo toward my room.

"You like it, Cleo?" I ask. "I fixed it up for you."

"Yes, I do," she says, and she pops a play-kiss on my cheek. She heaves her duffel bag up on the bed, and I see her biceps bunch and glide. I long to lay my palms along her gathered strength. When she notices my noticing, she grins.

"You've got mo' muscles, Cleo," is all that I can say. It's all that I can do to keep my hands still at my sides.

"I hit the pile a lot," she says.

"Huh?"

"That's jail talk. That means she lifted weights out in the yard." I jump a little, and then I turn around; of course Marla has done followed us all the way up into my bedroom. What made me think she wouldn't?

"Cleo," Marla says, and points at her. "Didn't Tammy tell you? Your auntie-dear is waiting for a visit from you."

Not right *now,* Marla, I almost say, though I bite my tongue before I do. Because if I do say it, Marla's going to insist—yes, right now. Right this red-hot minute.

"But you can relax a little if you want to first," Marla says. "I've got a ball game on the TV, so come on in here and have a sit-down. There's a can of Coke in the refrigerator, too."

Cleo sighs, rolls her eyes towards me, and plods heavily out to the living room.

Damn! Tears of pure frustration fill my eyes. I feel like beating on a wall. There goes my kiss, there goes my hug, there goes the love I have to give to her. Im'a have to drive back home tonight and go back to my teaching tomorrow, and Marla knows that she can hold me off until it's time for me to leave.

The game is boring, with UNC-C losing to State with a score so high it's getting to be embarrassing. I hate to see teams lose by lots and lots of points; it makes me feel sorry for them. They look so tired, galomping and galomping up and down the ball court even though they know they've lost.

Cleo's on the couch, scrunched so low her chest is only 'bout six inches higher than her sliding, swinging knees. That is one thing I'd forgotten about Cleo, how she never, ever will sit still, how she'll always be tapping, rocking, shifting, swaying as though it is her body that keeps her mind in gear, helps her keep her focus. She reaches for her can of Coke and slurps on it. Cleo's known for no home training, so I only squinch a little bit, trying to pretend that I don't care.

A commercial for a sports drink comes on, and Marla stands up from her easy chair. "I'm on my way up to the Eckard's for a new pair hose. Y'all want anything?"

Cleo lifts her can and shakes it. "'Nother can of Coke," she says.

Marla frowns. "Who you talkin' to like that? Get your own damn Coke." And she walks out the room.

One second later, when she comes back in, we have already turned toward each other; our hands are almost touching. "Im'a only be a minute," Marla warns. "That is all. Just one minute."

We wait until the front door slams before we move into a hug and then into a kiss, with Cleo's hands both on my neck, pulling me closer, deeper, and her tongue, yes, spicy with that Good 'n' Plenty, is moving in and out inside my mouth. I moan and come up for some breath. "Cleo. Let me fix you lunch," I say because I feel we really shouldn't be getting nothing started, it is just too frustrating, and fixing lunch for her is almost just as satisfying to me—for right now.

Cleo groans and rolls her eyes again; this time up towards the ceiling. "Country," it sounds as though she mumbles, but I ignore it. Call me country, I don't care—I know it is more easy to pry myself away from Cleo than it is from Marla's oversight.

So I walk out to the kitchen, and after a few minutes, Cleo follows me. I reach in the breadbox for the whole-wheat loaf and put two slices in the toaster. I poke my head into the refrigerator and pull out mayonnaise and bacon. Tomatoes on the windowsill, cheese inside the dairy bin. I close the refrigerator door, open up the bacon package and lay three long strips along the skillet, already shiny with fresh grease. By now, the scent of toast is filling up the room, and Cleo's sitting in the chair behind me—I can smell her hair dress.

"What you want on it, Cleo?"

I turn a little, and I thought I knew just where she was, but I didn't know she was right directly up behind me. Pressing her...you know...up against my behind. I feel a wetness spread inside my drawers. I reach behind me and...the back door opens.

Cleo moves away. "I wants lots of mayonnaise and a slice of that there cheese," she says in a somehow-normal voice as Marla walks into the kitchen with a plastic bag. She reaches in the bag and hands Cleo a can of Coke.

"Thank you," Cleo grunts.

"You are welcome," Marla answers.

"No lettuce?" I ask, amazed at how even my voice sounds. "No tomatoes?"

Cleo makes a face. "Nuh, uh. No."

"You still don't like you any vegetables?" Marla asks.

Cleo screws a tighter face. "They didn't give us none in there."

"That's how you know you need them. When'd they ever give you what is good for you?" Marla turns to go out to the living room.

The bacon snaps and sizzles. I turn it over, and the toast pops up. I pull a plate out of the cupboard, throw the hot toast down with just my fingertips, and reach to open up the mayonnaise. I smooth it over the toast, slice a tomato anyways, slice some cheese, drop the bacon on two paper towels, pat the grease away, lay the three strips on the toast, and close it all up like a sandwich. Cooking calms my nerves like nothing else.

"Here, Cleo." I turn to hand the plate to her, and she's grinning at me, has been grinning this whole time, lying back and slowly flapping both her knees. She rolls her tongue into the gap between her two front teeth, and my throat catches.

I put the plate in front of her, and she reaches for the sandwich and begins to eat.

At my elbow, Marla's telephone rings. "Get that for me, baby sis?" Marla calls in from the bathroom.

I pick it up, and know, by all the background noise, that I'm talking to a pay phone.

"Marla Moore?" Behind the voice, a siren wails.

"May I ask who wants to speak to her?"

"This is Johnetta Harper. I'm calling from the emergency."

One of Marla's clients. "Here she is, right now," I say, as Marla walks into the kitchen drying her hands in a towel.

She takes the call into the living room and stays on as long as it takes for Cleo to finish up her sandwich and ask me if we got some snack cakes.

I ought to tell her we got Moon Pies, like the country peoples that she knows we is. I am getting ready to say this, but

Marla's back here in the kitchen with the phone hung up and her bag and car keys already in her hand. "I need to see about Miz Harper's daughter." She puts the phone back on the counter and is already halfway out the door.

"Cleo," she points, on her way out, "Go and see your auntie." And she is gone so quickly that I can't help but think—forgive me, Lord—that this emergency is nothing but a blessing to me.

Cleo's more than grinning now. She is smiling so wide I have no trouble seeing her tongue caught in between her two front teeth. "Zippity-doo-dah, zippity day," she sings, dancing her fingers happily across the table top.

I giggle.

"How long you think she'll be gone?"

"If I'm remembering right, Miz Harper is the one with the daughter who was having pregnancy complications."

Cleo smiles and rolls her tongue again. "That means we got *hours.*" She spreads her legs; she opens up her arms. She slaps her crotch, and I feel my blush creep over my body. I feel how hot this kitchen is.

"Let's go into my room, Cleo," I say and grab her hand.

"Yo' room? I thought that you was giving it to *me.*"

"I am, but for right now, it's mines again."

"Meaning we playing house like Tamara want it played." She drops her arms. "Okay…I can stand to go that way."

I pull her up behind me, pull her to my room.

I take her hand and lead her to the bed.

"Nuh, uh," I hear her grunt.

I reach over and kiss her, right on the corner of her lips. "Come on…baby." I whisper that last, that "baby," 'cause I know that she ain't really ready for it. Not *yet.*

I squeeze her hand, and this time it's me pushing her down on *my* bed. I gives a tiny push, so that now she's sitting, and she puts her hands on my arms that are wrapping round her, like she's almost getting ready to maybe pull me off. I kiss her jaw, and she sets back to look at me with confused amusement drawing up her forehead.

She pulls my arms away, moves her hands down to my hips, and down some more, and gives a squeeze. "You ain't go' try and flip it on my ass now, is you?"

I give a little "tsk," and say what Marla says, "That is jail talk, Cleo."

"You ain't answering my question," she replies.

"You gonna have to let me touch you." I reach my lips toward her cheek and taste the velvety skin there, just where her two lips begins to plump to fullness.

She pulls back again to look at me. "Okay, baby," she says, and she's laughing like am I really up to this?

So I put my arms all around her, hold her like her mama oughta, hold her like I ought to have myself, long ago. I'm so glad to have her back; I'm so grateful to my older sister for getting Cleo back for me. My face is warming up with held-back tears, so I just let them go.

My warm rain is falling on her shoulder, and she reaches up to stroke my hair. "Nobody never cried for me," she says, in a small and distant voice; and she sounds so surprised.

And anyways, it isn't true—it's just that all the tears I'd cried for her, she'd never known about. They'd all been shed in my lonely midnight bed, into my bitter pillow, far away from her in prison.

I turn my head to kiss her cheek, and it is completely dry.

"She lacks the capacity to cry," Marla's always said, but I never could believe it.

I feel her squirm, but I make her lie back, and I cover her up with my love. Everyone at home has always, in all ways, loved me. Im'a show her what that feels like.

And if Marla were to ask me, What'd you do with Cleo last night, Im'a tell her:

We danced to "Smokey's Cruisin'"; we swayed and slow danced down to the bed where we undressed each other. I rubbed her over, slow, with warm cocoa butter till she shone like polished darkwood. She moaned, and my tongue went everywhere—yes *there*—while her hands tightened, twisted, through my hair. She moaned, and shook and heaved with what I recognized was dry crying.

Denouement
River Light

I undress and slip under the covers. The familiar feel of her flannel sheets caresses my skin, and as I burrow beneath the covers, the smell of wool and the musk scent that she wears invokes waves of memory. I can feel the tears prickling behind my eyes, before I force my mind away from the past, away from the future, and bring it back to now, to this moment.

I can hear her moving in the bathroom, turning off the shower. I imagine her standing in front of the mirror, running her fingers through her short wet hair. She will be inspecting her face while she brushes her teeth. The towel will be wrapped around her waist, and there will still be droplets of water on her shoulders and breasts.

I hear the water shut off. Then she is standing next to me, her skin looking even more tanned in the flickering light of the candles. For an instant I think I might shatter if she touches me, but I push that too from my mind and wait, frozen. It is no longer possible for me to reach out to her, and she knows this. She stands, looking down at me. She does not smile, but she does not have to.

"Let me see you."

I push the blankets from my body, my skin prickling at the almost tangible caress of her eyes.

"Put your hands above your head, spread your legs."

I do; the sticky lips of my cunt peeling apart for her. My breasts, belly, ribs feel vulnerable and exposed.

"Close your eyes."

And I do, aware now of the sound of her breathing, the cool touch of the air on my skin. I have lain like this for her, vulnerable and open, more times then I can count, and still my body responds—my skin tingles, warm with excitement.

"Don't move."

She reaches out for me but does not touch. Her open palms are so close to my skin that I can feel their heat. Her hands know me so very intimately, yet have never become blurred with familiarity. They move slowly along my body, tantalizingly close. Up my thighs, cupping the air above my bush, then moving on, brushing a single hair, sending shock waves through my cunt. She moves up my belly, over my breasts—my nipples grow hard in anticipation. When she finally touches me, it is to reach out and cup my face in her hand, tracing the line of my cheekbone with her thumb.

"What do you want?"

I flush red. It does not matter how many times she asks me this, it is still just as hard to answer. I try to turn my head away, but she holds me still, fingers around my jaw.

"Look at me!"

My eyes fly open.

"Tell me."

I know she will not touch me until I've spoken, but I squirm, feeling it impossible to get the words past my lips. She waits: patient, still, strong. Her eyes say she wants me, but I know from experience how great is her self-control.

I try to speak, stumble, try again, and manage a whispered, "I want you to fuck me." My body is burning, there is a touch of a smile on her lips.

"I can't hear you, slut. Tell me what you want. Tell me exactly what you want. Convince me."

"Please," I manage, my voice a little louder. "Please. I need to feel you. I need you to fuck me. I want your fingers in my cunt. I need you, please, I need you." I stop then, unable to continue, the edge in my voice a little too close to the surface. But she's heard it, and her face softens. She reaches for me, sooner then usual, and draws me into her soft embrace, into her strong arms. Her hand moves down my body, pressing into me, kneading my flesh.

The towel slips from her hips as she pushes her fingers into my cunt and her tongue into my mouth. I keep my arms and legs wide, but cannot stop myself from moving, from thrusting toward her, reaching for the depths of her mouth, the length of her fingers. Now, in her urgency, she reveals her passion. Her arms tighten around me, pin me to her. Her teeth find my neck, and she bites, just hard enough to catch my breath, to create seconds of stillness. Her fingers become more demanding as she reaches toward my core, exploring me, opening me. Then her thumb slips in next to her fingers, and in one exquisite movement she pushes her hand into me, her fingers curling into a fist under my heart. My breath catches in an almost-scream as I fold into her, curl around her fist and into the circle of her arms. I am consumed by her; she is all around me, and she fills me. Her fist moves, and I feel her presence in every cell of my body.

She hurts me just enough to sweeten the pleasure to almost beyond bearing, and when I come I lose myself, forget where I end and the world begins.

After, her cheeks are wet with tears as she holds me. I had not expected this. My face is dry. I have shed all my tears lying in my own bed, shaking with the agony of loss.

"I love you," she says and I believe her, knowing it to be true. This woman, who has made the decision to pledge herself, exclusively, to another, loves me.

"Thank you," I whisper.

Thank you for the gift of consciousness, of awareness. To be so lucky as to know it to be the last time, so that we can hoard the memory of each glorious touch, of every word. So that we can say goodbye in this most intimate of ways.

"I'm sorry." Her voice is gentle, loving. I slip into sleep, treasuring the feel of her arms around me.

A Girl Like That

Toni Amato

She's the kind of girl who brings out the worst in me. Coming on hip and cool and all into sex, rubbing some part of herself all up against some part of me every chance she gets. I'm not saying all the things my people taught me about women are so great, but I'll tell you what, where I come from, that kind of girl is called a cock teaser.

It's like there's this small thing, like those stars they talk about, those White Dwarves, sitting deep and low in my belly, and this girl comes along, doing her number, and that son of a bitch just goes nova.

She makes the worst part of me want to do the best it knows how to teach her a thing or two about fucking. A thing or two she thinks she knows all about, but doesn't have a goddamn clue. I know these middle-class types real well. See, it's like they think they got the nasty down pat, 'cuz maybe they've done it with a couple dozen different folks, in a couple dozen different ways, and they're like, liberated, you know, cutting-edge perverts.

And this girl, I can tell she's got a thing for hillbillies, biker trash, rough trade. Or at least, she thinks she does. She's read a couple of books, seen a couple of movies, and now she thinks she wants herself a roll in the hay with one of them low-class types. 'Cuz we're "such animals in bed."

But she don't know from animal, except for that one time someone made her take it on all fours. All cosmetics and watching themselves in the mirror, thinking how naughty they are or, what's that big word the college girls use? Oh yeah, transgressive.

Makes me want to teach her another thing or two she hasn't picked up yet, give her a couple of real life lessons—not all prettied up and theoried up. Couple of lessons she won't forget but won't be in such a hurry to brag about, either. Because it's all about control for her, all about another notch in her lipstick case.

But it ain't gonna be that way, when I get a piece of her. It ain't gonna be that way, 'cuz I'm gonna take all of her, and let me tell you, I know that girl ain't got a fucking clue what it really means to be taken. She don't know what they say, where I grew up, about how if you roll around with a pig, you end up dirty. That's what she likes to think her sex is, and that's what I'm gonna make her really feel like. Dirty.

Gonna get her alone, somewhere, don't care where, as long as she can make all the noise she needs to, as long as she can holler and scream and pound the walls. Gonna call her damn hand.

'Cuz I know that all it's gonna take is me looking at her a little longer, next time she starts that shit, just me holding her eye a little harder. See, she's sure she can get what she wants, whenever she wants in. Thing is, sometimes you got to be careful what you wish for.

Want to take that girl and slam her up against a wall, kiss her till her lips are raw, and till she's hoping I'll let her come up for air. Maybe make her bleed, a little, and get that good taste of blood in my mouth. Want to see her eyes get wide and wild and maybe a little not so certain what she's in for. Want to feel her teeth rattling against mine.

Want to suck spit out of her mouth, then give it on back to her, start right off pushing at her edges.

Want to rip her shirt off the way she thinks I'm supposed to do, on account of how hot she makes me. Wreck the damn hundred-dollar thing she went and asked me how'd I think she looked in it, when what she really wanted was to see if I was thinking how'd she'd look out of it. Then I'm gonna show her my knife, the one I've had since I was a kid, the one I've used to skin deer. Gonna tell her all about it, too, while I trace it down her, neck to belly. Tell her how you do it fast and deep, like, while the blood's still warm.

Then she's gonna be wondering what the hell she got herself into. She's maybe played with knives before—the pretty, shiny kind that ain't no good for nothing but show. But us hillbillies, we use tools, things you got to have to get the job done right.

I want to push that short skirt she's been waggling around in up over her hips and run my knife along the edges of her panties. If she's even got panties on. Want to tell her how much I like to see it all shiny with pussy juice. Gonna cut the crotch right out, quick and clean, and leave her with a cool breeze blowing on her. Slap the flat side up against her bush, run the handle up in between her lips, maybe even let her clit feel how sharp I keep it. Wanna watch her try to crawl up that wall.

And when she starts in like that, trying to get that sharp thing away from her tender spots, I'm gonna put one hand around her throat, gonna use the other one to put my knife between her teeth and tell her to hold it there. Tell her she's got an awfully pretty face and she ought to be careful. Gonna lift that girl up and pin her against my hips. She's small enough for it. Gonna push up against her so she knows what I got in my pants. Gonna make sure she knows how hard I am for her, gonna tell her my balls are hurting and she's damn well gonna do something about it.

Get her up against a wall like that, I'm gonna have her cute little ass sitting in my hands. That skirt, and the way she's been walking around in it was supposed to make someone like me wanna fuck that ass. And I do. But first I'm gonna work it. Gonna fill my hands up with her asscheeks and work it, while I grind into her, dry humping, biting at her tits. I'm gonna suck those tits like candy, like I'm the hungriest man alive. Pull some of that soft skin in between my teeth and leave her a mark or two to remember me by.

I ain't gonna stop till I feel her go limp, till I can tell that she's gonna need my help standing up. Play with her clit long enough till it feels like it's gonna burst, with her ass till it's making those little kissing moves. I ain't gonna stop till it's the last thing she wants me to do.

Then I'll let that girl fall. Hard. Let her fall to her knees and take a good look at the front of my jeans. Maybe she'll still be trying to be cool, then, but it won't be that way much longer. Gonna take my belt off and tie her hands together, behind her back. Gonna make her undo my button fly with her teeth. Bet she knows, how, too, a girl like that. Gonna make it hard for her, pushing up against her face till her back hits the wall again, till she has to keep her balance by leaning against my cock.

Then I'll take it out for her. Let her see what she's been toying with. Maybe slap her on the face a few times. With my cock. Tell her all about how that's her new best friend and how she damn well better make him happy. How being teased makes him kind of cranky. Run my thumb along her lips, pushing up under them and along her teeth. Nice teeth. Hate to see anything bad happen to them.

Wanna see her lipstick get smeared all along my cock, wanna see her lips get wide and full. Bet she gives damn fine head, a girl like that. Bet she never had anyone fuck her mouth till she gagged. Bet for all her selling herself as some new Linda Lovelace, she never woke up with the back of her throat sore.

Gonna let her suck me off till I'm almost there, till I'm where, if I were a real boy, I'd be coming in her face. Kind of wish I could, too. Wish I could see it running down her chin just so I could wipe it away and tell her how good she is, doing a good cop–bad cop mind fuck on her. Girl like that, you got to work at keeping her off balance, got to pull a trick or two on her to make her realize she ain't seen everything, yet.

Then I'm gonna put my knife right up under the softest part of her jaw and tell her she better stop. Pull my cock out slow and rub it all over her face, make it all shiny and slick. Tell her how pretty she is.

Gonna pull her up by her hands and spin her around. Take the belt off her and wrap it around my fist. Slap the end up against her pussy and make her lick it clean. Then I'm gonna wrap it around her neck, just tight enough to make her think. Gonna twist my hand away, making it hard for her to breathe, and tell her to bend over, tell her to reach down and spread that ass for me. Gonna tell her she better hope she got it good and wet, 'cuz I'm ready for a ride. Make her brace her hands against the wall and step in, wrapping my hands around her stomach, pulling her up against me. Gonna go so deep, she feels my jeans against her ass.

Yeah, girl like that makes me want to fuck her down and dirty, slow and deep and long enough to make my brain take a vacation. Want to fuck her till all I see is red, all I hear is my cock pumping in and out of her. I want to take her breath away from her and just long enough to make her struggle, feeling how she moves on me, then let her go, fucking her in time with the way she's gonna be gasping for air.

And I'm gonna save the best for last. Gonna save that sweet little asshole till I feel her pussy clamping down on me, till I feel her thigh muscles start to shake. Gonna wait till I know she's almost there. That's when I'll step back a little, pull her away from the wall, push her head down so she's bent over with her ass up in the air. That's when I'm gonna take her, for real, because there ain't nothing like feeling all of a big old cock working its way in to make a girl give it up. And that's what I'm gonna do, gonna make that girl give it all up to me, like she ain't never done before. Gonna stand there with my boots on and slide my cock into her sweet ass and out again till I know she's feeling every goddamn inch of it. Ain't gonna give it to her proper till she begs.

And I guaren-damn-tee she will. Because I'm gonna be that girl's back door man. Gonna fuck that sweet ass of hers until we both get to grunting and hollering and doing it nasty like she ain't never had it before. Till she don't know up from down from sideways and I got her heartbeat right there in the palm of my hand. 'Cuz a girl like that brings out the best in me.

Convince Me
Gitana Garofalo

The bar is usually too straight for my taste, but Rickie pours a generous drink, and I enjoy watching bikers of any persuasion—their rolling gait, the way they wear leather like a second skin. I transform the bikers into silver-haired butches to make my mouth water. The nearest lesbian bar is two hours away in a small college town. Here at least I can see people over forty and feel like I'm back in the city at my old bar.

"Hey Rickie, how's it going?" I call out as I take my usual seat at the end of the bar.

"Not so good. Those guys who were supposed to finish the bathroom two weeks ago have only finished the sink."

"That's all they've done?"

"They put the toilet in but haven't hooked it up yet. Everyone has to either piss in the parking lot or haul their ass next door to the motel," she says as she fixes my drink and sets it down in front of me on a thin white square of napkin.

Shifting on my barstool, I survey the dim smoke-filled room. Garish neon beer signs on the walls wash a brief patch of color over nearby faces. The light is a little brighter in back where lamps hang over two pool tables. I look around, my glance is thorough but noncommittal. The place is getting crowded, but there's no one interesting.

Then you walk in. I watch. You make your deliberate way to a booth in the back. You must be just passing through town because I'd have certainly noticed you. I see coiled languor and legs that go on and on. Leaning back against the dark green vinyl of the booth, you spread your long legs open and rest a careless hand high on your inner thigh, as if you had a million dollars tucked between your cock and cunt. Your body, like your boots and jeans, is worn but well cared for, and I can almost smell your leather jacket.

Looking away from you, I catch Rickie's eye and grin. I finish my drink before glancing back at you. I'm surprised to see a silver dog collar. It rides snug and low on your neck, a nice contrast to the dark green hanky flagging the left back pocket of your jeans. Provocative. So, are you a boy bottom or a Daddy Top this evening? You have my attention and know it. Meeting my eyes boldly, you look at me for a long moment before glancing away to inspect the rest of the bar. I take advantage of the pause to wave Rickie over and tell her that I'm buying for the butch in the corner. *I'll show you who's the Top tonight, boy.*

"And make sure that he knows that I'm the one buying," I add. Rickie winks. She loves drama.

I keep my back to you but am hyper aware of everything. I rehearse how I'll move toward you, the swing of hips under my miniskirt, the whisper of thighs encased in smooth black stockings, the stretch and pull of garters, long salt-and-pepper hair falling down my back, and nipples—hard and hungry under my leather jacket—leading the way. When Rickie gets back from serving your drink she lights a cigarette and gets ready to watch the show.

Leaning on the bar, over the carved initials and devotions of others, I meet your eyes in the mirror. You hold my gaze for a minute, then capitulate. I wait a moment or two longer before throwing a crisp twenty-dollar bill down on the counter and standing up. I make my unhurried way to the back of the bar; all of me moving in concert under fabric and leather. I pause at your booth only long enough to glance down imperiously before continuing on my way. It doesn't matter that the toilet isn't hooked up yet. The bathroom will do just fine.

I ignore the Out of Order sign on the door which isn't locked and swings inward. Perfect. I pull the door to, but don't close it completely. The bathroom is fairly large, about six-by-five feet. The light switch is located behind the door, but with the lights from the motel next door illuminating the room through a small frosted glass window, I decide that more light isn't necessary. Slipping out of my jacket, I set it aside, smooth my hair back over my shoulders, and wait.

You don't take long. Once inside, you pause. You're confused. Good.

"Lock the door," I say, soft and nasty. You obey, fumbling as you click the lock into place. "Spread eagle against the door," I hiss. You hesitate for a fraction of a second. "Now, asshole!" I bark, thrusting you against the door and giving you a quick body search. I don't need light to find the switchblade in your back pocket. Next I run one of my hands up along the inside of your leg and over your basket—hard and full. How delicious. I wonder what color dildo you prefer, basic black or perhaps you're a drag queen at heart and have a cock of gold or silver glitter. I draw my hand out from between your legs, dragging my fingertips along your crotch from front to back, cock to ass. You're already damp, and I can smell the salty tang of your excitement.

"You walked into this bar like you're carrying a gold mine between your legs, so I just had to see for myself what you've got down there. You going to be my million-dollar man tonight, baby?"

"Lady, if that's what you want, I..." you start to say, your voice ragged.

"Shut the fuck up! Did I say you could speak?"

"No, Ma'am," you answer quickly, pressing your face into the door.

"I thought not," I reply as I spin you around to face me. "Just because I'm shorter than you doesn't mean that I'm nicer. Got that?"

"Yes, Ma'am," you say, eyes cast carefully down.

"Good. I was afraid I might be stuck with a stupid bottom," I snap. This is my first chance to take you in up close. I can smell you—dampness from the rain outside, cigarette smoke from the bar, and your own odor mixed with a scent of aftershave and freshly laundered clothing. I remember that you favored your left leg when you came into the bar and so discard my original plan to have you down on your knees. Thoughtfully I draw my forefinger down your chest, over your belt, and along the length of your cock swelling urgently against the snug denim of your jeans. You stand perfectly still—eager, yet quiet—and wide open in a way that few are at the beginning. It feels like we've played together before, like you already know what I like.

"Q and A time," I inform you crisply, stepping back and crossing my arms over my chest. "My toys are clean, and I'm negative. I don't intend to stop this scene, but I do expect to know what I'm working with."

"I've tested negative and play as safe as possible, Ma'am," you respond.

"Very well. Hand over your switchblade."

The words have barely left my lips when you're pulling the knife from your back pocket and handing it to me without once raising your eyes. This show of experienced submission combined with your ability to anticipate what I want sends me. My stomach drops into my shoes and my nipples clench. *I'm going to beat you for knowing me so well and then fuck you for the same reason.*

"A well-trained boy I see. Now, take off your jacket and sit on the toilet facing me." You neatly fold your jacket and set it on the floor by the door before sitting down.

"Bend forward." Again you comply almost before I'm done speaking, putting your hands behind your back and spreading your legs, this time humbly.

"You're being such a good boy, but I'm still going to mess you up," I say as I walk over to you. I don't want to touch you just yet, but I can't resist getting closer—drawn to you where you wait with every nerve on end, focused on me.

"Do you want to be here?" I ask, leaning over so that we're almost touching. I speak quietly into your ear. I want you as aching and hungry for me as I am for you.

"Yes, Ma'am," you respond with alacrity.

"Are you here freely for my pleasure? Yes or no?" I murmur, almost touching the outer edge of your ear with my lips, making your body tense up and a groan escape. I love to ask a second time, to double check, to torture.

"I'm here to please you, Mistress."

"Then grab your goddamn ankles!" I snap. Startled, you hasten to obey. I reach down your back with one hand to where your black T-shirt is neatly tucked into the waistband of your jeans. Yanking hard, I pull it up and almost over your head and rake what little nails I have up your back. My nails are too short to do any real damage. Having found out early on that my small hands are a plus, I always keep my nails filed down to nothing. I make up for it by bearing down hard on you as I drag my hand over your skin. You're silent except to inhale, breathing deeply into my hand and embracing the sensation.

"You're turning me on just by breathing," I tell you. "I wish that I could take more time with you."

"Thank you, Mistress," you whisper.

"Close your eyes and face the wall," I reply.

Clicking open your knife I test the sharpness of the blade with my thumb. Knives are my favorite tool, so mysterious and neat, especially those with hidden blades unfolding into biting edges. Knives, so much more interesting and intelligent than guns, require physical contact and demand something from the person at either end of the blade. I stand over you, my chest tightening as it always does before I cut, and rest the tip of the blade against the bare skin of your back. Your skin ripples like a horse fending off flies. You'll have to do more than that to get rid of me.

"Count."

"Yes, Ma'am."

Time stops as you spread yourself out beneath me. I think of Gauguin boasting that he painted with his prick and see the knife in my hand as a cock that we've created together—a passionate brush to make you bleed and come, to change a part of you, and me, forever.

"I'm going to fuck you up so bad," I whisper lovingly and draw the blade across the skin to the right of your spine.

"One," you say, drawing a deep breath as I watch the tiny bubbles emerge in the wake of the blade. I feel the blood inside you racing up to meet the knife and have to fight the urge to run my tongue along that trail and taste you. Instead, I sweep the blade down and add another line below and roughly parallel to the first.

"Two." This time I pause, assessing your breathing and running my hand over your arms before cutting again.

"Three." Pause. "Four." Now I'm riding high—aware of the entire bar—Rickie emptying ashtrays behind the counter, someone sinking the eight ball, a young woman hitching up the bra strap that the man next to her will soon be easing off her shoulder in a motel room.

"Five." I barely give you a moment to catch your breath before quickly adding a matching set of five horizontal lines to the left of your spine.

"Just to keep you balanced," I tell you and note with pleasure that you forgot to count them. I smile, five perfect reasons for punishment later.

The sight of your blood races straight to my cunt. Suddenly I know that I'm taking you home to put my collar around your neck, mark your ass with my three-sided cane, and slowly fuck the ridges and welts on your back and buttocks—those horizontal lines dividing you into ten even sections. You're my venetian blind. I'm going to twist you open to see what's on the other side. *What do you have in there, boy?*

Without a word, I impatiently push you up into a sitting position and yank your shirt down. You watch as I wipe the blade with your hanky and close it before handing the knife back to you.

"Stand up," I order and back you against the wall. I hold your eyes with mine as I begin to tease your cock with one hand while slipping the other under my own skirt.

"You want more of me, baby?" I ask, panting a little as I rub my clit just enough to bring me to the edge. This is where I love to be, on the brink—swollen, urgent, and yet possessing all the time in the world. Wordless, you nod eagerly as I firmly knead your dick, my hand matching the rhythm of your hips. I pull my other hand from between my legs and use my damp palm and fingers to cover your mouth and nose. I alternate between smothering you and giving you trickles of air laden with the scent of my pussy—a scent that you must draw into your throat, lungs, blood, heart. You're now plunging into my hand, hips dipping down and forward to meet my fingers. I slide my other hand off your mouth, releasing your harsh gasps, and hold you against the wall as I continue to wind your body impossibly tight and then tighter. You surprise me, not by the way you come in a series of jagged peaks of movement and sound, but by the following implosion of your body—a melting that almost causes me to lose my grip on you.

Pressing my hands against your shoulders, my heart is in my mouth as I stare up into your face so raw and open. It's been a long time since I've met a butch who was man enough to be touched, let alone fucked, like this. I don't move a muscle as I wait for your breathing to slow and your eyes to focus on me.

"You think you can handle more of this?" I ask, my hands still pinning you to the wall. You look at me for a long moment as if you know all about the collar, the cane, my hunger. You finally respond by slowly bowing your head. I didn't realize that I'd been holding my breath. Exhaling makes me feel light headed and high.

"In that case, darling," I respond, stepping away and heading for the door, "you'll need to collect my things, meet me at my car, and convince me to take you home."

There's a pause and then a rush of air as you slam me against the door so hard that I lose my breath.

"Don't you dare talk to your Daddy that way," you hiss in my ear. Flipping me around to face you, you secure both of my wrists over my head and roughly kick my feet apart, separating my legs so wide that my skirt rides up my thighs.

"Well, now we're playing by *my* rules," you smile as you slip your free hand between my legs, over my stockings, and on up to my pussy. You find me far beyond the preliminary stages of wet and so hungry that I try to force myself down onto your fingers. You pull them out of reach, laughing. Then, abruptly silent and furious, you wrench my arms even further upwards, pinioning my wrists so tightly that tears well up in my eyes.

"Go ahead and cry. I like that," you say. I look up at you, my shoulders and wrists aching, my eyes full of tears. Then, as if to take the sting out of your words, you rub first two, then three fingers along the length of my cunt. "No panties?" you say in surprise. Tears spill down my cheeks as I squeeze my eyes closed in pleasure and the vain attempt to hold still. I sigh, but then, just as quickly, cry out when, without warning, you force four fingers up into me. Then you pull your fingers out just as fast, leaving me unsatisfied and ajar.

"You think that you want Daddy now? You haven't seen anything yet," you say before slapping me, first on one cheek and then the other. My ears ring from your blows, and I can smell my pussy juices on your hand, on my cheek. "That's for teasing me. You think that just because you leave your panties at home and lead me back here, I'm going to take you with me?" You suddenly release my arms which have begun to tingle and step back to look me over, as if noticing me for the first time and not liking what you see. Mortified, I'm at a loss for words.

"It's up to you to convince Daddy that it's worth his while to take *you* home," you tell me. This immediately loosens my tongue.

"Oh, please, Daddy," I implore. "Don't leave me behind. I don't want anyone else, but you." I try to keep my voice calm yet seductive. I want to bottom for you as well as you did for me but fear I'm failing when you simply stare at me impassive and unimpressed. I take a deep breath and try again, "I can be whatever you want—the one you've always dreamed of—shy or hungry, scared or horny, resisting or insatiable, surprised or always ready. Oh, please."

"I don't believe you mean it," you say and turn to the door.

Desperate, I fall to my hands and knees. Arching my back to raise my ass in the air I get between you and the door and fervently lick your boot. The contours of your foot under my tongue combined with the sudden brush of air on my pussy makes me moan, but I don't stop. You're silent except to order me to do your other boot as well. I comply and am finally rewarded when you bury your hand in my hair pulling my head slightly back.

"Not bad," you say thoughtfully and then add, "get my coat. We're leaving."

"Yes, Daddy," I reply, quickly getting to my feet and retrieving your jacket before following you out the door.

Just wait until I get my hands on you, boy.

Black Vinyl
M R Daniel

When I first started doing erotica readings, women who didn't really know me came up afterwards and said, "Gurl, I had no idea! I always thought you were such a good girl." They would do a mildly tortured-looking Pollyanna grin on the "good girl" part. "Now you acting all wild, reading about fucking in all these different positions. Damn!"

Then they would call out to a friend, "Hey girl, can you believe that was Cecelia up there?"

Poised to put in her two cents, the friend would cock her head, "Okay?! I was on the edge of my seat—I just couldn't believe my eyes!"

Then girlfriend number one would counterpoint with, "You remember when she first moved here? She was so quiet and proper acting!"

Girlfriend number two parried back with, "Didn't I *say* I almost didn't recognize her?!"

It was like being at a family reunion, trapped between two aunts who since time immemorial had been dueling over who was the first on the scene at your most vulnerable or humiliating moment:

"Well, I was there when she was delivered, first baby in the family born bald as an ape's behind!"

"Well, I was the one who helped her when she had her first period and bled through her drawers while we were opening up the Christmas presents."

"Oh, please, everybody was there for that, but I was the one who drove her to her first dance and saw her get her first kiss from that Eric-what-was his-name-isn't-he-in-the-army-now? Cecelia you and him coulda made some pretty babies."

"Don't listen to her Cecelia girl. Now, he does have a sister...."

The only relief is in the recognition—often just before you de-evolve into a state of twelve-year-old, preteen humiliation—that you're just this moment's fuel for a verbal duet that began long before you were born.

But at least these two sistahs were ready to believe I might truly be the person they saw on stage. *My* friends acted like the cousins who expect you to still be the goofy one years after the end of adolescence (not to say goofy is bad, I can get behind a goofy-sexy woman—she's not afraid to fall off a table and stay on the floor to get you on your knees.) In my family, cousins cultivate the spoken read like nobody's business, emulating the verbal sparring they saw around the holiday tables of their youth, when the previous generation would come together to pick apart turkey and childhood foolishness. Like making up new names for the cousin who as a toddler used to invade the compost pile and dress up in banana peels. Or acting out the tale, with full sound effects, of the sibling who at five years of age ripped down part of a wall when wearing nothing but Wonder Woman underwear and a sheet tied around her neck as she jumped off the back of the sofa while holding the curtain cord proclaiming herself Panty

Girl, come to free all children from the tyranny of nap time and lima beans.

Somehow without consciously attempting to do so, I find my closest friendships are with girlfriends who seem to have made a priority of acquiring these same oral skills. No development goes unnoticed, and they give me grief about every change I make, taking my self-consciousness to new heights. There are times when I feel I am walking into a high school reunion with nothing on but tit clamps and a G-string. I don't mean to say there is an absence of love. They have my back and love me dear, but you know, on occasion, girlfriends can be a little too attentive to each other's lives. We have all been there; sometimes it's just more compelling to get all up into someone else's business than to be concerned with your own. Like when you know you need to be thinking about applying to school or changing your career, taking a computer or art class, but instead you're worrying if Sheila has the right beeswax candles for her romantic date? Or is that gold ball really what Jordan wants dangling from her labia? And if Micaela blindfolds Gertie and takes her off for a fuckfest at the beach, has she scoped out their rendezvous point so that they won't be bothered with that annoying sandy-pussy problem? Admittedly, I was changing, but not as much as they seemed to believe; I was just becoming more myself.

Avoiding their banter was my aim in coming to the club alone. The other times when I had come with J. J. and Samara it was ridiculous: on the last occasion they had kept up a running commentary the whole time. Since they both had been dating recently, and I hadn't, they'd decided the evening was all about finding a fuck for Cecelia. That's what I get for going out with two ex-lovers who are now best friends. In the end they'd been all over each other ("a bit of lusty nostalgia," Samara said.) But by that time in the evening they had rated my outfit, my come-on lines, and, much like my protective aunties, had managed to loudly appraise every woman in the place before I could as much as say boo to anyone. When I dropped them off they were licking each other's juice off fingers, snuggling and humping toward the sidewalk (oblivious to puddles), and barely avoiding slipping on the slick, rain soaked steps to J. J.'s apartment. Adding insult to injury, the pungent scent of *their* good-time sex-smell seemed to have soaked into the damp backseat, and the car heater recirculated the remnants of their pleasures the rest of my pissed-off ride home. "Never again," I said to myself. It's too much to go out for some anonymous sex in the company of sistahs who have shared your lipstick, and the other side of your bedroom wall, and don't care who knows it.

At the club by myself, I could leisurely take in the textures and curious smiles of the women coming toward me. For once feeling bold, like "What the fuck? What's the worst that can happen?" Since I had gained weight and my *tetas* were spilling out of my laced up charcoal leather bustier, I felt more grounded in my body. Some of the extra inches even had the foresight to go to my behind, which was looking smoky, black, and buoyant—a round shadow in my skin-tight velveteen miniskirt. Anyway, I reminded myself, "Cecelia, no one sister, no matter how fine, is attractive to everyone every day of the week." So letting go of that fear, before I came I promised myself that I would meet the eyes of every woman who caused my nipples to harden and who sent a paralyzing twinge down to my clit. Usually, I feel like I can't put one foot in front of the other cause my brain forgets how to send the message. I always end up looking down, disoriented and embarrassed, lamenting the loss of what I take for granted as a basic bodily function. I pray that no one notices me furtively trying to make eye contact with my feet in the hope that it will help my brain remember where to fire those neurons.

I decided that instead of freaking out because I couldn't feel my legs, I'd just take a deep breath and look forward, undaunted and unafraid, and breathe low—from the diaphragm baby, just a pause to let me get my bearings and fully appreciate the passing view.

Still, my hands felt gangly and unwieldy—I couldn't figure out what to do with them. I ended up unconsciously fingering the drawstring of my skirt with one and caressing my leather-bound breast with the other, absentmindedly caressing the skin on my arms, the exposed skin on my thigh, in between my laced-up stretch mini and my thigh-high hose. As a virgin I used to feel the slick smoothness of myself in the shower. I was studying my own pleasure, wanting to know in advance where I desired a stroke, a squeeze, a grasp, and how good my body felt under my fingers. I took the opportunity to give myself luxurious kisses wherever my tongue and lips could reach, the water flowing, dripping from mouth to skin and making my lips feel full and silken against flesh. The minute after I got some sex I gave up my water rituals, and I forgot about the value of my own caress. Now I don't mean fingers to clit, I could wear myself out on that, I mean the significance of touch: skin to skin, body on body.

Some attractive women passed by, but their presence didn't generate that slow burn under my skin. And then, I could hear the blood in my ears. The treble in the club's soundtrack seemed to fade back, and I felt the bass in my knees. *Damn!* Big 'fro, ow baby, black vinyl tank with breast zippers, stomach showin' with a little bellybutton ring, and black vinyl hip-high pants. Work me, girl!

Something about her reminded me of the first woman I had a crush on. Truthfully she wasn't really a woman, I was eight or something, and she seemed like a woman of the world to me: sixteen! But she was probably only fourteen; after all we were both at a summer day-camp. Girlfriend was tall, bittersweet-chocolate dark, slender, and kind of muscular. Her effortless grace and power plays back in my mind, as I see her striding down the sidewalk wearing a pale pink, almost ankle-length cotton sundress and black-and-white Converse high-tops, giving off an intriguing combination of early black boho mixed with a butch/femme androgynous vibe. But I wouldn't have known anything about that back then. I just knew that she didn't look anything like the relaxer-coiffed-up, heavy-lidded-eye-shadowed, Bonnie Bell lip-smacked girls at school and choir practice. She had jet black hair, long and kinky and coarse, like Chaka's was in the '70s, and a shock of dark hair coming out of each armpit, which probably accounts for my thing for underarms—not licking on some Secret or Sure, but a fresh hollow that's just started to get moist with a fine sheen of new funk.

There was a really hot afternoon during that day-camp summer when we were holed up alone in a car, one of those late '60s American models with the you-can-do-it-to-me-all-night-long, ribbed-for-pleasure bucket seats. My bittersweet girl-woman was a vision of knowingness and cool as she kicked up her feet on the dashboard. She pulled out a pack of menthols, and with a display of good, if misguided, home training glanced to the backseat and, in a husky liquid-burnt honey voice, offered me a cigarette. I barely squeaked out a trying-to-be-cool "no thank you," and that sensuous arm with the languid fingers withdrew from the top of the seat. Then without bothering to scope out the adult supervision, she lit a smoke in the front seat of the camp counselor's car. And of course there were those rebellious underarms.

But getting back to Our Lady of the Luminous Black Vinyl. The sistah in front of me was honey-brown complected and had more curves than my girlhood crush. But her vibe, let me tell you... that tank top went up to her neck and gave me little chills. I imagined my come caught between her shiny creases and slicking down the teeth of her zippers. She stood against the wall next to a doorway. Shit, and here was the test: she was giving me a look like, "You want it. Let me see you come and get it." I wished at that moment I could fly, 'cause pushing off and taking flight seemed a lot easier than the prospect of making my legs work for the whole of the time it was gonna take me to get across that hall. The feeling was starting to come back into my toes, so I put my hips into it—my body picked up the rhythm and began to follow. It occurred to me that the dare to come and get it might have given her a chance to see how I moved and to get the blood back into her *own* toes. That second thought gave me the courage to speak first: "My, you look very shiny and delicious tonight." Damn, she was licking her lips, not self-consciously, just as if it was an afterthought. They were full and brown and that pink tongue looked agile, like it might have a mind of its own.

"Thank you. I like your lacing. Is that a double knot?" She had a full, sweet voice—a big ole saucy pepper, with a little bit of honey to taste.

"Hmm, well I hope not, since I have a hard time taking out tight knots. I'll probably get a cricked neck trying to work this one by myself." I put on a crooked-coy little smile.

"Oh?" She flashed me a big grin, pretty teeth and a little overbite. "Well, here let me test it." She hooked her index finger through the two loops of the tied laces and led me through the dimly lit doorway. There were pillows on the floor and a futon or mattress of some kind with a black rubber fitted sheet; nearby there was a table with various sex supplies. This time I got to see how *she* moved; those full hips were working me, and I did see the hint of a powerful booty. She leaned me into the wall and took one end of the bow between her thumb and index finger. A little snap of the plastic tip against a rivet, and I felt the knot come undone.

"Lucky that was easy; you must be relieved." She smiled and arched her eyebrow. Cocking her head to the side she asked, "So you like my vinyl?"

"Yeah," I said gazing at the light playing off the zippers and the shiny blackness as she moved. "I'd like to lick it."

My mouth was parted in silent laughter, but I was looking directly into her eyes. Like a dare. They seemed to get big for a moment. I thought maybe she wasn't used to women having a thing for vinyl, or not while *she* was wearing it. But then her eyes went sharp and curious.

"So do it," she said.

I came up off the wall. I didn't touch her. I put my lips forward and kissed the shiny material right below her collarbone. I had to turn my head to the side so I was directly under her chin. I stuck out my tongue and licked her up to the edge of her top, just nicking the skin above her throat. I went lower, licking near the zippers, circling the outside of them. The vinyl was smooth and slick against my tongue. I left little islands, little peninsulas of saliva on her; they separated into clear drops of light. Going lower I had to bend my knees; a shadow outlined the hollow of her stomach as she caught her breath. I looked up at her as my tongue grazed her stomach and circled the loop of her bellybutton ring. She was watching me, her mouth a little open. She pulled me up, unraveling my laces and putting her fingers between my breast and the leather. I felt my muscles tense and release as she worked her fingers around me. She was pulling sounds of pleasure from my throat. I bent my head again to stroke the other side of the zippers with my tongue. I wanted to tease myself with the anticipation of the size and taste of her nipple and tease her with the attention I was going to give it. I began sucking her through the vinyl. I sucked her on both sides and let out a moan of satisfaction it felt so good. The material bore the twisted imprint of the force of my lips around her nipples. I raised my head and began to work my tongue on the little bit of exposed skin on her throat. She began to moan with me, putting her fingers in her mouth and putting them back in my bustier.

As I put my hands on her hips for balance, she said, "Now. Unzip me."

Sometimes…sometimes, I like to do as I am told. I pulled down the right breast zipper and pushed aside the flap, diving onto her with my full mouth. I noisily filled my mouth with her firm breast. We sank to the floor; we didn't quite make it to the bed. I was on top of her working that other zipper. She had my bustier practically off, and we were sideways sucking and licking.

As I was bent over, hardening her nipples into little balls, she outlined my ears and painted my neck with her tongue. When I sucked harder she bit my shoulder. She pulled away and drew back from me, smiling mischievously. I looked at her, curious, and rolled to my side, rising up on one elbow. She cupped my chin in her palm and drew her thumb over my lips. Suddenly she sat up, came closer to me, and caught my lower lip between her teeth. She bit me some, just hard enough to make a mark—something to let me know she'd been there. Her teeth parted quickly, and her lips held me. I sucked her tongue into me, and I could taste that peppery sweetness as I undid the zippers that led on both sides from her neck to her shoulders. Finally free, she pressed against my leather, rubbing her nipples against the laces. Spit covered our lips as we slowly, forcefully wrestled with each other's tongues.

She began to work the second set of laces, the ones that went up the front of my skirt. I had chosen not to wear any underwear so I could feel less restricted and, of course, bold as fuck, but now I was having second thoughts as her naked hand was getting closer to my pussy.

"Oh, we, we need some gloves, baby."

Her voice was muffled, her juicy, firm mouth still against mine. We did a sensuous and hungry mouth-fucking (I was right about that tongue), tit-rubbing, walking-on-our-knees two-step over to the table of plenty, lined with toys and various forms of latex. With sidelong glances we figured out where the gloves were and with a little teamwork both got one on the appropriate hand. She undid enough laces to get comfortably at my pussy and began working the juices around my labia, running two fingers through my folds at once. Then going in for more juice and running them back again, narrowing them against either side of my clit as she slid back up.

"I'm a sensitive one," I breathed.

"That's okay," she whispered back. "I'll just have to work my way to the edge of your pleasure. *You* tell me when to stop."

"Oh shit," I moaned, as the tips of her fingers came closer to my clit and then quickly dove, circling in between my increasingly sensitive cunt lips.

Not to be outdone I worked my digits into her hip-hugging vinyls. I went for one of the side zippers, stripping back the material. There was skin and a nappy bush, shining damp with sweat. I felt the curlicues of her hair beneath my gloved hand and inched my way to the part between her bush to her pulsing little mound. My fingers found her well creamed and hard, and she shoved her crotch onto my thigh.

"I like the pressure," she said, coaxing me with her deep brown gaze.

Her raspy moaning and the feel of her fingers stretching inside me gave me incentive to push my hand deeper into her tight pants and get to her pussy. She pressed her swollen clit into my palm and rode the length of my thigh, rising up and trembling, and back down again. I looked at her face, high on her own rhythms and mine, as I pushed into her deeper. She was straining against my palm, and my thighs were wrapped around hers.

"Wait! I don't want to come yet," I said.

"What is it?"

"I want..."

Ever so slowly she drew her fingers from between my legs, and I almost came on her hand.

"Mmm, don't come yet, baby."

Fuck. The way she drew out the word, she could call me "baby" all day long. She smiled and drew little circles on my breast with my pussy juice.

"I want you to get on your hands and knees."

Would doing as I was told a second time make my wish come true? She began to loosen the third set of laces that went down the back of my skirt. I heard her sigh.

"Your cunt and ass look so good through that lacing. Damn, you're so wet and swollen, it's making me want to fuck with you."

She was like a wolf at my door. I felt her biting and fingering me between the thin cords, heard her sniffing and breathing me in deep. The breath of her exhale was jagged as she ravenously dug her teeth deep into my behind and then traced the bites with her tongue. My skirt came completely undone under all this attention and she moved it to one side as it fell on the floor. As for me, I was so wet she could have spun me around the floor on my cunt.

With my naked ass up in the air she asked, "Now baby, I want to know: Have you been bad?"

I closed my eyes, feeling an unspeakable fury of heat—a desire that was raging beneath the skin of my ass.

Pausing for only a second, I growled, "Baby," my voice a low rumble, "make me *wanna* be bad."

Her hand came smack on my ass. She drew her wet mouth over the searing where her hand had been and then smacked me again until my ass felt hot and electric. Humming, like every nerve was alert, like they could individually receive each sensation she was giving my ass as she bit and nibbled me, drawing her nails down my butt as she trailed her tongue to the edge of my crack and slapped me again. Then I felt the cold sensation of lube dripping between the cheeks of my buttocks. I heard the snap of the old glove coming off and a crinkly sound as she adjusted a new one. It made my nipples hard all over again. I shivered as she spread the lube over my anus.

"Are you feeling like you wanna be bad yet?" She teased the rim of my asshole with her finger.

"Mmm, oh, almost," I moaned as the finger probed my hole.

She pulled out her finger and grabbed some of the toys and latex from the table. I felt her working what seemed to be a butt plug into my asshole. She was biting my cheeks and rubbing and spanking me again. "What about now?"

"Unh..."

The plug started to vibrate, and she began to push it in deeper. "What about now?"

"Yes, unh, mmm!"

"What?"

"Yes!" The word roared from my pelvis.

"Say it louder!" Her rasping voice was insistent.

"YES!" Now I was screaming, my ass wildly bucking trying to find more of the butt plug.

"Say you want it." She was pulling the butt plug out so just the tip of it was against my rim, pressing it in a little deeper and then pulling it out again.

"I WANT IT! Fuck! give it to me, give it to me now, DAMMIT!"

She thrust it in me deep, and my ass swallowed it whole. I didn't hear the zippers while I was pleading for her to ram it up my ass again. But she must have taken her pants off cause the next thing I knew she was flipping me over on top of some pillows and sliding against my thigh. And I was slippery against hers, and she was biting my nipples while I was twisting hers and hanging on as we crammed into each others thighs and hips. She had that damn butt plug on high and her teeth were on my lips while I was screaming my come, and her mouth covered mine as we howled into each other.

You Know What?

Cara Bruce

I work in a place "nice girls" don't usually visit. Starting about four in the afternoon I enter a black-covered doorway underneath a flashing marquee that reads: "Live Girls—All Nude." I am a performer, a dancer, an exhibitionist. And I like it.

Sometimes I strip on stage, but mostly I work the booths. The booths in my joint have a tiny bit of glass at the bottom. They are open so I can see everything the john is doing, and he can see me. If a girl wants to make some extra money she can let the guys touch; there is also a security button if they get out of control.

I like it this way. I like to watch the men jerking off. I like to look right in their eyes as I shake my tits and move my shaved pussy up and down in front of their faces. Some girls hate to know what the customers are doing, but not me. I'm causing it; therefore I own the reaction. I want to know what I own. This is why I make the most money.

I don't usually let anyone touch, I just like the watching. Just the two of us, making each other hot as hell in a space as big as my bathroom closet.

146

One day I was working the booths, it was pretty slow. A couple of guys came in, one just sat there, staring at me. I don't like it when they just look. I want participation. Makes me feel as if I'm doing a better job. One guy jerked off, came in about two strokes. Made me feel as if I was doing *too* good a job. Then this woman comes in. Now sometimes we get lesbians or prostitutes with dates, and once in a while there are girls who come in with their boyfriends. Usually these women won't even look at me, they look at the floor, their feet, their boyfriend, or they try to make out to distract themselves from the show. It's like they're embarrassed for themselves and for me. I always try and dance harder to force their attention. The couples never stay long.

So anyway, this woman comes in. She is hot. I look at her, dressed in her chic black business suit, little skirt, blouse, and matching jacket. And the first thing I think is that she might be a cop, but she sits down and puts some quarters in. The lights come on, and I can hear a faint beat of music from whoever is dancing outside, so I start to grind my hips and toss my hair.

The woman stares right at me, as if she's daring me to show her what I've got. So I do. I look right back in her eyes and start fucking an imaginary body, real slow and sensual like. And she keeps looking. She drops more quarters in, and she spreads her legs.

She's not wearing anything underneath, and I wonder if she went to work like this. Her legs are spread wide, and she's shaved bare as well, giving her big and thick lips plenty of air. Now I'm thinking maybe she's in the business, and I start sort of showing off for her.

I bring my cunt down right in front of her face, and you know what she does? She breathes on it. Real hot breath coming out and almost making me lose my balance. So I keep dancing, grinding real close to her face. She starts unbuttoning her blouse, no bra on. She lets her tits fall out, then she starts rubbing and pinching her own nipples.

She's trying to outdo me, I think. I shake my head, that bitch is trying to steal my spotlight. So I reach down by my feet and pick up my prop: a big pink vibrator. I'll give her something to feel herself about, all right. I take the toy and draw it slowly through my mouth, lubing it up. She licks her lips, still staring right into my eyes. I bring the vibrator down and tease my clit with it, knowing it'll pop out hard and full, giving her something to stare at. So I start moving the vibrator around, turning it up a notch and breaking a sweat.

She has her skirt around her waist now, her long legs spread wide. She tilts her hips up, and starts jilling off.

She mimics me, each stroke I make with my vibrator she copies with her finger. It's a masturbation duel, and I'm not sure if the objective is to come first or last. Without missing a beat she puts more quarters in.

I slide the vibrator up inside me. She matches this with her fingers. I'm squatting, using my palm to stick the vibrator up, then releasing my muscles to let it fall back. Her digits are diving in and out, with the same gentle rise and fall. I shake my head; I'm on fire now, this woman is making me hot. Her pretty head is tilted back slightly, her lips parted, her eyes stuck on mine.

Suddenly it hits me. I want to fuck her. I don't usually do customers, but I want her real bad. I get up in her face, my whirring cunt is inches from her mouth, and I say, "You want me."

She smiles, her hand never stops, and she says, "*You want me.*"

"Fuck me," I tell her, and my voice quivers a little with the excitement, even though I'm trying to sound stern.

She takes the vibrator in her mouth, and she starts fucking me with it. I'm squatting above her, and she is fucking me with my own vibrator in her mouth. Meanwhile, her hand never stops moving. She's getting lipstick all over my toy and juices from my dripping slit are sliding down and gathering on the corners of her red lips and she is still staring at me. My legs are trembling, because she is fucking the hell out of me and herself at the same time.

"Yeah, honey, fuck me, fuck me," I pant and I can almost see her smile.

I wrap my hands around her head and push her deeper into me. I'm moving her head and every time I look down those eyes are staring at me. My legs are shaking and my cunt starts to clench and I feel my insides begin to boil and I look down and she winks at me. I can't believe it, I lose my shit. I start to come, shaking and crying I fall over on her.

"Please stop, stop, stop," I cry, but she won't. That vibrator isn't moving, but it's still deep inside me. I reach down to grab her hair but then, the bitch, she starts to come and I get off again, just feeling her shaking and moaning under me. It's too much.

She's done, and finally she pulls out the vibrator. I climb off of her, and she turns off the toy and places it down on the little stage. I'm spent, I feel like I've been fucked for the first time in a long time, and if the floor wasn't covered with spent jizz maybe I could crawl up and go to sleep there.

She's still looking at me, that smile that's more like a smirk on her face, and she's buttoning up her blouse and pulling down her skirt. She stands up, looking like nothing ever happened, and she walks over and you know what she does? She kisses me. Plants a big wet one right on my mouth while she slides a twenty on the stage; then she turns and walks out.

I can't believe her. The nerve of that slut, I know her type, the kind that always needs the last word. I shake my head, some people are just crazy, you know what I mean? I get back on stage and wait for my next show.

from *The Great Bravura*
Jill Dearman

"Ladies and gentlemen! Pre- and post-ops! Welcome to the Zucchini Lounge! Tonight we have a very special treat for you...the amazing magician and mind reader extraordinaire: The Great Bravura!"

The cheer of the crowd was my cue. The announcer passed me in the wings, and her lush beard brushed against my neck. We silently acknowledged the moment, then I lunged onstage and scanned the crowd. A veritable house of stylish freaks! Men in pearls and women in leather and lace. Drinks everywhere and a hookah pipe in the center of it all. Enough smoke and decadence for everybody.

I turned to the far wings and looked at her. Even in shadow she radiated electric blue light. A delicious red satin dress wrapped around her curves and secrets, just as I wanted to. I was only flesh and blood after all! Her liquid blue eyes sparkled like a luscious rare liqueur. The stage lights seemed to gravitate to those eyes, making them bigger than life. I knew I could drink from them till the end of my life. She blew me a silent kiss, and I caught it deep within my soul. But it wasn't my soul that felt her presence first, it was a much more provocative part of me. Oh, my darling Lena. How beautiful she was. Could she ever find me as dazzling as I found her?

I bowed to her and waved her to the stage with a flourish. The audience ate her up, as I wanted to. Oh my friends, you can laugh at my youthful ardor! But you would have felt the same way. She was alive, this girl! And she brought me to life the first time she shared the stage with me, on that very night.

"Thank you! Thank you! My, what a naughty audience we have tonight. Oh yes! I sense a sexually twisted woman out there in the dark! Tell me: is there someone here tonight who just had a ménage à trois with her ex-lover..."

I concentrated hard.

"...and a lion tamer?"

A yummy lass on the fourth row aisle raised her hand, shy but proud. She was all blushed and spankable. I looked over at Lena. She was already thrilled by my prowess. Thrilled but not surprised. How I longed to surprise her then. With my hands and my mouth and every part of my flesh.

"Ahh...and how was it my dear?"

The lass gave a timid but excited thumbs-up sign. The audience laughed and applauded, already giddy from the show. They could only imagine what she used that thumb for, but I knew. I saw a vision of her stroking the inside of that lion tamer, keeping the beast at bay.

"All right. That was a fine warm up. Now I want a real challenge. Are there any nonbelievers out there? Come on! I want a real cynic. Come, come. Do not be afraid. It will only hurt for a little while. Then it will start to feel so, so good. Ah! You there. You really don't believe in magic at all do you? Please, come up to the stage. That's it. Come to Daddy."

Susie. My old partner. My right-hand man. My past. What a sweetie. I winked at her as I leaned down to kiss her hand. On my way down I noticed her extraordinary furry boots, and the way they seemed to move like a sleepy pair of animals.

"Cigarette? Water? Fine," I said. "Now, I can see that you don't believe in magic. That's a shame really. Life can be so dull without it."

"So, my dear," I began, edging closer to Susie. I could smell "Cognac," the cheap perfume she favored. It was sweet, like the smell of a familiar old dog. But I longed for the smell of Lena, who seemed more of a luxurious pampered cat than a musty old dog. Oh Susie! How I took that dear girl for granted in those days. Out with the old second banana and in with the new. Susie was jealous of Lena from the very start, and she had good reason to be. Susie was just the appetizer. Lena would be my main course. Youth is the time to be cruel, isn't it? I was drunk with my own power.

"You work with your hands and with your mind, but your heart is empty. You broke the heart of someone who loved you deeply, and you've been punishing yourself ever since. How'm I doing so far?"

"A little too well," Susie replied. Her mouth seemed tense, but I paid no attention to that. I knew she loved to have her mind read, if only onstage. During our affair, I never read her mind. We were too busy working. By the time Lena joined our act that night I was ready for something to transform me, something to take me away from the ball and chain that had held me too hard and fast to the ground.

Not Susie, my friends. I can't blame my pal, old partner, and ex-lover for anything. I once believed, briefly, that she had broken my heart. But it was just my pride she had wounded. She chose our work over our affair. But soon my obsession with work stopped me from truly flying with the spirits.

"You have a secret, don't you? Something you've never shared with anyone else."

"Look," Susie cried, visibly upset. She feared I might throw a little real life history into the act. "I had those warts removed two years ago, and my last four pap smears have been just fine!"

The audience laughed in bawdy unison. Why did I feel compelled to torture Susie in front of hundreds of onlookers that night? I see now how much I resented her. For she knew the old me. The earth-bound me. The me I had grown bored with. Lena stood on the other side of the stage and saw a different part of me. A more omnipotent and bold me, and I admit now, dear friends, it was Lena, my irresistible obsession, whom I really wanted to impress that night.

"No! No! No! It's something much deeper. When you were a child you wanted to be a magician, but something stopped you!"

I backed Susie against the stage left wall. I could feel her breasts beneath mine as I leaned into her body. They still felt good. Not miraculous anymore. But good, nevertheless. Supple, full, and most of all, willing. She tried to smile at the audience as she gave me frightened "stop it" looks. No safe words had been agreed upon.

"Yes. Ha, ha! A magician, sure. Whatever you say!"

"You were afraid of something. You were afraid of the dark. You were fine when the lights came up, but those brief moments in the dark, before each performance...they frightened you. So you gave up your dream and never looked back!" I yelled.

"Yes, it's all true except..."

"Yes?"

"I have looked back."

I knew then that she still loved me. Dear, innocent Susie. It's a good thing she couldn't read *my* mind that night. For if she could she would have known that it was her love that gave me the confidence to love another, to love the most ethereal and sexy woman I'd ever encountered, save for my mother. Lena. The beauty for whom I was performing this bizarre show.

I took Susie's arm and kissed it, all the way up to her neck. Her skin felt tender, as if each kiss touched a wound inside her, invisible but not quite healed. As I kissed her I spoke, to the audience more than to her.

"The past is gone. But I see more and more magic in your future!"

"You do?"

"Yes! In the very *near* future."

As I pulled back from Susie's body I saw Lena. She'd appeared in my line of vision and gave me the lewdest of looks. She slowly licked her own lips, like she was kissing and seducing herself. I'd never made love to Lena, and now I was on fire. My desire knew more than my mind, or my six senses.

I spun Susie offstage, grabbing Lena along the way, and said, "Dear girls, I will need you both. Do not travel far."

I turned to the audience. They were enthralled by me, and I was even more enthralled.

"And now, the moment you've all been waiting for. I will saw a lady in half!"

The audience screamed, unable to hold back their enthusiasm. I knew that feeling well enough, but I kept going. I guided Susie as she wheeled the black box onto the stage. A lovely young artist had painted secret symbols beneath the black paint. Constellations from the zodiac. Animal spirits. Mothers and daughters. They were barely visible to the naked eye, but their presence made me feel all hot and revved up inside. I never felt such heat looking at those painted curves and secret signs before. But tonight they worked like a drug, raising the temperature inside me and stirring up the hot, dark forces within me. That heat lead me to Lena, all cool and powdery as I opened the box for her. She stepped in, trusting me completely.

"Lena, in case anything goes wrong tonight, let me tell you now: You've been a *great* assistant."

"Legs please!" Susie yelled, interrupting the moment, goddamn her.

Susie knelt at the far end of the box as a pair of feet slipped through the large round holes. Susie pulled the legs out a little so the audience could see them clearly.

The lights shifted and the crowd simmered down. Susie and I went through the motions of turning the box all the way around so the audience believed they could see it all. Lena's head hung down, exposed outside one end of the box, and she watched every move I made with contained lust and dripping fascination.

When the moment was right, on my silent count, Susie and I dropped the large mirrored blade through the middle of the box. The audience gasped in horror and excitement.

At that moment I froze, and all time seemed to stop. I looked down at Lena's face between my thighs. The top of her head nuzzled quietly against my belly. Her long golden hair fell against my legs.

In my mind I heard her speak clearly, *"I am so turned on right now."*

"I really want to make love to you," I answered back with my mind.

This was no game. We were one mind. In all my years on the stage, my friends, I had never experienced the real thing before. A complete psychic connection with another mortal. If she was indeed mortal. This I still cannot be sure of.

I didn't give a damn about the act at that point. All I knew was Lena. I zipped through the rest of the performance then ended the show as quickly as I could. The audience was annoyed, but I knew I would win them back. I'd worked my whole young life for them, until I didn't have a life anymore. Now, they would just have to wait. Lena was too important.

She gazed up at me and reflected my wildest desires. Nothing else existed for me then but my longing to be all that she expected of me. A sexual magician.

After the disgruntled audience finally left, it wasn't easy getting rid of Susie. She insisted I give her notes on her performance. Instead, I slipped her a generous wad of cash and told her to buy herself a good time; I said that I'd catch up with her later. She begrudgingly left, furry boots, grease paint, and all. What a great kid.

"G'night, Bravura," she said softly, a touch of either longing or exhaustion in her voice. I wasn't sure which.

"See ya, Susie."

Something streaked down her face. Sweat or tears? Either way, I'd make it up to her another time.

Lena appeared then, from nowhere, like a spirit. I was leaning against the saw-in-half box, smoking a cigar and drinking a little whisky from my flask, as I did after every show. But I knew tonight would be richer and realer than any performance I'd ever given in my life. At long last, I would have the greatest partner in the world.

I put the props down on the floor and stared at her.

"Lena," I said. Her name tasted like honey on my tongue, like an ancient pagan ritual that I had walked through a million times and would walk through again and again until I learned its true meaning. I kept saying her name until a voice inside my head that sounded just like Lena's told me to stop. "Call me Mama," the voice said. And when I looked into her eyes again, I saw my mother, as she once was, beautiful, mysterious, and welcoming. All those things she was before the drink and the phony magic of my father, "Señor Bravura," had ruined her. Did he even have Latin blood in him? Or was his name a mere charade, too? I didn't know. I just took the name and made it my own because she wanted me to. And whatever Mama wanted, I wanted, too. All those thoughts swam around in my head and brought intense pain to my heart and tears to my eyes.

"Oh Mama, you're so luscious, so perfect," I said aloud. She smiled then. Lena, I mean. A sad smile of empathy that quickly turned sexy hot.

"Tell Mama," she said aloud.

But when I opened my mouth to speak she raised her hand, both threatening and protecting me.

She put her hand on my lips to quiet me. I let her graceful finger slip over the gap between my teeth. Then I licked at it, first vertically then horizontally, making the sign of the cross. No symbolism would be lost on this young lady, I knew. My tongue reached outside my mouth and licked her finger, luring it in, as my arm slipped around her waist and pulled her to me. My hands lingered on the small of her back, and as my lips brushed against hers I felt a wave of heat, hotter than any spotlight, pass through my body.

When our mouths came together completely, I shivered a little, unsure of my fate. I sucked on her lower lip, which was full and inviting, and hunted around in her mouth with my tongue, looking for answers that I knew would elude me. But, oh how I enjoyed the search!

Our kiss lasted longer than some of my past relationships. I pulled my mouth away and looked into her eyes—the blue of my dreams. I stared at her with a hunger that was no performance. It was real. I devoured her neck, passionately, then gently, savoring the cool, sweet taste. Part mocha and part exotic fruit that I could not name. I took my chin and nose and pushed her white pearl necklace into her skin, teasing her, tickling her, hurting her, and most of all, surprising her and surprising myself. My body could not ignore one single centimeter of her body. I had to feel every part of her and know that she belonged to me. The surprising part was that for each kiss, each lick, each touch, I felt two simultaneous tugs at my heart. One pulled me towards light and beauty. Towards the delicious transformation of passion. The other pulled me towards darkness and death. For when I opened my eyes, between kisses, I saw not just Lena in all her cakelike deliciousness, I saw my mother, too, in all her devastating need and loneliness. I tried to communicate with my eyes and with my body the longing and fear that I felt, and I believed, kind friends, that Lena understood.

She took my hands and kissed them, never breaking eye contact with me. She put my newly baptized magician's hands on her breasts and gave me the permission I needed to go to the dark side. I crossed over very slowly. It was as if I had died a little death and hovered like a ghost over my own earthly form.

I bit into her voluptuous breasts through the satin of her dress. I leaned her back against the box and watched with animal arousal as she lifted her arms over her head, arching her back, begging me to remove the earthly material that separated us. She wore dark gray lingerie that sparkled blue and silver under the stage lights and felt as sexy and rich as the most delectable creamy, chocolate dessert. Her tights were black and thin like a membrane of invisible flesh.

I wrapped my burgundy velvet cape around her body and pulled her to me, humping against her as I kissed her every pore. I could feel her insides throbbing for me as I slid down past her most womanly part, only teasing her with the top of my head. I shimmied slowly back up her body like a cat stretching in the dark and then stood over her, holding her hands back against the box.

"Oh, Bravura," she said, growling like a little wolf. "You do have magical powers. I knew it the first time I laid eyes on you."

I smiled at her then, seemingly confident but inside sweating with fever. I felt overwhelmed by the attention she gave me. I did not know who she really was, this dark lady in the pale, blonde form. But I knew who she wanted me to be. I tore off my shirt but kept my cape on. I liked the way the cool satin of the inside lining slid against my nipples, hardening them, and stirring me up even further. I gently picked up her smooth, almost fleshy foot, unmarked by years of walking on the ground like the rest of us, and rubbed it against my face, taking my time on each toe, licking, sucking, and nuzzling. Now warm and wet I took that graceful foot and slipped it into my velvet pants. I let her toes explore my clit. They moved easily inside my shorts, guided by wetness. I felt hard and ready for her now.

I slid down and reached inside the box for one of my most important tools of the trade. Power comes from within my friends, but every magician needs her props.

We rocked together for what seemed like a lifetime, and dear friends, let me tell you in all honesty, I was sure then, as I am now, that I'd known this woman for many lifetimes. As a lover, as a mother, as a daughter, as a daddy, and as an enemy. I loved her hard and passionately for each incarnation and each unfinished lesson from our past. I could feel her heart rate speed up as she grew closer and closer to climax. My own head was spinning as if I might pass out at any moment. But I kept going till she came and came, simultaneously pushing me away and pulling me towards her. I loved her then, as I knew she loved me.

Still, I knew I was about to find out the true extent of her love, as she allowed me to untie her restraint and then pushed me against the box. This was no little girl push either. Her shimmery gold hair and delightfully curvy body screamed "femme" but Lena had the hard edge of butchness deep inside her. She just kept it very well disguised.

I laid back against the box and opened my lips gratefully as she poured some whisky from the flask into my mouth. I swallowed hard then opened my lips again so I could kiss her and taste the combination of the dry but strangely sweet sandpaper of the booze with the warm fruitiness of her mouth.

She kissed her way down my body, lingering long and luxuriously on my breasts and belly. She rubbed my stomach for luck, and I prepared myself to grant her wish. For I knew she was about to give me something that would give her the kick of a lifetime. Overpowering a magician is no mean feat, my friends, but if anyone could do it, and do it right, I knew it would be Lena, my sweet, sweet Lena.

She nipped at my thighs with her teeth and licked her way inside me. She teased me with sadistic abandon, sometimes stroking, sometimes licking and sometimes just rubbing her knee up and down, keeping the road slick, till she was ready to speed up for the thrill ride of my life.

She was gorgeous to me, in an unreal yet completely lifelike way, like a painting done by true master. I stared at her, my insides still throbbing, dying for more, as she leaned over and thrust her breasts over my eyes and mouth. I unsnapped her bra and tossed it over the box. My lower lip followed her nipple wherever it went, pulling me deeper and deeper into my own fantasy world. She *was* my fantasy, and she knew it. This knowledge was our secret, and there were more secrets I had yet to discover, I was sure. She climbed onto my face and wrapped her thighs around me. I explored her navel and the soft belly that delighted me with its every curve. I teased her still wet clit with my lips and tongue, which only made the hotness between my legs and in my very heart grow more intense.

When we were both groaning and writhing in pleasure, just savoring the magical energy between us, she finally worked her way down to my center. The place where every trick and every true act of magic began for me.

When she had me where she wanted me she rocked her head back and forth, her mouth gently but possessively sucking on my clit. As I tried to hold back my explosion, she slipped fingers inside me that stated firmly: "You have no power here. The torch has been passed." I held on still, dear friends. I wanted this moment to last forever, and in a way it has.

When I came, it was like a divine act. A promise of miracles to come. And let me tell you now, just so we're clear, I had never believed in anything as hokey as miracles before that night.

Now I can't stop believing.

My climax never peaked. It kept moving deeper and deeper like a child being pulled out to sea by a powerful undertow. Inside I knew how dangerous those waters would be for me, but the waves were so lovely and promised safety and immortality, if only I'd believe. I was still coming when she moved away from me, stood up, and lit a cigarette. She placed a tender hand on my mouth and put the lit end of the cigarette inside her own mouth as I watched, in amazement. Her tricks could be frightening, but were impossible to ignore. That was all part of her allure. She blew smoke at me, which added to the rush of my seemingly inexhaustible orgasm.

As she stood over me I screamed and pounded the box with my hands, my body and my very being completely out of control, as never before.

When it was over I pulled her to me and kissed her hard and long, reclaiming her as mine. This was the creature I had conjured up from my darkest and brightest fantasies, and I had now earned the right to keep her forever, or so I thought.

We lay together in the afterglow, smoking and cuddling and nuzzling each other. This was the happiest night of my life, but in a way the most tragic. As I stroked Lena's soft body I felt euphoria slipping away. It was as if I was now stuck like a sleepwalker in a dreamy nightmare, a person who unconsciously refuses to wake up. Still, I must be honest now and say I don't know if I would change a thing, even if I had the power to. Even if I still had the power. It was a long while before either of us spoke. At last, there were only a few words to be said, and as if speaking from a script that had been written and rewritten over and over again, only to remain the same in the end, we finally allowed the words to escape our lips.

"You must've read my mind, darling."

"And you, mine, lover. And you, mine."

Long and Lean

Robin G. White

"Hmm, love that smell," Carolyn thought to herself as she shut the tailgate of her SUV. She lifted her nose toward the mist that had just begun to rise from the softball and soccer fields. The scent of newly turned earth and freshly cut grass mingled with the sweet aroma of a late fall rain. She closed her eyes and inhaled deeply, drinking in the air that burned her nose, tickled her throat, and filled her lungs to capacity. A smile spread across her face as she exhaled and started across the empty parking lot toward the gated athletic fields and the short wooden fence that surrounded them. She loved this time of day. Peaceful. It was earlier than most people would get up for an outdoor workout. The sun hadn't risen and wouldn't start showing hints of its color for another half hour. Carolyn listened to the familiar sounds of birds chirping their morning greetings to one another. She had learned early not to become startled by the rustling they made in the bushes alongside the track where she alternately walked and jogged each and every morning since moving to this pristine southern suburb.

Again she smiled to herself. How much her life had changed from her former northern self. Some things about her old life that seemed so crucial dissolved once she had settled into her new digs in the suburbs of Atlanta. She had successfully fought off homesickness by calling her friends almost daily and then less and less until she only called two friends once weekly, which was more than enough.

"Thank God for five cent Sundays," she giggled. "Okay, pull it together, Binky. You're slipping." Carolyn placed her toes at the edge of the curb along the walkway and lowered her body, feeling her weight stretch the muscles in her thick calves. This exercise and the bananas she consumed daily were the only things keeping her from the painful charley horse cramps that had plagued her since childhood. Up and down, up and down, she felt the muscles relax. She stepped forward and rotated her neck, torso, hips, knees, and ankles until her joints began to loosen. "Old age, whoever thought you could be so stiff?" Lifting one leg over the horizontal beam of the fence, she leaned forward, grasping her ankle in a full stretch. She did the same with the other leg before beginning her lunges. Since she had been stretching thoroughly before working out, she had suffered fewer injuries. Even her back and knees, which had always given her trouble, were feeling better these days.

She headed to the softball field. Walking through the gate, Carolyn was surprised to see the lone figure of woman, running along the fence and through the mist. "Funny, I don't remember seeing any other cars," she thought to herself.

Just then, a car pulled up along the fence, slowing next to the figure. She could hear a voice over the crunch of gravel. "You sure you'll be okay out here? It's pretty dark and..." The runner interrupted, "Frank, thanks, but don't worry. I come out here all the time, and I can jog home. It's just over the hill."

"Look, I'm not trying to give you a hard time. Just one cop to another. I have to remind you that any park can be dangerous when it's dark. Don't go thinking you're Superwoman just because you carry a badge now."

"Frank." The female figure stopped jogging and moved toward the fence. Frank stopped his car. Carolyn could make out the writing on the side: DeKalb County Sheriff Department. She relaxed. They were always out here in the morning. And it sounded as though that fine body up ahead might be extra company and extra protection this morning. "I'll be fine." The soft voice continued. "Besides, I'm not the only one here." They looked in Carolyn's direction. "Okay, okay. Just looking out for my deputy sis."

"Scram, baby brother." The car rolled off down the access road and of the park. Carolyn watched the car head off, its taillights flashing in the distance.

"Brothers are a trip!" The woman jogged up to the fence where Carolyn was stretching. "I'm Trish Hughley."

"Carolyn. Carolyn Means."

"I see you out here all the time. Well, I did when I was on third shift. My partner and I would sit back there doing our nightly reports on the laptop, and here you'd come, just like clockwork." She waited for a response. Carolyn couldn't decide whether she was annoyed by or welcomed this woman's company.

"Well, I've got to keep moving if I'm going to stay warm. Are you jogging or walking this morning?"

"Jogging, but I need to walk a few laps first. It helps build my stamina and gets the adrenaline going."

"Well. Okay. I'll see you later." The young woman headed off. Had Carolyn sensed disappointment in her voice? "Hmm," thought Carolyn as she strapped weights onto her ankles and wrists. When she'd first bought them they seemed so cumbersome. Now she loved the way her limbs felt when she removed them after a workout. It was like floating. As she began to walk on the sand and gravel outfield, Carolyn watched Trish move with ease and precision around the red clay earth of the batter's box, heading along the foul line toward first base, her feet pounding the soft turned clay into red clouds. She watched her while her own limbs gained rhythm and momentum. Barely into left field, Trish flashed past her, her lungs pushing clouds into the damp morning. Carolyn looked after the woman and watched her arms pump, the mist closing in around her, her feet pushing the earth away, her body defying gravity with enormous stretch.

"*Wow.*" Carolyn couldn't catch the exclamation before it passed through her lips. Her body began to catch the fever, her strides became longer, her arms too pumped at the air, her feet pounded the earth, and she could feel the heady adrenaline coursing through her veins. She may have been forty, and fifty pounds overweight, but right now she didn't feel her age or her weight. She could hear Trish's steady beat pulling up behind her and then the sweet voice, "How are we doing?"

"Fine," Carolyn exhaled. She had just mastered breathing and couldn't talk, breathe, and run at the same time. Trish slowed her pace and turned to face the older woman to offer a gentle reminder, "Don't overdo it." Carolyn nodded and smiled as Trish resumed her pace.

The sun rose in brilliant oranges and fire reds, blazing in flames through the atmosphere. The skeletal trees of darkness came to life under the sun's glowing color. The mist quickly dissipated as the daylight suddenly shined on the two women racing around the softball field. Carolyn realized that she had been out there for a while. How many laps had she run? She tried to think back. How many warm-up laps had she walked? One maybe. Uh-oh. She began slowing her pace, but it was too late. The pain started in her right calf first and followed almost immediately in her left. She went down.

"No, no, not now." Carolyn felt like a complete idiot. She knew better than to run at that pace. She hadn't moved like that since her distance days in college. And that was a very long time ago. Oh, and now she's out here trying to impress this young sistah. And how was she to do it, rolling around screaming in pain. What a dope. Trish heard the yell and raced over.

"Carolyn, what is it?"

Carolyn put on her brave face and fought back the tears.

"My calves...charley horse." Trish reached down and felt them. The muscles were so constricted they were hard as rocks. She bent over and undid the weights from Carolyn's ankles and unsnapped the pants up to her knee. She helped Carolyn sit up and lean against the fence.

"Now listen. You have to relax. Breathe with me. I'm going to try to rub out the muscle, but you have to concentrate on relaxing it." Carolyn nodded through her tears. She looked up into Trish's comforting gaze and began to relax. Trish's voice was so soothing, "Now breathe. Come on, Carolyn. You can do this, breathe again. Softly exhale." Trish blew air into her cupped hands and rubbed them together. Placing her palms on Carolyn's muscle she began to rub. The heat from her hands relaxed the constrictions as Trish continued to knead them. Carolyn knew she felt better when the warmth of the massage began to move toward her groin. She looked carefully at the young woman kneeling beside her with her sweats pulled up to her knees, the thick black hair covering her caramel colored leg, her long fingers carefully pulling at the muscles in her strong hands, her lips full and puckered as she deeply breathed her own exhalations, her gray eyes now staring back into Carolyn's; she was beautiful.

"Thanks. I'm better now." Carolyn attempted to rise on her own. Her muscles were tired and sore and barely supported her. "Umm, would you mind?"

"How about I drive you home?" Trish offered. "We can get some coffee and, umm, talk until you feel better and can drive me back home. If that's okay."

"Yeah. That's fine." Carolyn was grateful for the redemption. As they headed to the car Trish grabbed her bag from the stands. Carolyn tossed Trish her keys, and she got behind the wheel as Carolyn settled into the passenger seat. Pulling out of the parking lot, Trish commented on how the traffic seemed to be particularly slow on Route 20. Carolyn mentioned that it was rush hour. "Yeah, but that is the way home for me; I live about four exits up. It may be a while for me to get home." The morning traffic report confirmed her suspicions. There was a major accident on Route 20 at the 285 exit. A truck full of mayonnaise had over-turned and backed up the traffic into the next county. It would take hours to clean up.

Carolyn looked at the driver, sorry now that she had so foolishly injured her leg. "We can take the back roads when I drive you home." She offered.

"Maybe I won't want to leave at all." Trish looked sexily at her passenger as she pulled into the development.

"Why, Officer, are you coming on to me?"

"Most assuredly."

"Well then, let's get busy."

Trish pulled the car into the last parking space in front of Carolyn's building. Trish carried her bag and took the steps two at a time ahead of Carolyn's limping frame. They smiled a greeting at a neighbor ushering her child out of the door. "Hurry up, chile, or you'll be late!" The long-faced child pushed past them in the breezeway. Carolyn pushed open her door and quickly surveyed the room. Had she left the place a mess? No, everything was tidy and clean. She pulled back the vertical blinds to let in some light.

"Coffee?"

"Sure." Trish looked around the living room and sat in an overstuffed chair in the corner. Carolyn offered the steaming mug of coffee and munched on a banana.

"Will you eat me that way?" Trish went right to business. After all, she had been waiting months for the chance to get this close to this brown-skinned beauty. She licked her lips as she watched Carolyn's eyes for a reaction. She was not disappointed. Carolyn deftly slipped the length of the banana into her mouth. After swallowing, she answered, "The bedroom is this way." She turned and marched down the hall past her office, the guestroom, and the bathroom, and flung open the doors to her sanctuary.

The room was everything that Trish had hoped it would be. The cherry wood of the four poster bed was draped with sheer fabrics. Fresh flowers filled crystal and porcelain vases everywhere. The mattress was high, and bed stairs rested against the sideboard. A large beveled mirror hung over the bed and matched the ones throughout the room. The room felt lush and lived in. A door was open in the corner of the room. Trish peered inside and stepped into a large walk-in closet. Lingerie draped out of drawers as though tossed aside by a careless lover. A large vase on the vanity in the corner was filled with eucalyptus, its fresh aroma filling the space. Another door revealed a bathroom with a garden tub and double sinks. Carolyn was right behind her.

"To use one of your phrases, 'Wow!'" Trish turned and winked, the corners of her mouth turning upward at her joke. Carolyn blushed, "So you heard me?"

"Yes, and I liked what I heard. I'd like to hear more." Trish reached for a towel from the rack. "Shall we?"

"Shower or bathe?"

"Let's start in the shower and see where it leads us." Carolyn unzipped her jacket and pulled it off and the T-shirt underneath to reveal a royal-blue spandex sports bra. Trish unsnapped Carolyn's nylon pants and pulled them off. She pulled Carolyn to her with one strong sweep of her arm. Their musk mingled into a heady aroma. Carolyn could feel her heart pounding in her chest as Trish planted her velvet soft lips against Carolyn's and sucked in her breath. Clothes were flying. Trish pushed off her sneakers and peeled away at the layers of sweats and cotton liners. Why had she worn this many clothes? She pressed her hungry body into Carolyn's and squeezed the firm butt cheeks that rested in her hands. She had admired this woman for months, watching her day in and day out walking and jogging around and around the track. Her pounds had melted away and her stamina had increased. Damn. Even her partner commented on it. She had looked good to her in the beginning, but now, *wow* was right.

"I have to tell you something."

"Okay, what? You want to know if I've been tested? Yes. Or were you going to tell me that you haven't been?"

"What? No. Of course I've been tested. Yes. I'm negative. What about you?"

"Negative. So what were you going to say?"

"Well. Look, I wasn't kidding when I said that I'd seen you every day. In fact, I have been watching you. I mean really watching you. I was so impressed by your consistency and effort. I mean, you really try to take care of yourself. It takes real commitment to do what you are doing. I thought that you were beautiful before when you first started coming out to the park in the mornings, but after seeing you month after month, well, I really began to like what I saw and wanted to get to know you. That's why I was out there this morning and why my brother was giving me such a hard time. He was just teasing me. Anyway, I thought that you should know the truth."

Carolyn stepped back and looked at the young woman.

"I already knew."

"What? How?"

"Honey, anyone could spot you a mile away. I would see you in the squad car watching me. Sometimes I would see you leaning up against the vehicle, and pacing back and forth. Many a time, I wanted to just walk up to you in that getup you wear and ask you for your number, but you always had your partner with you."

"I don't now."

"Well, baby, now I've *got* your number." Carolyn moved to the shower stall and turned on the water. Flipping another switch, Erykah Badu's voice filled the room.

"Oh yeah, I can get with this," Trish stepped into the steaming water. Carolyn knelt at her feet, wash cloth and soap at the ready. She lathered Trish's crotch and buttocks and reached up to lather under her breasts as the triple-headed shower sent water and soap cascading down her body and onto Carolyn's head. The water felt so good, and the rough cloth tingled her skin. Trish moved out of the direct force of the water and pulled Carolyn's face toward her pussy.

"Now how did you eat that banana? Show me." Carolyn opened her mouth and hungrily took what waited at her lips. The clean scent of Dove reached her nostrils, but it was Trish that she wanted to smell.

"Baby, can we take this to the bedroom?" Carolyn asked.

Trish nodded her agreement and moved out of the stall first as Carolyn finished showering. When Carolyn walked into the room, the curtains were drawn and Trish lay in the bed waiting. Carolyn crawled beneath the covers to finish what she had started. Trish grabbed her face in her hands and said, "Be good and there may just be a treat for you." Carolyn smiled in acknowledgment and dove under the covers. She slid easily between her lover's thighs and began to kiss them just above the knees. Trish could see her head moving under the comforter. Carolyn stopped just as she reached the spot where the vagina should have been. Instead there was something long and thick. She started to lift her head and heard an admonishment from above the covers, "Be good and show me how you eat a banana now." Carolyn swallowed. She knew she was physically no match for the woman whose legs she lay between. She felt the covers move slowly across her back. The light revealed the dildo and the athletic frame to which it was attached.

"Is there a problem? You seemed so eager earlier."

"I've never done this before."

"Good. Neither have I. But we both will today."

Carolyn felt a flush go over her body. She wanted so badly to give in to this woman. But she didn't know anything about her. Trish must have sensed her nervousness because she stopped her bad boy behavior long enough to offer some con-solation.

"Look. I am just experimenting. If it isn't okay, we can stop. I just thought you liked the tough guy/jock sort of thing. And I am sort of enjoying it myself."

Carolyn put away her fears and got down to business. She started at the base of the dildo and worked her way up, flick-ing the tip with her tongue. Then quickly she wrapped her mouth around it, taking in as much as her throat would allow. Her head bobbed up and down over it, and she could feel her saliva spilling from the corners of her lips and down the sides of the hard cock.

"Oh yeah, baby, suck my dick. You know how turned on I get watching you race around that track, don't you? You know when you get home what you've got to do. That's right. You take care of it. Suck that cock."

The words were music to Carolyn's ears. She felt her own juices heating up inside of her. She wanted to ride this bad boy. Trish thrust the head of the dildo deeper into Carolyn's mouth. She grabbed at Carolyn's hair and pumped her groin against her face. Pulling back on her hair, she pulled her off.

"You want this? You want some of this, don't you? I see your ass down there humping. I'll give you something to hump. Turn around and hold onto the bed."

Carolyn turned her back toward Trish and grabbed hold of the board at the foot of the bed. Trish cozied up behind her and reached between her legs. Her pussy was so wet that the cum was dripping down her thighs.

"I want this pussy." She stuck a finger in and rotated it. Tight. Carolyn softly moaned at the intrusion. She pushed her ass back toward the invader. Trish stuck another finger into her vagina. This was going to be hard. She wondered if Carolyn could take the eight-inch cock and all the passion that Trish had built up in fantasizing over this woman.

"I want whatever you've got." Carolyn moaned. Then added, "And don't hold back." She surprised herself with that last request. Trish pushed up against her and whispered in her ear.

"If I take this now, I'm always going to want it. And I will always want it my way. Whenever I come for it, you'd better be ready to give it to me, or you will be severely punished. I promise."

"Will you spank me if I'm bad?" Carolyn knew she was getting in deeper.

"No, I'll spank you if you're good." With that, she sent a hard slap crashing down on the fleshy buttocks of the woman before her. Carolyn spread her legs.

"Good girl." Removing the fingers from her vagina, Trish spread the warm cum onto the hard cock at her vagina. She licked her fingers and commented on the salty taste before she pressed the head of the cock against Carolyn's waiting pussy lips. Carolyn pressed back anxious to feel the hard cock fill her. Trish reached down and placed her hands on Carolyn's ample hips. She forced the head of the cock into the soft velvet pussy. Carolyn's breath became heavy; she was panting.

"That's right, you can take all of me inside." She watched the contorted face of her lover agonizing with the strain of the dildo forcing its way inside of her.

"Good girl, just a few more inches." The tears burned Carolyn's cheeks as they coursed down her face.

"Good girl, you've almost got it. There." She was snugly inside.

But being filled was not enough. Carolyn could feel her muscles begin to contract. She pushed back onto the dildo as much as she could. She gasped as she felt Trish pull the cock nearly all the way out and then force it back in. Trish began fucking Carolyn slowly at first and then harder and faster. She watched as Carolyn's face changed from tears to pants.

"Yes!" Carolyn exclaimed between breaths. Her nails dug into the hard cherry wood. "Please, baby, I'm good. I'll be good."

Trish's slaps came down like rain upon Carolyn's ass. Carolyn's juices flowed faster with every one. Trish's trim athletic body showed no signs of slowing. She pumped harder and faster watching Carolyn's expression change with every move. Carolyn raised her ass higher in the air to greet the slaps as they came down. She was truly enjoying the experience.

"You like that? Let's see if you like this." She moistened the thumb of her right hand with her mouth and slid it into Carolyn's anus. Carolyn became unglued.

"Yes. Oh yes, baby. I like it. I like it. More. Please. Oh more. I'll be good. I promise. I'll be a good girl. Please take me in the ass. Please." Her pleading filled the air as Trish reached for the lube on a bedside table. Stepping around to the end of the bed she grabbed Carolyn's hair.

"Kiss the tip of my dick. That's right. Just the lips. Now slobber all over my dick you pretty little bitch." Carolyn willingly did as instructed.

"Now be a good girl and take what I'm going to give you. No begging, no pleading. Just take it." Before moving back onto the bed Trish locked her silver cuffs onto Carolyn's wrists. She had little room to move. She looked up and saw a wild woman staring back at her from the mirror. She liked the way this woman looked—fettered and out of control. The shock of the cold lube against her ass brought her back to the moment. She raised her ass high to accept the lube. She pressed her body down onto the bed and spread her legs open wide.

"That's a good girl." The enormous head of the cock in her hand, Trish pushed into the anus quickly and painfully.

"Should I take it out and try again you disgraceful little bitch?" Trish said, coldly.

"No. No, I'm sorry." Carolyn sobbed. "I'll be good. I'm sorry."

"That's better. Now let's see if you are telling the truth." She forced the cock farther into Carolyn's anus, ignoring the panting woman if front of her. And then she began to ride her, pulling and pushing Carolyn's hips to-and-fro, rocking her body back and forth on the dildo. The base of the dildo pressed against Trish's clitoris as she rocked, bringing her closer to her own orgasm. Trish looked up at the gentle face in the mirror. Carolyn's head was hung but she was no longer crying. Instead she was moaning softly.

"Let me hear it. Let me hear you moan," she demanded. Carolyn's moans filled the room. She pushed and pulled against the cock stuffed inside her ass, her muscles contracting against it.

"Please let me touch myself. I've been good. Please let me touch it so you can hear me moan," Carolyn pleaded.

Trish relented and unlocked one of the cuffs. Carolyn dragged her still shackled right arm underneath her body and between her legs. The metal of the bracelet snatched her pussy hair as she rubbed her clitoris. She felt the frenzy behind her growing as Trish began to explode.

"I'm cumming. I'm cumming in you. I want to pump your ass, you little cunt. I want to fuck you, fuck you...." Trish's voice trailed off in a list of obscenities as Carolyn screamed her own orgasm into the morning air. Trish withdrew the dildo and pulled the woman beneath her closer. She could feel her shuddering still, and it turned her on. Lying on her belly she pushed her face into her partner's cum-filled vagina and began to lick. Carolyn could only twitch in response, her orgasm having spent all of her energy. She meekly trembled through one more orgasm before drifting off to sleep in Trish's arms.

Trish awakened to find herself bound to the bed spread eagle and Carolyn parading around in Trish's uniform.

But we'll save that story for another time.

A Real Life Superhero

Kate Dominic

I want to be Xena.

Actually, I don't want to *be* Xena—except in my fantasies. Maintaining a body like hers would be way too much work. I just want to be a strong, sexy, all-muscle-no-fat warrior woman with royal connections—someone everybody knows will save the world, every time.

In other words, I want to be a real life superhero, one named Jeena.

And I want to have a sidekick lusting after me. Not Gabrielle. She's taken. I want one who's all mine and who changes from week to week to meet my latest fantasies.

I've decided my sidekick will be Arielle. She has long blond hair, and is very feminine—voluptuous, even—in a muscular, superhero, sidekickish sort of way. Good with swords, a worthy companion, someone whom I can always trust to protect my back and fight at my side. We're totally in love, of course, touching each other whenever we want, even in broad daylight, in the middle of a village. Nobody minds. After all, we're their heroes, their defenders. We can do no wrong.

In one of our first adventures, Arielle and I are perusing a stand of ripe fruit in a typical medieval village's typical open marketplace. As we walk along, I run my hands along the smooth, bare flesh below the silk short top that struggles to contain my lover's full breasts. Yes, I know silk doesn't travel as well as leather, but I like the way silk feels, and it's *my* fantasy, so Arielle's top is silk! Anyway, as I'm looking at the apples, I reach up under her short leather skirt and caress the curve of her luscious bottom. Her skin is round and smooth, and I like to bite it. Arielle never wears underwear. She wants to keep herself available for me. Which is a good thing, because I'd demand it anyway. Being able to reach up under my lover's skirt and fondle her ass in public really turns me on. The villagers laugh encouragingly when I slip my fingers into Arielle's slick folds and draw out fingers dripping with her sex honey. I bark an order at the baker. She hands me a loaf of hot, fresh bread. I smear the sticky juices on it. I take a bite, then share it with Arielle. She licks my fingers appreciatively, spreading her legs wide for me to prepare another slice.

The women in the village nod and look knowingly at their girlfriends—some even at their husbands. "*That's* the way you're supposed to do things. Like Jeena does!" they say. Then there's a rush on the baker's cart, followed by the rustle of skirts being lifted, the contented moans of women being fingered, and the sounds of people chewing as everybody has a midafternoon snack. Afternoon snack becomes a new tradition in the village—and they prosper forever after because everyone is so happy and energized.

We have several adventures in that country. In another of my favorites, I teach the local nobility the proper way to negotiate a peace treaty. The meeting takes place in the castle of one of the feuding overlords. The combatants are a mixed crowd, some women, some men—most of them highly impressed with their titles and armiesand not so sure they want to listen to the warrior woman their thoroughly disgruntled king has sent them.

As I enter the room, the assemblage rises from their seats at the great table—the women aloof in their satin dresses and silken veils, the men prim and proper in their velvet clothes. There's a collective gasp as I saunter over to my chair—wearing nothing but my boots, weapon harnesses, and jewelry. Arielle walks at my side—barefoot, shoulders erect, naked. As I sit down, Arielle kneels beside me, resting her staff against the back of the chair. While the others are still reeling in shock, she starts licking my breasts, and I start to speak.

"We'll get nothing accomplished if our minds stay focused on our anger and our differences. So I'm going to insist that everyone remove their clothing and get comfortable. That will put us all on equal footing." I shiver as Arielle licks a particularly delicious spot. "Then we're going to settle this matter once and for all. You're laying waste to the countryside, and it's going to stop. Now strip!"

No one resists Jeena's orders. Pretty soon, veils and shifts and tunics are dropped on the floor. An army of servants suddenly appears to salvage the clothing before it needs to be laundered. And since my second-in-command is servicing me, nothing less will do for the others—soon their sidekicks kneel quietly at their sides, waiting to see what I'll say next.

"A properly negotiated treaty will be in everyone's best interests." As I speak, I let everyone see how much Arielle's ministrations are turning me on. My nipples are hard and erect, dark with desire, glistening with my lover's saliva. There's another collective gasp, followed by a loud murmur of stunned disbelief as Arielle moves between my legs and licks her way downward. When her hot, probing tongue slides between my labia, I hold up my hand for silence.

"Excuse me a moment," I say, purposefully letting my voice quiver with pleasure. "My sidekick's tongue is quite delicious. I must indulge myself for a moment before I can concentrate on business." With that, I open my legs wider and slide farther down in the chair.

I shudder visibly, then take a deep breath, looking pointedly at the other sidekicks. "I said get comfortable! Everyone will negotiate much more effectively that way." I rest my hand on the back of Arielle's head. "If you don't know how, watch Arielle. Pay particular attention to how she's sucking my clit while she fingers her own." With that, I close my eyes and lift my boots up to rest on the edge of the table, snuggling comfortably into my chair as Arielle settles herself between my wide open legs.

I watch surreptitiously out of the corners of my eyes as shocked murmurs give rise to appraising glances. Then one of the overladies leans back in her chair, followed by another, then another. Pretty soon all the former combatants are comfortably ensconced, their seconds-in-command between their legs, studiously following Arielle's sterling example. Before long, the hot smell of good sex and the general sound of contented slurping fill the room. I close my eyes all the way and enjoy as Arielle's hot tongue teases an orgasm from me.

When my breath settles, I start speaking again, motioning those who haven't yet climaxed to continue and participate as they're ready. "This is how we're going to do business."

The conference lasts all day. I don't keep track of the number of times I climax. Sometimes I take breaks, lifting Arielle onto the table in front of me so I can bury my face in the honeyed feast between her legs. Later on, I eat my lunch off her belly, feeding her with my fingers as I address yet another point in the negotiations. I savor her pussy, then give her mine for dessert. As the negotiations draw to a close, I lift Arielle to her feet and kiss her soundly. She picks up her staff and stands behind me—sturdy, proud, her face glistening with my juices and flushed from her many climaxes. She's every bit a true superhero sidekick—one who's been instrumental in the development of a lasting peace treaty. She blushes deeply as the sated negotiators thank her with a round of thunderous applause.

Of course, not all our adventures are as trouble-free as that. After all, Arielle is a sidekick, so she sometimes doesn't follow orders. She'll go off on her own path, which—as is always the case in superhero tales—creates problems. So I have to punish her. Arielle expects no less of me, and my justice is always swift and fair. One day she wakes up grouchy and, in a fit of pique, spills the breakfast she's cooking. Superheros are big on courtesy, and we don't tolerate tantrums. So I sit down on a log, pull her over my knee, and spank her bare bottom until my incredibly strong superhero hand finally gets sore. By then, her backside is bright red and hot and she's crying and kicking and promising to be good. So I let her up and go off to sharpen my sword, ignoring her sniffles as she recooks breakfast and tends to the horses. Eventually, she sets a plate of steaming pancakes next to me, lays her head in my lap and whispers, "I'm sorry, Jeena. Please forgive me." So, of course, I do. After all, she's my sidekick...and I like spanking her.

Another time, Arielle is rude to me in front of a shopkeeper. As a wise superhero, I've made friends with the local craftsmen, giving them the tools and technology they need to fashion superior quality sex toys. I'm shopping in one of my favorite establishments when Arielle makes a snide comment that one of my choices must be for me because it's definitely too large for her petite derriere. Arielle knows better than to pull a sassy sidekick stunt like that in public. So I buy the plug, making a point of telling the shopkeeper Arielle will be wearing it before we leave the store. The shopkeeper is very matronly. As Arielle pouts, the shopkeeper pats her hand and says, "There now, dearie. Be glad you have a woman who knows how to pleasure your bottom. It took my girlfriend years to learn."

Arielle blushes. She blushes even more as I set our purchases out on the counter. I bend her over the display case, lift her skirt, and nudge her legs apart with my boot. Then I pick up the new jar of cream, lube a smooth string of large duotone balls, and slide them firmly up her pussy.

"Jeena," she whispers. "That feels so good. I'm sorry I was sassy."

"Apology accepted," I say pleasantly.

I put a large glob of cream on my finger. She jumps, yelping, as I touch it to the puckered pink hole between her cheeks.

"Now take your punishment as befits a sidekick."

Arielle whimpers and moans as I work the lube into her anus—slowly, lovingly, and very deliberately stretching her tight little sphincter open. Soon her pungent pussy juices trickle out around the bead string. Other women come into the shop as I minister to my young sidekick. We discuss the latest news, ignoring Arielle's groans of pleasure as we share our opinions with the shopkeeper. Within ten minutes, every toy similar to the ones I've bought has been sold out. Superheros have impeccable taste—and much influence.

When Arielle's anus is finally relaxed, I pick up the new plug, slather it with cream, and touch it to her pucker. As she moans my name, I start working it slowly up into her. It takes a while. The toy is bigger than anything she's used to. I wiggle it around, pulling it in and out as she gasps, as she gradually loosens. She yelps when, with one final, tiny push, I slide the plug in the rest of the way and her anus snugs up around the neck.

The room erupts in applause, and I pull Arielle to her feet.

"Does that feel good?" I ask, pinching her nipples.

"Yes, ma'am," she whispers, blushing as she smiles at the appreciative group around us.

"Is it too big for your 'petite derriere,' as you were so certain it would be?"

"Oh, no, ma'am." She shivers, clenching her buttcheeks as she thinks about the size of the plug up her bottom. "Um, I think it fits just right, just as you said it would."

The shopkeeper chuckles, and Arielle blushes again.

"Good," I laugh. "Then we will leave immediately for Argentown." As Arielle's eyes widen in shock, I say sternly, "Don't even think of taking those toys out. You asked for this. I want you ready and willing for me tonight."

Her hushed "yes, ma'am" is lost in a round of appreciative giggles as I take my other hand, lube up a second set of beads, and slide them up my own pussy. Then I grease a respectably sized plug and, squatting comfortably back, slide it up my own behind.

"I have plans for us tonight, Arielle. Don't screw them up."

To a round of thunderous applause, I wash my hands, then march my bemused sidekick out of the store. I toss her up on her horse, then carefully mount my own mare, setting off at a vigorous trot so Arielle will have no illusions about how the trip is going to go.

I stop a couple miles out of town. Arielle's flush lets me know she's miserably turned on. While I want to teach her a lesson, her little display doesn't warrant a true punishment. I pull my horse over to her. Her green eyes are shiny with unshed tears.

"What's the matter, love?" I ask, brushing her hair back from her face.

"I want to come," she says softly, leaning into my hand. "I need to so badly I can hardly breathe. The motion of the horse is almost more than my pussy can stand. Please, Jeena, please, may I come?"

"Certainly, love," I whisper. I reach over and untie her top. She shivers as her soft breast falls into my hand. I lean over and lick. "Touch your clit, sweetheart."

Her horse whinnies, shuffling a bit as Arielle squirms at my biting. "Quiet," I command. The horse obeys, breathing heavily but maintaining her position as I suck my lover's nipple. All animals obey Jeena. Using just my knees, I nudge our mounts forward, very slowly, my lips locked on my prize, my pussy quivering as the toys rock inside me at the rolling gait of the horses.

Arielle whimpers, shivering. I can see her butt muscles clenching as she responds to the unrelenting stimulation of the plug in her anus.

"Make yourself come, Arielle." With one hand steadying Arielle's horse, I hold my own reins in my other hand, the thin leather straps tickling my thighs as my fingers rub my mons. "Come for your superhero lover, the way a good sidekick should."

Arielle lifts the front of her skirt, her fingers moving in a frenzy as she fingers her clit. She moans, shuddering, crying out softly as she comes. My own pussy answers. As my breathing steadies, another climax already starting to build, I sit up, tweak my lover's nipple, and move my horse away. Arielle smiles sheepishly.

"Is that better?" I laugh.

"Yes, Jeena," she blushes, still panting softly. "That felt really good."

"I knew it would. You have my permission to come as many times as you want between now and when we arrive at the outskirts of Argentown."

"Oh, thank you," she purrs, closing her eyes as her fingers start moving again.

"Superheros get to have super sex," I say crisply. "Now, close up your top, and listen to my plan for dealing with the burghers tomorrow." I gasp, shivering deliciously as I climax again. This time, Arielle's laugh rings through the clearing. I urge my horse forward, setting us off at a good pace to cover some ground.

We sleep soundly that night, wrapped in each other's arms. The next day, however, Arielle's self-confidence from a day of pleasure apparently overcomes her good judgment. She deliberately disobeys my direct orders, the negotiations collapse, and we end up having to defend ourselves and the good townspeople in one of those smoke-filled battles that only look good on TV. With the city finally in good hands, we beat a hasty retreat, still pursued by angry bands from the factions whose coup I've foiled despite my sidekick's antics. I'm furious. And scared. Arielle has nearly been killed a dozen times during the day.

I've only really whipped Arielle a few times. In each instance, I've done it because she's openly defied me, thereby causing problems that took me a whole episode to correct. While I like saving the day, I get really pissed at having to draw my sword and use my gymnastics for stupid stuff.

We escape with the twenty noblewomen hostages we've rescued, riding hard until we're certain we're safe. As night falls, we make camp. I don't even wait for dinner. I take off my sword belt, double it over, and march Arielle off to the stump that holds my saddle. Arielle's face is already wet with tears of remorse and trepidation.

"Take off your clothes," I order as the women gather round to witness.

"Yes, ma'am," she whispers. She doesn't try to argue. She knows she's earned her punishment. She lays down her weapons. Then she unties her top, her firm, heavy, young breasts falling out as she shrugs the smooth silk over her shoulders. When she hesitates, I nod peremptorily and snap the belt. She's sniffling loudly now. Arielle unties her belt. Her skirt falls open and drops to her feet. Then she leans over and unlaces and pulls off her boots. When she's naked, she slowly hauls her gorgeous, sorry butt to the saddle and bends over.

Arielle stays in position, yelling and wiggling and dancing on her tiptoes, as I very methodically set her ass on fire with my belt. None of this holding-back-because-she's-a-lady crap. Arielle's a superhero's sidekick, so she gets one helluva strapping. Every crack of that belt kissing her skin echoes through the forest. Almost as loudly as Arielle's howls. I make sure she really learns her lesson. I strap her bottom until it glows hot red in the setting sun, and I see the other women reach back to rub their own behinds in sympathy.

Afterwards, Arielle is properly remorseful. She is a very trustworthy sidekick. I lie down in my sleeping blankets and draw her into my arms. She snuggles against me, trying to get her blazing sore bottom comfortable under the scratchy wool. When she wiggles too much, I swat her.

"Owwie!" Her tears are still close to the surface.

"Settle down," I say sternly. "Your backside's supposed to hurt. That's why it's called a punishment." As she tucks tearfully up against me, I tug my top open for her. Her lips nuzzle around for a nipple—licking, sucking, kissing. When she's settled in against me, when her mouth and tongue are comfortably suckling, I stroke her hair with one hand and finger my myself to a raging orgasm with the other. Our misadventure has really scared me, so I take a very long time, letting the sweet tug of her mouth awaken the need deep inside me before I let myself come. Then we go to sleep. Arielle knows better than to ask to come when she's being punished.

The next morning, since everyone in camp is female, I make Arielle go around naked, wearing only her nipple ring, nipple clamps, and a lightly pressured clamp on her clit. Since I really want to draw attention to her flaming rear, I hang weights from the clamp, so she has to walk with her legs wide open. The weights swing back and forth, tugging mercilessly on her clit, making her juices run down her leg as her hips roll with each step. I invite the women to inspect her rear. After all, they were also endangered by her behavior. And I want them all very aware of what happens to anyone who disobeys me; however, since Arielle has paid for her sins, I also invite them to admire her body. After all, she is beautiful, and she likes showing off her body. She's strong and sexy and worthy of being a superhero's sidekick. And she loves having people finger her nipples and clit and the smooth, naked folds of her vulva.

By the way, Arielle keeps her pussy shaved for me—except for the rare occasions in winter when I'm cold and in the mood to kiss soft, fur-covered lips.

After she kneels and apologizes to each of the women in turn, they show her their forgiveness by lifting her carefully into a sturdy leather sling they've hung on a nearby tree. They cluster around her and lay their hands and mouths and bodies on her in blessing. Arielle moans as the clamps are removed, first from one breast—a blue satin glove reaches out and sharply twists the oversensitized nipple, working it hard as the feeling surges back into it. Arielle's groans die to whimpers as the pain passes and the sore flesh is sucked tenderly into a hot, wet, waiting mouth. Then the other nipple is released. Then the weights on her clit— one at a time, so that she feels each rush of blood in exquisite detail. Finally the clamp itself is removed—quickly. Strong lips immediately suck hard on her pulsing clit, working the awakening hood back and forth over the swollen nub beneath. Arielle yells, thrashing, her arms held tightly, lovingly, by other women. Fingers, too many to count, some gloved, some naked, slide over her folds, exploring her outer lips, her inner ones, moving deep up into her cunt. Some of the wisest curl up inside her, pressing hard, until she begs for release. Others, coated with butter, cup and massage her sore, well-punished butt cheeks, sliding up and down her crack, teasing her open, then sliding up inside.

I love hearing Arielle's continuous cries of pleasure as she submits to each respectfully questing touch.

"Jeena!" she begs. "Please! Please—I want you!!"

Arielle is now almost insane with lust, filled with the warm, loving, passionate absolution bestowed by the strong hands that restrain her. I pull off my warrior's clothes until only the leather straps of my sword harness cover my body. Then, facing the minions, I straddle my lover's face, groaning in pleasure as Arielle's hot tongue licks up my slit. I shiver as her cry vibrates against me, as I share in what I know is one of many orgasms sweeping through her.

Arielle knows just where to press, where to suck and lick, to make my juices flow onto her face. Women all around me follow my lead, taking off their flowing silk and satin gowns, helping each other from velvet robes—pleasuring each other with touch as they bare their skin. A young woman with short red hair steps to my side, runs her fingers up my arm, and kisses me as I grind against Arielle's face. The young woman kisses her way down my neck and over my shoulders, licking hotly, tantalizingly, over the curve of my breast. She rubs her cheek against my nipple, teasing a response from my already hard nub. Then she looks up at me, her dark brown eyes laughing, and slowly sucks the tip, then the entire areola into her mouth. And she keeps it there, suckling as I gasp with pleasure. I spread my legs wider, feel Arielle's tongue snake up inside me, licking deep into my cunt. Naked women take turns at each of Arielle's pleasure sites, kissing each other as they fondle her cunt and ass, fingering each other's vulva as they suck her breasts and clit. Someone new—I see only luxurious swirls of golden blond hair falling from an errant comb—reaches up and slides her fingers between the legs of the woman at my breast. The red-haired woman shudders, sucking harder, just as Arielle again sucks my clit. I yell as an orgasm resonates through my body.

My cry sets off a frenzy of motion. Another woman is at my other breast. I feel a hand trace my buttocks, then the hot lick of a tongue sliding up into my crack. I squat back over Arielle's face, quivering as the tongue slides over my sphincter, then licks determinedly, relaxing me, working its way in. A finger teases next to Arielle's lips. I shiver as my lover moves up, concentrating mercilessly on my clit. The finger slides into my cunt. Farther and farther. Pressing deep, curling forward, teasing the core spot deep inside me that sings with my most heart-stopping orgasms. Arielle's climaxes are almost constant now, her cries continuous. I look down to see her chest heaving as she gasps for enough oxygen to feed the fire of her passion, to meet the need devouring her. She arches to meet the questing mouths pulling her passion from her.

Suddenly, Arielle shudders hard beneath me. In response, the women at my breasts suckle deep and long, like they are drawing nourishment from the strength of my body. The tongue between my nether cheeks pokes in hard, fucking me with ardent, ladylike glee as I shiver deliciously. The finger in my cunt presses relentlessly, stroking the fluid source of my sex. Finally, Arielle shrieks, licking once more, then taking my clit fully in her lips and sucking, mercilessly working the hood of my clit over the nub beneath.

I scream out my war cry. My whole body shudders as my cunt contracts, my whoop of release deafening. Arielle howls against my cunt, arching up hard against me, convulsing like her body is exploding with pleasure. My ears ring with the cries of joyfully shared orgasms all around me.

I lift Arielle from the sling and into my arms. We kiss each other and slowly collapse onto the sweet grass beneath us. The smell of well-licked, well-serviced cunts fills the clearing as the rest of the women join us and the morning sun rises higher into the trees.

We nap together, all of us, our faces resting between each other's legs and against each other's well-suckled breasts. Arielle and I especially sleep soundly. After all, another superhero adventure will be upon us when we wake up. We need to be ready.

The Princess and the Outlaw

Jean Roberta

There was a full moon over the kingdom that night, and the scent of summer flowers wafted up from the palace gardens to the balcony where Princess Irene stood gazing into the night sky. Her thin cotton gown clearly revealed two firm nipples that were hardening under the caress of the evening breeze. Long black ringlets tumbled over her shoulders as she pulled the jeweled pins from her hair, one by one.

At twenty, the rosy-cheeked Irene was ripe for marriage and childbearing, according to her old nurse who frequently advised the king to find his daughter a husband. Many a prince had courted the lively heiress to the throne, but she found fault with every suitor and sent them all home disappointed. She had no intention of marrying a man who would usurp her power as soon as she became queen.

For weeks, there had been nervous talk in the palace about a peasant uprising. Irene had seen strange horses and unaccustomed activity in the nearby village and knew that something would happen soon. Although she was afraid of the violence of an angry mob, she felt strangely elated at the thought of her father's rule being challenged by the peasants who had been overworked and underfed for too long. She knew that she had been raised in pampered luxury at the expense of others. Once the throne was hers, she intended to bring in an era of peace and prosperity for all.

Irene wished she could meet the legendary Yora of the Forest, who was already being called The General and the heroine of the revolution. For years, Yora had lived as an outlaw with a small band of followers, robbing any rich travelers foolhardy enough to enter the forest that she regarded as her own preserve. Rumor had it that Yora was riding through the countryside on her swift mare, Lightning, to recruit men and women into a rebel army that grew bigger every day.

For some reason, Irene shivered pleasurably when she thought of the female outlaw. The princess pictured Yora in a rough, manly jerkin of deerskin, with trousers that did nothing to hide the shape of muscular thighs and womanly buttocks. Irene marveled at the fate that had made the outlaw her enemy, although the princess knew that if she had been born in a hut where the goats and the chickens shared space with humans, she would probably have joined Yora's band.

To the eyes that watched her from the foliage below, the princess appeared both delicate and voluptuous. The tight lacing of her gown accentuated the crease between her full breasts as she leaned forward and listened to the leaves rustling and the birds calling from the trees. The exuberant curve of her bottom was only slightly disguised by the graceful expanse of skirt that covered it. The eyes that watched her would have liked to see the round cheeks and the slender waist cruelly laid bare at the whipping post in the town square.

Sensing danger, Irene strained to hear every sound coming from the grounds below. Too late, she stepped backward as a sinewy arm clutched the balcony railing, followed by the shrewd, sun-browned face of a woman who spent much of her time in the open air. Suppressing a scream, Irene tried to rush into her chamber where she could lock the peasant woman out of her life.

With amazing speed, the intruder threw herself feet first over the railing and seized the princess by one wrist. Struggling desperately, Irene found herself gripped around the waist from behind while a rough hand covered her mouth. The hand smelled of earth, venison, sweat, and gunpowder. "Be silent," hissed a slightly husky voice into one of Irene's small pink ears. Irene gasped when the arm that clutched her waist slid upward and the strong hand rudely grasped one of her breasts as though it were a fruit in the market.

Before she fully realized what was happening, the princess had been pushed into her chamber by a vigorous woman of about thirty who looked out of place amongst the velvets and brocades of a royal boudoir. Turning to face her, Irene forced herself to look into the clear green eyes of her assailant. "I know who you are," whispered the princess. "They call you Yora of the Forest. I will not call the guard if you promise not to harm me." Irene jerked when she felt the cold steel of a hunting knife held against her throat.

"Your Highness," sneered Yora, "alert your servants, and they will find you dead. I need your jewels. The people need them." Sensing that the princess would do as she was told, Yora suddenly released her captive, allowing Irene to gaze at the figure before her. The princess noted that the queen of the outlaws was slimmer than she was, with skin that showed creamy white with freckles wherever the sun had not tanned it.

On impulse, Yora bowed low to the princess, trying to hide her genuine admiration in a sarcastically muttered "my lady." The wild woman of the forest pulled off her green cap with a jaunty feather in it, exposing a head full of short reddish-brown hair that stuck out at various angles like rooster feathers. Glancing into the full-length pier glass, Irene could see her own glowing reflection along with that of the strong woman whose body seemed to exude such energy that the air around her almost crackled. Looking quickly at Yora's small, firm breasts and compact hips covered by deerskin, the princess felt her heart begin to melt, but she was determined not to surrender completely to a lawless peasant whose honor had not been tested.

With perfect self-control, Irene strode to her dressing table and unlocked a large ebony case, inlaid with mother-of-pearl. The light from the candles set in sconces around the wall lit up the jewels that sprang into view as soon as the princess lifted the lid.

"Whe-e-ew!" whistled Yora. "So that is how the royal family spends the people's tax money. To make a lazy wench beautiful." Her cool, green-eyed gaze traveled slowly, deliberately from the hem of the younger woman's floating gown to her tight waist to her young, full breasts straining against the thin fabric. The princess knew that the outlaw's gaze was meant to be insulting, and she felt herself growing hot with shame and suppressed excitement.

Yora plunged her hands into the glittering jewels to hide her confusion. She had hated the royal family and all it stood for ever since her father, as a groom in the royal stables, had his right hand cut off for a theft he had not committed. From her aunts and her sisters, Yora had heard of seductions and ravishments inflicted on defenseless maidservants by idle courtiers in the palace. She had decided at a young age that the hard life of a low-born woman was not for her. Before she was seventeen, Yora stole a horse and set out to make her own way in the world, a way that sometimes included sharing the pallet of a woman of easy virtue or the lonely wife of a sailor at sea.

Yora had never before had such close contact with a noble-woman, and it made her uneasy in spite of herself. She wondered whether she were truly born to serve women like Irene, and the thought enraged her. What would become of her quick wit and sound instincts if she lost her heart to a vain young princess? Yora fought off her growing curiosity about Irene. As the descendant of ancient warrior queens, had she a depth of spirit belied by her luxurious surroundings?

The older woman would not admit to herself why she wanted to see the tender flesh of the ripe maiden before her exposed to the humiliations suffered by village girls trapped by the king's soldiers. Yora smiled slyly, and Irene knew that her smile boded ill.

"That is not all, my lady," muttered the outlaw. "Surely you have other treasures than these, perhaps on your person." The princess gasped in shock as she guessed Yora's intention. Three fast strides brought Yora to the outer door of the boudoir, which she quickly locked. Then she turned to Irene, who was gazing in dismay at the handle of the knife that Yora carried in a sheath at her hip. The princess knew that it would be dangerous to struggle against the outlaw. Deep in her heart, the princess had no wish to summon help if it would endanger the woman who was known as the hope of her people.

Irene blushed but did not resist as Yora unlaced her gown and ripped it from her shoulders. "You must be thoroughly searched," Yora informed her harshly, "as my sisters in the village and the fields are stripped of their modesty when their lecherous masters call them thieves." Tears trembled in Irene's eyes as the outlaw chief pulled the lace petticoat from the soft pink curves of her hips and backside and pulled her stockings down her legs. The robust young woman stood trembling in the flickering candlelight that cast shadows from her dancing nipples across her bare body. Many a suitor had wished to see what Yora saw.

Pulling the princess close to her, Yora felt a pang of pity. "Little one," she murmured, softening, "this will be no worse than the touch of a lover. If you still have your maidenhead, I will handle it gently."

Irene could no longer control her anguish. "You are no better than a drunken guard, Yora!" she whispered as loudly as she dared. "I do not deserve such punishment from you when I have never harmed you or yours. I give such counsel to my father and his ministers as they will accept, but they dismiss my concern for the common people, saying I am still a soft-hearted child. I promise you, General, that when I am queen there will be justice in this land."

The forest woman looked up from massaging the princess's heavy breasts and roughly squeezing their hard nipples. Yora was filled with a new respect for the young woman she was tormenting. For her part, Irene pressed her thighs together in a vain effort to break the spell that Yora seemed to have cast on her, which made the young woman want to beg her seducer for pleasure and relief.

Yora's sense of honor was touched, and she knew that she owed the princess satisfaction in any form she chose to take it. "Lady, I will not let you go," murmured the outlaw, "but ask of me what you will." As a token of her newfound humility, Yora deftly shrugged off her jerkin, exposing her well-developed arms and small shapely breasts to Irene's curious gaze.

Without a word, Irene tugged at the outlaw's trousers. Yora's breathing became irregular as she stepped out of her last item of clothing. Together, the two women tumbled onto the large, canopied bed that stood in a corner. Their lips met in a long kiss as arms and legs intertwined. Eagerly the princess opened her mouth to Yora's exploring tongue. As waves of excitement traveled from the young woman's mouth and breasts to her rigid clitoris, she moaned in Yora's arms.

A voice deep in Yora's mind told her that this communion was meant to be and that somehow Irene had always known whose promised bride she was. The outlaw was not often moved to pity or to wonder, but the princess's trust in her was unlocking her heart.

Irene gasped with pleasure when Yora's strong left hand opened and filled the wet cave between her legs. The princess's buttocks lifted off the bed as Yora began to frig her with slow, deep strokes intended to bring her frenzy to the climax she craved. Irene felt lightheaded as her warm dark eyes met her ravisher's light green ones. The princess writhed in ecstasy, and Yora's name burst from her lips.

Irene came in a series of sharp spasms that made her cling to Yora for support. Much as she wanted to leave her blood-stained fingers deep in the young lady's fiery well, Yora withdrew her hand enough to cup the tender mound until its spasms stopped.

"I am no longer a maiden," whispered Irene in a sadly resigned tone. "Who would marry me now?"

"No man, if I can prevent it," her lover whispered back. "You are not meant for such a marriage. You are betrothed to me now." The princess smiled in answer, suddenly feeling tired. Yora stroked Irene's silky raven tresses as though soothing her own daughter to sleep. "Pretty one," whispered the outlaw, "I will protect you."

Irene chuckled, raising herself on one elbow to look once more into the knowing eyes of the older woman. "Have you forgotten who I am?" asked the princess aloud. The woman at her side was reminded that Irene was accustomed to having her will obeyed. "My dear queen of the forest, I could have you killed for treason. Do you really believe you could have seduced me if I had not wanted you?" Yora found Irene surprisingly strong when the young woman rolled from underneath and lay atop her fierce lover.

Yora found herself strangely willing to be commanded by the woman who was to be queen someday. A delicious feeling overtook her as the princess stroked her back, her sides, her breasts, and her flat belly with the confidence of one born to rule. Irene's long, manicured fingers found the button of flesh she was seeking between Yora's legs and exposed it to her manipulation. The hungry outlaw's resistance melted as the princess slid down her muscular body and began hungrily licking the wet seat of her pleasure.

Yora gasped as her young lover teasingly licked the hard clitoris that screamed for relief and darted her pointed tongue into the hot, pungent depths of Yora's vagina. Getting the response she wanted made the princess eager to continue, and she thrust three fingers into Yora's welcoming inner space while stroking the hard button without mercy. The rebel woman was completely outmaneuvered, and she announced her surrender by howling into a silk pillow that she clutched hastily to muffle the sound.

The princess rolled off her lover, smiling to herself in triumph. "Now the score is even," she teased the older woman. Yora was caught between conflicting desires to slap the spoiled brat for her effrontery and to nuzzle her bouncing breasts. The outlaw had never been beaten by an enemy of either sex. Yora told herself that she had given the willful princess her way because she did not want to break her spirit, but the time had come to show her who ruled the countryside beyond the palace walls.

Yora smiled to herself as she surveyed the chamber for suitable objects. Laying on the mahogany dressing table were a matching brush, comb, and mirror, gleaming softly in the light from the candles and the moon that shone through the window. Yora could not tell if the articles she admired were made of brass or gold; she only knew that they gleamed with a deep yellow luster. The thought of what she was about to do made her shake with amusement. The outlaw nimbly slid to the floor and strode across the room, then seized the brush with its long slim handle and returned to bed. "Lady," she said roughly, turning the princess onto her belly, "my search is not over. Your body is mine to explore at will." Irene struggled to see what Yora held in her hands, and the queen of the forest gave her captive's buttocks a resounding smack with the back of the brush that excited both women. "Lie still," Yora commanded.

The princess squirmed when she felt the cool bite of metal entering her still-virgin anus. Waves of pleasure flowed through her body from the site of her latest seduction, and she gave herself up to the spiraling motion of Yora's penetration. "Oooh," she moaned into the silk coverlet beneath her. Her hips moved uncontrollably as she arched her plump bottom backwards onto the thin, smooth handle. Yora seized the opportunity to reach between the spread legs of her passionate victim to find and caress her nub of pleasure.

Yora was pleased to see how well the young noblewoman accepted her prodding in a place that was not used to such attention. With royal graciousness, Irene seemed willing to reveal all the secrets of her innocent body. Yora rode her mount as though she were a bucking horse and kept her place when Irene thrashed in climax. Her entire lower region continued to throb after Yora gently removed the instrument of her conquest.

Sighing with contentment, the young beauty nestled in Yora's strong arms. Irene wished she could keep her lover with her forever, but she knew that the rebel chief who had stolen her heart could never be kept within the walls of a palace. "Yora," breathed the princess, savoring her name, "are your people planning to overthrow us? I must know."

Yora felt as though she had been stabbed in the heart. How could she have forgotten her plans so far as to tumble recklessly with the girl who was supposed to be her enemy? As an honorable woman, the outlaw queen would have to tell the truth. "Yes, little one," she said sadly. "You were all to be killed. But sweetheart—" As though struck by lightning, the princess jerked away from the woman she now saw as a monster.

Irene quivered, but her voice was steely. "Let me warn you, peasant," she hissed. "If you kill us, we will not be forgotten! My death will be avenged. Drive me into exile, and I will return with an army to take back my throne." Yora was moved by the determination she saw in the eyes of the young woman who now looked like a proudly naked goddess at the moment of creation. Yora realized that the maiden's submission had indeed been a valuable gift.

"Irene," sighed her lover. It sounded like a prayer. "My love, power is meant to be shared. You know I could never harm you after what has passed between us." The princess softened as she realized the truth of Yora's words. "The Amazon tribes of old were always ruled by two queens. Sometimes they were lovers. We will revive that tradition."

Irene was appeased, but she needed to know all that was in her lover's mind. "Am I to be a sop for the loyalists?" she demanded. "A figurehead queen to give the appearance that nothing has changed while decisions are made by someone else?"

Yora laughed at the young spitfire she held in her arms. "No, my lover," she assured her. "It is your destiny to rule, and you will. Some of your friends must have their power taken from them because they do not use it wisely, but your people need you, Irene." Yora paused for breath. "I need you," she added quietly.

"Wild woman," laughed the princess, holding her lover's experienced face in her hands. "No more than I need you." The full moon still flooded the room with silvery light, and the lovers accepted it as a blessing. Under the eye of Lady Moon, the two woman began to move in unison as they each yearned to take and be taken, to fill each other full, and to send their cries of joy to the night sky like incense from an altar.

They pleased each other until the early dawn summoned Yora to escape from the palace as quietly as she had climbed the young lady's balcony in what seemed to her like an earlier age.

Little Buttons
Danielle Carriveau

You have always had a fascination with little buttons rows of
tiny fasteners carving between my breasts so i wear my
little white shirt with the little plastic buttons and you lick
your teeth with expectant salivation my sister's teeth
shined like that once when she made six ripe peaches disappear with slippery swallows until she was nauseated
you're like that you will eat my ripe skin so fast you'll get
allergic and then what will you do on a wet and moonless
night when my juices are sticky like summer sex like the
August i lost my virginity in those purple panties with the
big white dots stealing around my ankles, every bite then
was like swallowing pieces of summer itself, now i'm just a
halo of tiny hairs in a little white shirt begging you to
suckle my circumference, as i watch you through aureole
irises all i can taste is the smell of me in your morning
breath kisses makes me push my nose into your mouth like
a cat sniffing tuna fish exhales the scent peels my peach
fuzz skin cleaving my seed like you used a watermelon
knife i

am

anxious—

and you know exactly how to push.

Choke
Dorian Key

I know I'm in trouble when I start thinking about a boy's cunt. When I want to uncover him slowly, feel his sweet raw under my thumbs, the strongest muscle wrapped around my fist.

And that's how I've been thinking about you.

Just pausing between words here and watching my hand grip this pen makes my fingers tremble, my skin, my fingertips wanting to trace you and not these weak words.

It's hard not to rush. Slow down, boy; I caution myself. So I begin with the beginning, the bottom, the street you're standing on. I love seeing things and starting from the ground up. On my belly or back, doesn't matter. Both are equally fascinating, equally frustrating, taking me so long to go where I want to go.

It was very hard not to sink to the street yesterday while you fumbled with your chaps, your jacket. I was torn between wanting to help you with your multitude of zippers and snaps, to bundle you up and keep you warm, and my need to sink downward so I could work my way up you.

You weren't packing, but still I couldn't keep my eyes from your groin and the place waiting for your boycock. The slight pouch of your button fly made me imagine what your hard-on would be like, how it would feel between my teeth and how I would hold you up from below by anchoring you deep in my throat.

But you're really the one who'd have me trapped, a trick on the ground. And I'd stay so willingly, so stunned by a boy who comes gunning, running himself down my throat. And now I know by the look in your eyes that you know the words I've written here as surely as if I'd spoke—

I hope
to choke
on you.

Giving Thanks
Wendy Becker

You took me to your bed, then to your church.

In your quiet way, you let me know that we'd spent a sacred night together, and now it was God's turn to hear our rapture down at the Evangelical Mission. I shook in my ryebread body. Jews from Queens don't know Jesus, though we've seen him at the Marconis' for years, hanging next to the Virgin Mary, her sad eyes and dripping candles protecting the honor of uniformed Catholic girls, his hands bleeding the blood of the righteous.

You could come to synagogue with me, we could meet the rabbi, she's a really liberal reform and very nice, you know. But she'll still be happy you're a doctor. That's a joke. And Sammy Davis Jr. is Jewish; you wouldn't be the only one. Really? This Friday? This is great! Thank God. I mean, thank YOU.

What? Oh, yeah, I guess it is only fair that I go with you, too. Mrs. Washington looks white, you say? I won't be the only one? Don't tease me, this is serious. They killed my people over religion. Oh, yeah, guess you'd know about having a history of persecution. Sorry. I'm just nervous. Yeah, I'll wear the yellow shirt. Yeah, I'll meet the pastor. What do you mean he'll be disappointed I'm not a doctor? Oh. I get it.

Cinderblock walls. Fluorescent lights. Worn gray linoleum under brown folding chairs. The smell of bleach and AquaNet envelopes twelve women in choir gowns, disciples backed up by a band with a bass, all standing in front of big felt banners with messages of hope. And damnation. The coat rack at the back is full. I have nothing to hang my expectations on. None of the saints I'd run into casually at the neighbor's back in Queens are in attendance today.

A fat woman in a navy blue dress reaches out to you. Chile, how have you been? So sorry about your grandma. And Miles has been asking after you. Again. That boy won't take no for an answer, he'll keep after you till you marry him, or someone else, mark my words.

In a sea of bobbing hats, tongues cluck agreement. You tell me, now don't be put off. They know I like sisters, but they hate the sin and not the sinner, and most of them don't even go that far, because their own closets are jam packed with skeletons too. And church is family, and family's family, and they just want what they think is best.

Aunt Sylvia. Uncle Ira. Make your old aunt and uncle happy. Just meet the Katz boy and go to the Jewish Singles club once in a while, is that too much to ask?

Yeah, I say to you under my breath, it doesn't hurt anyone if they try, huh? Your hand in mine is my thanks and their cue to look away. This is more mysterious than sex, scarier than red blood on white underwear in the seventh grade.

The preacher takes the stand, or is it the altar, or the podium? I am too embarrassed to ask you the name. Afraid to call attention to my lox-colored face, to use my scratchy, dry matzo voice. You sit next to me, running your fingers through my hair, seeming not to worry that you brought a woman to your bed, a Jew to Jesus' house, a butch in crisp pants to a sea of print dresses.

I whisper that I'm nervous. Hot breath and steamy words hit my ear. Just follow along, it will be fine. This is a part of me, baby. It's inside of me. Like you. Like last night.

Pray for Mrs. Mulah, whose arthritis prevented her joining us today. And for Brother Aikens, who is fighting cancer. I think of Grandpa Sol's swollen joints, cousin Hilda's tumor, and of last night. Last night, when I felt our sameness through miles of smooth skin and hard nipples, pink tongues and dark, hopeful eyes. The thousand beautiful words I summoned for the color of your skin have slipped away, and I am left alone, pale, as the pastor gives thanks.

We stand. You take my left hand in yours, and I think you are trying to reassure me until a teenager in a Raiders jersey and baggy cords says, "Ma'am?," his large hand extended. Like yours, his hand is warm, dark and dry. Like you, he knows the words. This is not my native language, and my tongue trips over unfamiliar cadences as it calls names my God does not respond to. Still, I find myself agreeing with the message of goodwill that I mumble, because, as we found out in a tangle of sheets and fingers and tongues and sighs, peace and love can live anywhere.

The pastor asks: What do *you* love the most? What are *you* thankful for? Shout it out! he commands. Everyone speaks at once. Your hands drift towards the ceiling and in the flurry of words I hear my name. You speak it like you did last night, when my mouth touched your wetness, when my arms wrapped around your hips. I say your name, quietly, so you don't hear, giving thanks for the join in your legs and the tips of your fingers raised in prayer.

It is suddenly quiet, except for the voice of an old woman who has fallen to the floor. She is yelling, sounds rushing from her lips like air from a punctured tire. I don't understand what she is saying. Tongues, you say, and I imagine my mouth on yours, tasting holy words I don't understand. Miss Gillian, she gets the Lord every Sunday, you inform me. Do you understand her? I whisper urgently. Yes, I understand her. She's had a hard life. This is her time to shine. That's not what I meant. Oh, you say slowly. Do I understand the words? I understand that the Lord is here. He's in her. Your words from before echo: This is a part of me, baby. It's inside of me. Like you. Like last night.

Like last night. Polished cherry, chestnut, iced tea, sarsaparilla, redwood, terra cotta, topaz, fudge; more original than ebony, chocolate, coffee or cinnamon but still unable to capture your thousand layers of brown, your hundred shades of pink. Your eyes are dark like mine, heavy lidded but smiling as you reach for me, your fingers long like twigs, warm like July and soft like chamois. I give thanks as white teeth framed by cocoa lips find my nipples. My legs open slowly, beige against your deep red sheets. I am full with your fingers, warmed by your words in my ear, chilled as my hands find the long, raised scar he gave you when he found you with her. Our lives have been as different as our hair: yours, long and wild; mine, short and severe. Your mouth on my stomach, your tongue brushing my thigh, reminds me that our wetness is the same milky color, our clits the same hard buds, and that it would take more than a man with a knife to cut you off from your passion.

Something cold and metal hits my skin. It's the small gold cross you wear around your neck. Jesus, he watches over me, even in bed, you say. Especially in bed, you say, laughing. You stroke me harder, faster. My stomach tightens, my hands clench into fists, an orgasm washes over me. Spent, I collapse into your arms. You pull me close, and then I am above you, my tongue exploring your mouth, my hands clasped behind your head. For the past three years, I have seen you. I have heard your voice. I have even, on occasion, smelled your perfume and sweat, and once or twice, quite by accident, I have touched you. But never have I tasted you. I lower myself between your legs, my fingers opening you, my tongue finding your wetness. Your hips rock. My name escapes your lips. I hold you as you shake and moan.

I love you, I whisper. Amen, sister, you breathe back.

Center of Attention
Dawn Dougherty

There was something about being out with her family that
made me want to fuck her.

Maybe it was how better looking she was than the rest of
her family. Maybe it was the fact that I couldn't have her that
made me want her so bad. All I know is that when we all sat
down to dinner at the restaurant I could barely look at my
menu from wanting to slip underneath the table and unzip her
pants.

Her parents had just gotten back from an extended vacation when they called to invite us to dinner.

"Please don't make me look at pictures," I pleaded as we
got dressed. I twirled my hair around my fingers and knotted
it up on top of my head.

"You don't have to look at pictures," she said as she pulled
her shirt over her head. "But you do have to keep up with the
conversation."

I let out an exasperated sigh as I sprayed my curls in place
and slipped my earrings on. "I'm ordering a very expensive
meal."

"Yes, honey."

"And if your brother makes one comment about church I'll let him have it."

"Yes, dear."

"Are you even listening?"

She came over and gave me a kiss on top of the head. "I'll be downstairs."

The minute we got to the restaurant and she hugged her parents I was wet. By the time the waitress took our order I had my hand on her thigh. As her brother droned on about the new secretary at work I wrapped one of my black leather boots around her pant leg and started to inch it up towards her knee.

She smiled and nodded her head at her brother and gave a little smirk I knew was meant for me.

"You okay?" she asked quietly as the waitress dropped a bowl of steaming pasta in front of her.

"I could be better."

After we ate she got up to go to the bathroom, and I stared at her ass she walked away.

"So how is your family?" her mother asked, interrupting my thoughts.

"Oh, they're fine." I managed to keep them entertained until she came back.

We kissed them good-bye after cappuccino and tiramisu and drove out of the parking lot.

"Why is it that when we go out with my parents you can't control yourself?"

I wiggled my way over to her side of the car and stroked the outline of her breast. "I don't know. It's the same way at parties. You look so good when you're talking to other people."

"It's because I ignore you, and you know it," she looked down at me. "You can't stand not being the center of attention. Admit it."

"I don't know what you're talking about," I said as I kissed the side of her neck. I was thinking about how good she smelled when she pulled the car over to a rest area.

"What are you doing?"

She stopped the car and turned off the ignition.

"Do you have to pee?" I asked. "I don't think they have a bathroom here."

"Do me a favor and get out of the car."

Two men had just raped a sixteen-year-old boy at a rest stop a few months before, so I was a little apprehensive. I got out and she met me around on my side. It was a dark, and there was only one other car parked almost half a mile away.

"Honey, this isn't exactly safe."

She ignored me and grabbed both my arms and pulled them around my back and kissed me hard on the lips. She snaked her tongue inside my mouth, pulled my wrists back hard, and held on to them both with one hand. She continued to kiss me as she grabbed the hem of my skirt with her free hand and pulled it up just under my ass and squeezed.

Several cars whizzed by, and I looked up to see if anyone was pulling in.

"Pay attention, babe," she said. With a smooth motion, she let go of my skirt, grabbed the top of my underwear, and pulled it down to my knees.

"It's really too busy here," I said. She wasn't listening. I wondered how many people were about to see my ass hanging out.

She put her entire mouth over mine and gave me a hot kiss, pulling back only to bite down hard on my neck, collarbone, and shoulders. I was sure she was leaving marks. She pushed me up against the passenger door, and I yelped as the handle dug into my hip. I'd be bruised from head to toe before the night was over.

She unbuttoned the first three buttons on my sweater and unsnapped the front of my bra. Then she pulled up the hem of my skirt and tucked it into the waistband leaving my ass and pussy fully exposed. I felt like a fool with my underwear still around my ankles, but she didn't seem to notice as she stepped back and checked me out. I was glad I wore my black boots. They looked great.

She opened the back door and told me to sit on the edge of the seat. When I did, she knelt outside the car, pulled my underwear off, and spread my legs. The wetness between my legs kept my lips from parting. She took my left ankle and placed my foot on the armrest. My right leg stayed planted on the ground. My lips spread wide and the air on my cunt felt cool.

She leaned back on her heels and took a slow, even breath. As she did I saw someone's headlights flash across the car. I sat up halfway, startled and nervous.

"Shit!" I said.

She didn't move. "Wait," she whispered. "They may just drive by."

The car stopped about thirty feet behind us.

We both sat frozen waiting for something to happen. They had to be able to see us. The car stayed there for almost a minute, then slowly backed up to about fifty feet away and turned their lights off.

Through the rear window I could see it was a man and a woman. They watched us for a minute, and then they turned to each other to kiss. In a minute her head disappeared into his lap.

We both looked at each other.

"I don't mind if they don't mind," she said. "Besides, they'll never even see your face, honey." She leaned forward and pushed me back down on the seat.

I lay back tensely, and she had to press my knees apart until they rested in an open position. I wondered how much of my legs they could see. I wondered what the women at work would think if they knew my girlfriend fucked me at a rest stop while some guy got his dick sucked and watched.

Then with total precision the very tip of her tongue grazed just the edge of my clit. I forgot about the voyeurs as she shot her tongue out and hit me again. I moaned and pulled my thighs in towards her head. She pushed them away and kept her hands planted on the inside of my legs.

"Do you like them watching?" and her tongue was at my clit again. She flicked her tongue over my clit four or five more times then stopped and pulled my hips a little farther out the door. This time she slowed down and used her tongue in small, tight circles. My pussy was arched up off the seat to meet her. My tits lay open across my shirt and bounced to the rhythm of her tongue.

She stopped.

"Roll over."

I did, and she pulled me down so my knees and ass were outside the car. They definitely had a full shot of me now. Then she pushed my skirt up to my waist, and I heard her unzip her pants. I looked back to see her slide a fat dildo out of the crotch of her pants.

She had packed for dinner out with her parents.

I smiled.

She pushed my knees farther apart and my boots scraped across the dirt. She bent her head down, pushed my cheeks apart, and slid her tongue into my ass. Her movements were slow and juicy, and I practically dripped onto the ground I was so wet. I loved to get fucked up the ass.

She dipped her tongue into me and rimmed me hard. I pushed my ass into her face and used my own hands to spread myself even wider. She groaned from deep inside her throat as she met my resistance with her entire mouth.

After a minute she slowed and then stopped. She spread my ass farther and placed the tip of the dildo outside of my asshole. She dropped it down and pushed it slightly into my cunt to get it wet, then brought it up again and slowly started to push into me.

I lay still while she worked it in. She placed both of her hands on my hips and used them for leverage. After a few minutes of slow rocking the dildo was all but an inch in. She paused then pushed the last inch in hard and held it there tight inside of me.

She brought her hands up to my shoulders and pulled them back as she started with slow short pumps. She gradually increased her speed when she felt me pushing against her. I felt the leather smack against the inside of my thighs. She was on her knees between my spread legs with her hand on my shoulders fucking me up the ass with my favorite dildo. I was in heaven.

She took one hand off my shoulder and brought it around to the base of my cunt. She moved up to my clit and started to massage me. My ass tightened around the dildo, and I gritted my teeth. She bent over and rested her head between my shoulder blades and whispered in my ear.

"Come right here, baby, with me up your ass and these two getting off on you."

She clamped her teeth down on my neck and bit and kissed me while she stroked my clit. My ass loosened, and she moved into strong pounding strokes. I grabbed the edge of the seat as I came. My body jerked hard as she pushed and continued to rub her fingers over me.

I imagined them watching me come and wondered if they'd ever seen two dykes do it before. I bit my lip and strained my arms as I held onto the upholstery.

She slowed and lay on top of me for a minute breathing, catching her breath.

"Whore," she joked. I pictured how we must have looked from fifty feet away.

"You're the whore! This was totally your idea."

She sat back and slowly eased the dildo out of me. My muscles contracted with the final pull out, and I relaxed. I pulled my skirt back down over my ass as she took the dildo off and threw it onto the floor in the back seat.

"I hope we don't get pulled over."

I'm sure the cops would love to confiscate a dildo off of two lesbians.

"Can you see them?" she asked looking back. She was wiping the dirt off of her knees.

I nodded my head. I didn't particularly want to see them. What if they were totally gross and disgusting? I wanted to imagine them as gorgeous and bisexual.

As I got into the front seat I felt the stickiness between my thighs and squeezed them together tight. My ass hurt as I adjusted myself and put my seat belt on.

"They're driving by."

I looked in the rearview mirror, and sure enough their car was inching towards ours. We both sat waiting to see what they'd do. As they passed they just smiled and nodded. The woman's was fixing her hair. The man just grinned. They didn't look gorgeous or bisexual.

As she started the car, I curled up around her arm.

"We need to go out with your parents more often."

"We sure do," she said as she pulled out onto the highway and headed home.

Always

Cecilia Tan

Morgan was always the one who wanted a child. Even when I first met her, before we got involved, before we got engaged, always the talk of motherhood with her, of empowering Earth-mother stuff and of making widdle baby booties. I, on the other hand, had always said I would never have children, was sure somehow that I would never decide to bear a child, and yet I had always thought about it, secretly. So when I fell in love with Morgan, and she fell in love with me, and we had a hilltop wedding where we both wore white dresses and two out of our four parents looked on happily, I figured I was off the hook on the parenting issue.

This was, of course, before John, and way before Jillian. But I'm getting ahead of myself.

Back up to the summer of 1989. New England. Cape Cod. Morgan and I are in a hammock in the screened in porch of her aunt's summer house. The night is turning smoothly damp after a muggy day, cars hiss by on pavement still wet from the afternoon's rainshower, the slight breeze rocks us just enough to make me feel weightless as I drowse. I am on my back with one foot hanging out each side of the hammock; Morgan rests in the wide space between my legs, her spill of brown curls spread on my stomach and her knees drawn up close to her chest. The hammock is the nice, cloth kind, with a wide wooden bar at either end to keep it from squeezing us like seeds in a lemon wedge, not the white rope type that leaves you looking like a bondage experiment gone wrong. Morgan's hands travel up my thighs like they come out of a dream. It never occurs to me to stop her. Sex with Morgan is as easy and natural as saying yes to a bite of chocolate from the proferred bar of a friend. Before her fingers even reach the elastic edge of my panties I am already shifting my hips, already breathing deeper, already thinking about the way her fingers will touch and tease me, how one slim finger will slide deep into me once I am wet, how good it feels to play with her hair on my belly, how much I want her. With Morgan, I always come.

Imagine afterwards, lying now side by side, holding each other and sharing each other's heat as the beach breeze turns chilly, when I decide to propose to her. I am gifted with a sudden and utter clarity—this is the right thing to do. It has been six years since I came out as bisexual, three years since I began dating women, but something like ten years of getting into relationships with men and constantly trying to disentangle myself from them. It's not that I don't like men. I like them, and love them, a-proverbial-lot. But I've never been able to explain why it is I've always felt the need to put up resistance, to define myself separately, to have my foot on the brake of our sex lives, with a man. I always do.

But here, with Morgan, the urge to resist is not even present. Maybe it has nothing to do with men versus women, I think, and maybe it has everything to do with her. She's the right one. And she says yes.

So we got married, that part you knew. Marriage for us did not mean monogamy, of course—rather we defined it as "managed faithfulness." We had our boundaries, our limits, our promises, and our outside dalliances were allowed. But when you're happily married, who has time or energy for all the flirting and courting and negotiating with someone new? Neither of us did for several years. And that's when John came into the picture.

Morgan always toasts the bread a little before she makes cinnamon toast. Always two ticks on our toaster oven's dial, then on goes the butter and sugar and cinnamon, and back in for the full six ticks. I've tried making it without the pre-toasting and can't tell the difference, but she insists.

A raw spring day in Somerville, me in galoshes and a pair of my father's old painting pants with a snow shovel, cursing and trying to lift a cinderblock-sized chunk of wet packed snow off the walkway of our three-decker. On the first floor lives our landlady, one frail but observant old Irishwoman Mrs. Donnell, on the second a new tenant we haven't yet met, a single guy we hear walking around late at night and never see in the morning. Hence me trying to shovel the late-season fall, two April-Fool's feet of it, because I'm pretty sure no one else will. Morgan inside rushing to get ready for work, emerging soap-scented and loosely bundled to plant a kiss on my cheek as she steps over the last foot of unshoveled snow onto the sidewalk (cleared by a neighbor who loves to use his snowblower). She's off to catch the bus to her job downtown as facilities coordinator at the Theater Arts Foundation. I heave on the remaining block of snow with a loud grunt and perhaps it is my grunt that keeps me from hearing the noise my back must surely have made when it cracked, popped, "went out" as they say.

I am hunched over in pain, cursing louder now and not caring if Mrs. Donnell hears it, when another person is there, asking if I'm all right. His hands are on my shoulders and he slowly straightens me upright. It is the new tenant, wearing an unzipped parka and peering into my face with worry. I tell him I'll be alright; he says are you sure. I say yes but I'm clearly not sure—it goes back and forth the way those things will until it ends up somehow with me in his apartment drinking some kind of herbal tea and then lying face down on his formica counter with my shirt on the floor while his thumbs and palms map out the terrain of my back.

In the theater world a backrub is a euphemism for sex ("Hey, come upstairs I'll give you a backrub." "Oh, those two, they've been rubbing each other's backs for years.") So you'd think I'd know. But no, there's no way obviously that he could have planned that I'd try to lift too much snow. No, it was an honest case of one thing led to another. Maybe a couple of resistance-free years with Morgan had dulled my old repeller-reflexes, and we...well, in specific, after they had done their magic with my spine, his hands strayed down to my ribs, and he left a line of warm kisses down my back. He had longer than average guy hair, straight and tickly like a tassel as it touched my skin. I moaned to encourage him, my body knowing what I wanted before my mind had a chance to change the plan.

Morgan always says I plan too much.

My father's oversized pants slid to the floor and kisses fell like snowflakes onto the curve of my buttocks, feather light, and then a moist tongue probed along the center where it went from hard spine to softness. We got civilized after that, and went to the bedroom and it wasn't until we were lying back having one of those post-coital really-get-to-know-you talks that Morgan came and knocked on the door. No bus, saw your galoshes on the second floor landing she explained at her seeming clairvoyance, to which I replied This is John.

John always says "How do you do" and bows while he shakes two-handed when he's formally introduced.

Our first threesome happened right away, that night after dinner fetched on foot from the Chinese restaurant on the corner. On our living room floor, the white waxy boxes and drink cups scattered at the edges like spectators, the elegant curve of our bay windows standing witness to his hand between my legs, Morgan's mouth on his nipple, my lips on Morgan's ear, John's penis sheathed between us, my chest against his back while he buried himself in her, her tongue on my clit, his nose in my neck, my fingers in her hair, our voices saying whatever they always said, mmm, and ahh, and yes. I didn't know if this was going to be one of Morgan's experiments in excitement, or one of my few dalliances, or one of John's fantasies come true. What it was, which I didn't expect, was the beginning of something more solid, more intricate, and more satisfying than any twosome I had known.

John always buys two dozen roses on Valentine's Day, which he gives to Morgan and me one rose at a time.

When was it, maybe a year later, when Morgan became director at TAF and John, who was in computers, had a discussion with Mrs. Donnell about buying the building. Morgan always loved housewares, I've always loved renovation and design. The idea hit us at Christmas dinner, Morgan's parents' house in Illinois, her mother on one side of her, me on the other, John on my other side, and all manner of relatives near and far spread down the two long tables from the dining room into the ranch house living room, in folding chairs brought for the occasion in minivans and hatchbacks. Turkey so moist the gravy wasn't needed, and gravy so rich that we used it anyway. Wild rice and nut stuffing heaped high on John's plate, shored up by mashed potatoes, his vegetarian principles only mildly compromised by the addition of imitation bacon bits on green salad. Family chatter and laughter, Morgan's father sometimes directing men's talk at John. And somehow the discussion turning to Mrs. Donnell and her plans to sell the house, and somehow our three hands linked in my lap, under the table, and John announcing to everyone, suddenly, that the three of us would buy the house together, voicing the thought that was at that moment in all three of our heads, even though until that moment we'd never contemplated the idea.

I always clean the toilets and the sinks but I hate cleaning the shower and bathtub. John, who has a slight paranoia about foot fungi, loves to do the shower and tub. If only we could convince Morgan to do the kitchen floors.

If my life seems like a series of sudden revelations, that's because it is. The most recent one was watching Jillian walk her stiff-legged toddler's walk from one side of our living room to the other. I knew then what Morgan looked like as a child, what her exploratory spirit and her bright smile must have been like when she was knee high.

The night we made Jillian we had a plan. We didn't always sleep together, or even have three-way sex together, but we knew all three of us had to have a hand in her creation. For months we had charted Morgan's period, her temperature. We cleared a room to be a new bedroom and put a futon on the floor, lit the candles and incense (we're so old-fashioned that way) and made ready. Imagine Morgan, her long brown curls foaming over her shoulders, her back against the pillowed wall, her knees bent, framing her already seemingly round Earth-mother belly, watching us. John kneels in front of me, naked and somber-faced. I will not let him stay that way for long.

I begin it with a kiss. I kiss Morgan on the lips and then John and we pull away from her. I take his tongue deep into my mouth, my hands roaming over his head and neck, and he responds with a moan. My hard nipples brush against his— my hands on his shoulders I continue to kiss and wag my breasts from side to side, our nipples brush again and again.

Then I am licking them, my teeth nipping, my hands sliding down to his hips, one hand between his legs, lifting his balls. He gasps and throws his head back. My mouth is now hovering over his penis, hardening in my hand. I reach out my tongue to tease. Instinct begins to overtake the plan, his hands are reaching for me, he pushes me back, his mouth on mine, his tongue on my nipples, his fingers seeking out my hottest wettest places and finding them. He knows my body well, he slides two fingers in while his thumb rests on my clit.

Morgan watches, her belly taut, her hands clenched in the sheets.

He is slicking his hand wet with my juices up and down his penis, and then he climbs over me, my legs lock behind his back, and he settles in. Tonight there are no barriers between us. I let go with my legs and let him pump freely. If I let him I know he will grant me my secret wish, to make me come from the fucking, from the friction and rhythm and pressure and slap and grind. I am sinking down into a deep well of pleasure, his sweat dripping onto me, as he becomes harder, hotter, faster, tighter, his jaw clenched, and I become looser, and further away. The turning point comes though with a ripple in my pelvis, and then every thrust is suddenly bringing me closer to the surface, up and up again, drawing me in tighter, closer, until my wish comes true. I break the surface screaming and crying, and calling out his name, and thinking how good it is to have learned not to resist this....

His eyes flicker with candlelight as he strokes my hair and jerks from me—the plan is not forgotten after all. His penis stands out proud and red and wet and the strain of holding back is evident in his bit lip. Morgan's nostrils flare and she slides low on her pillows. I go to her, my fingers seeking out her cunt which is already dripping, my mouth smothering hers, our tongues slipping in and out as I confirm what we all already know. She is ready.

And I put myself behind her, my hands cupping her breasts, my legs on either side of her, as John lies down between her legs. My fingers sneak down to spread her wider, to circle her clit and pinch her where she likes it, while he thrusts slickly, my teeth in her neck, her hair in our faces, the three of us humping like one animal, all of us ready.

Morgan always comes twice.

There's nothing like a grandchild to bring parents around. So Jillian has six grandparents and none of them mind enough to complain about it. We always have them here for Christmas now, we've got the most bedrooms and the most chairs. Jillian will always be my daughter. John always shovels the snow. And Morgan always says we could make Jillian a sibling—that it could be my turn if I want. I don't know. I just know that I love them always.

Fetish

Terry Wolverton

Bruise on my ass where you bit hard
skin purpled the shape of your mouth
still marks the pearled moon I view in mirror
like a flag planted in a colonized orb

Skin purpled, shock of your greedy mouth
set loose the body's rumbling tide
grateful to be colonized, pulled into orbit
after drifting so long in deep space

Borne on the body's shuddering tide
I wear these marks like jewels
no longer hidden in shadows of deep space
I want to gleam with emeralds, amethysts

I wear these marks like precious jewels
on my shoulder, neck, my collarbone
guard them like rare emeralds, amethysts
but still want everyone to see and envy

Shoulder, neck, hip, collarbone
tokens that remain when you've gone
if everyone could see, how they would envy
the depths at which you've touched me

I search for tokens when you've gone—
thumbprint on my thigh, vermillion nipple
conceal the depths at which you've touched me
the splayed viscera that seeks your entry

Thumbprint on thigh, vermillion nipple
I see them with my nerve-endings;
my splayed viscera wills your entry
flesh requires opening, transgression

My vision now resides in nerve-endings
and so I stroke the mark on pearled moon
flesh pleads for opening, transgression
bruise on my ass where you bit hard.

Thalia

Kathe Izzo

The entranceway was filled with a small twister of Chinese restaurant flyers, broken leaves, and weird random trash. There were three buzzers and a little speaker on the wall near the door, but when I pressed the top buzzer, there was no answer. I started to bum and turned around to leave when I heard the muffled thud of someone shutting a door somewhere inside. A tall, pale beyond belief, scary looking girl came down the stairs, her hair bleached empty white, looking like it was torn instead of cut. She looked old to me, like she could be thirty or more; I don't know. She was wearing a tiny faded T-shirt that said GIRL and was still big on her, her arms sticking out like razor sharp twigs. Her jeans barely touched her hips, leaving the bone of them exposed, skin barely covering them too. A large white spiraled snake tattoo with an ornate head covered the long stretch of her abdomen and disappeared into her pants. She had multiple piercings on the inside of each forearm, tiny gold bars. In the center of her lower lip was a silver ring, with a point on the end sticking down over the lip and a ball on the tip coming through the hole just below. She pushed open the door and leaned out without saying anything, with just a sarcastic smile, like something about me made her laugh.

"Hummer?"

"Yeah, um, are you Thalia?"

"Yep."

She turned and threw her long frame up the stairs ahead of me, taking two steps at a time. I could barely keep up with her. She pushed open a door on the top landing. The apartment inside was empty. I mean empty. No furniture. Well, not really, there was a table in front of us in the kitchen when we walked in and two chairs, but none of the other kitchen stuff, like any food that I could see, or plates, cups, or anything like that. There wasn't even any trash or take-out containers. There was one pot on the stove, the table and the chairs, and off to our left, in the living room, piles and piles of books. Taped to the wall were some large sheets of paper covered with pale pencil drawings you could barely see of hinged limbs, trees, and body parts, and tiny scribbled writings. In the corner of the living room were two closed doors. Everything was ultra clean, like I said, the apartment empty of any trash, any clutter, anything extra, painted white, with the floor in the living room covered with what seemed like twenty or more layers of red paint, thick like rubber, and the kitchen floor a muddy brown linoleum.

Thalia stretched out against a window frame in the living room and looked at me. Pigeons or doves surged behind her, gray against a gray sky. There were no curtains. She looked at me. I stood in the threshold of the kitchen with my coat on, my hands still in my pockets, alternately clutching a matchbook and mindlessly pulling apart a seam in the lining. She locked her water-colored eyes on mine. I was sweating. In the other piercing and tattoo parlors I had been to, you came in, like you were going to get your hair cut, and there were pictures and jewelry on the walls. You asked for what you wanted, you got it and then you paid for it.

"So what do you want?"

"I wanted something on my stomach. Not a navel ring, but more like..." I touched myself through my coat.

"You want it in the gut, right?" She laughed a little. At me. Again. "How old are you anyway?" She didn't look me up and down but continued to stare without blinking. I was still standing in the doorway.

"Eighteen."

I realized, with horror, that I was beginning to blank out, looking at my feet and staring through the floor. I jerked my head up.

She squinted at me, shifted her weight slightly, and went on, "I'm clean, one of the cleanest. I work here because I just like to work by myself, I don't like to be restricted by a studio. After you leave this room, you know you're going to have to take care of yourself. I mean, you don't look like you're going to give me any trouble, but I don't want to hear from you, you or anybody else, about you, in the future, not about this anyway. You're on your own. You got that?"

She lifted her shoulders a little and rolled them back toward the window. I could see the pointy bones at the base of her throat pushing up into her T-shirt. She stretched her neck to one side.

"You ever have any complications with any of your other piercings?"

Her eyes fixed on me again.

"No, everything healed real fast. I have a couple of tattoos too. Everything healed really fast." I started to pull up my sleeve to show her the boxing girl tattoo on my forearm, the one with the red gloves, but my coat sleeve was too tight to show much more than the ankles.

"You have anything, any other piercings, any other place than your face?"

"No."

"Well, it's not going to want to heal, so you better be prepared for that. The belly is one of the most sensitive places, really. You wouldn't expect it."

She crossed her arm in front of her, placing her palms on her almost nonexistent tits, spreading her feet hip-width apart and moving her balance away from the window sill. She continued.

"Your jeans will rub against it. You can bandage it, but it's going to need a lot of air. You're going to have to figure at least six months for a complete heal. That's if you stay on top of it. You want a ring right? We can look at some bars too, but I have to see your stomach first. I'll get the jewelry."

She disappeared into one of the back rooms. She moved gracefully for such a harsh girl, like she was too light for her feet to touch the floor. I was still standing there with my coat on. I felt stupid in more ways than one. I wished there were somewhere to sit down. It was crazy how I missed her, even though it was only a few minutes. I wanted to stay close to her. When she came back into the room, she held a large velvet board with rings and bars of various sizes on it against her leg. With her other hand she removed my coat, brushing the back of my neck with her long fingers and moving so close to me I held my breath, drawing in the smell of her; a heavy animal smell I devoured even though I didn't expect it. She was so skinny, so pale. Even so, she was almost a head taller than me. She put the coat in the kitchen on the back of one of the vinyl covered chairs.

"Come in here and lie down on floor so I can see what I'm dealing with."

She opened the other door in the room and reached into a closet, pulling out a thick towel almost the size of my body and laid it on the floor. Then she just stood there. I wasn't sure what to do. I didn't know whether to take my pants off and then lay down or to open them once I got down there. She stood there and watched me without moving. No one had ever found me that interesting before. I looked at her, and she looked as if she would wait forever if it took that long. How can I explain it—that there was absolutely nothing else in the room, nothing but her waiting and my fear. Somehow the silence made me feel alive. It was thrilling. It was as if I could stretch out in it, stretch out and do something I never did before. Unfortunately I didn't know what that something was.

I floated above the two of us for a moment, but the room began to decompress almost immediately, and I ended up smaller than I was when I had started. One thing I knew was that I didn't want to show her my stomach. I didn't know how, but I had somehow managed not to show anyone except for Tash—well, except for a few asshole fucked-up boys who were so focused on the hole they didn't see anything anyway. Actually one of my least complicated emotional thoughts is that I have earned every one of those fucking scars. I wanted this new mark so much, I found a way (again) to make myself lay down and unzip my pants, again, again damn it, found that way of concentrating on being somewhere else that I swore I would never do again, swore I would not put myself into another position that I would have to do it. I wanted this girl to see me; I wasn't sure why but I did. That's pretty unusual, pretty rare. It's just any other way would just have taken too long, like forever, like I would have had to totally unravel myself. I mean I know she was patient, but I'm pretty sure she wasn't waiting for me to move in or anything. She knelt over me on one knee, bowing her head down low before my stomach and then close to my face.

She took a deep breath and spoke in a low voice, reaching her palm out; the goose bumps on my belly pushed the fine hairs up to meet her.

"I am glad you came here. I can appreciate this in a way that somebody else would not. Do you understand?"

I nodded.

"Don't let them tell you that it's wrong. You just need to learn not to be ashamed. That's when you hurt yourself. You get that?"

I nodded again and blinked hard. I looked into her pale eyes and tried to relax my stomach muscles. I felt like I needed to pee. She looked at my belly again and ran her hand over it with a slight pressure. She looked at the card. I closed my eyes.

"I think we have to go with a heavy gage hoop. Something like this." She pointed to a silver open hoop about three-quarters of an inch in diameter with a ball on either end.

"I think I have some points you can put on the ends later, if you want. You can fool around with it. They're screw-on. Did you have some idea where you wanted it to go?"

I tried to speak but could only point to a small clearing to the lower left of my navel, on the incline of the mound of my stomach inside a deep-V-shaped scar. I had gotten creative with these scars, they were some of my most recent, and I had rubbed cigarette ashes into them. They were thin but raised and slightly darker than the rest. She got up and walked over to the window and leaned against it, her foot on the sill. She pulled a crumpled pack of Luckies from her pocket and lit one.

"Do you need to smoke first?"

I was so grateful. She sat cross legged on the floor next to me and lit two cigarettes, placing one in my lips while clenching the other in her teeth. We smoked together. She pulled an ashtray off a pile of books and put it on the floor between us. On the top of the pile, underneath where the ashtray had been, was a worn paperback book *Addiction: A Cure* by someone named Jean Cocteau. On the cover was a fragile line-drawing of the back of a naked figure holding itself, the spine drawn in cartoonish detail, a heavy head tilted to one side. I slid my eyes down other book titles: *Nobody Nowhere, In Memoriam of Identity, Chelsea Girls, The Diary of an English Opium Eater, Kiki Smith, Gender and Science, The Serpent and the Rainbow, Les Guerillieres, I Was a White Slave in Harlem, The Sheltering Sky.* There were many copies of *Body Arts* and tattoo journals piled up, a copy of *Babel* by Patti Smith, a tiny tattered book, *The Gnostic Bibles,* and lots of comic books, all cut up. I smoked without moving. I followed the veins in Thalia's arms, unfolded and flat against her knees, through the arrows of her piercings. I followed a curl of smoke rising to the ceiling. I finally let myself look at her, really look at her. I only stole a moment. She was, of course, waiting, smoking, watching me under dark bushy eyebrows, making her all eyebrow and pupil, everything else without color—disappearing irises, her translucent skin. It made me wonder, as I often did, what we all looked like before we started changing ourselves.

"I'm ready."

She touched my arm. Her hand was warmer than I thought it would be. From where I was lying I could see the small naked knobs of her breasts underneath her shirt. I could see her ribs. My blood was pumping. I didn't get it. She was hardly a girl at all, but she was totally screwing with my head, with the new Hummer gospel of sexual truth. I mean, I thought I had it straight now, that all I needed my whole life was girls and to learn how to fuck, but right now this wrangly boygirl was the beginning and end of it all. I wanted to turn my head to her, to curl into her body, to lay there, and wait for my life to begin. I didn't move. She rocked slightly above me. She looked down at my blond boxing girl tattoo above my left wrist, an old-fashioned Kewpie nudie girl tattoo I had managed to keep hidden successfully from my mother. Thalia smirked.

"Well this shouldn't hurt *you* at all, sailor," She laughed and bent deep into me again. She whispered, "What you've done is really beautiful, you know that. I don't say that to everyone. Hardly ever, really."

She made me sit up and took the towel from under me. She went into the other room and brought back another one. She left the room again and came back with a clamp and an aerosol can of antiseptic in one hand; in the other she held a bottle of Jack Daniel's. She flicked on the bare bulb in the middle of the high ceiling with the back of her hand. Standing over me, one leg on either side, she took a swig and rearranged the ring in her lip with her tongue as she brought the bottle back up to her lips. She took another, swallowed, and bent down, still moving the ring with her large white teeth.

"I think we're going to have to pull these down a little bit. You don't want them to get in the way."

She put her hands on my hips and pulled my jeans down gently; I raised my butt for her without thinking.

"Good girl."

She smirked and pushed my hair away from my face. I wondered if I was smiling. Then she stood up and pulled a box out of the closet; she crouched on the floor and opened it, her long limbs bent insectlike, her feet flat on the floor. The box was filled with surgical steel medical instruments. She pulled out a thick hooked needle, sprayed it with the antiseptic, held it up into the light, squinted, and slid a thick ring on the hook. She sprayed the whole operation again, sliding the ring back and forth in the light without touching it.

After cleaning the surface of my belly with the same process, peering closely, she pulled a roll of skin up and pinched it, sliding it inside the clamp and holding it tight. I was embarrassed to see my excess flesh held in the raw bones of her fingers, pulled away from me into the light and held out in that clinical way. It looked so soft and girly. Like I would like it if it wasn't mine. Against her touch I didn't know who I was, and I didn't care, I just didn't want to be me, I wanted to be something else, I wanted everything I was to go away. I wanted to evaporate, and yet I wanted to watch, I believed in watching, always. I had to stay and see the needle entering my body; otherwise I would almost be wasting it, it almost wouldn't count. All I could see was the amazing spiral scar on the back of Thalia's neck, just below her hairline, as she bent over me. It was jagged with knots in it, a tortured looking scar, a half-inch thick in some places. Suddenly I felt the burning shot of the needle in my gut, and I jerked into her thighs. She reached out and pressed into my shoulder, hard, her thumb was on my throat.

"Down," she growled.

I felt my body spreading beneath me in that hot calm of coming again and again. I was sweating, burning up, but, yeah, it was going to be okay. I had the vague feeling that the rest of my cuttings were taking me over, and I could rest now, really sleep, like they would watch over me like no mother, no lover, ever could. The vision died like a dream, and I woke up way too fast. It was over. The burning had moved into my whole body, but I knew it was over. This wasn't the way it used to be. It used to last longer. My body was pissed off now and hungry, starving. I wanted to be new again. I wanted to see. I wanted it to always be like this. I never wanted to leave.

Thalia was leaning over me, her elbow pressing lightly on my rib cage. I could smell the bourbon on her breath. She pulled the hoop back and forth a little through my skin, spraying it again and dabbing it gently. Then she stood up without looking back and left the room.

I lay in the middle of the floor, in the empty room, and stared at the lightbulb above my head, listening to the water running in the kitchen. For the first time in a long time, for the first time since I started this whole thing with girls, for the first time since I knew anything, I knew I wanted someone, something, big inside me, hard, slamming hard, inside me. I knew without knowing, I knew with only wanting, wanting to be full in that reckless, I-wanna-die kind of way. I thought I was going to start bawling from the want, crazy like a baby, isn't it so weird, bawling like I thought I was going to cry forever, since I was born, since my dad left, since Tash didn't call, I could feel it coming up like the rise of puke in your throat, but it was a false alarm. I wanted, needed something from someone, but I was freaked to let anyone see this mess. I stumbled around, pulling my pants up, wincing with pain and shame, not knowing whether to zip up my pants or wait for her to return, but she stayed in the kitchen, she just left me there by myself for an eternity. By the time she came back into the room, it was as if nothing had happened. She seemed bored and restless, perched on the window sill, smoking. She gave me a few instructions of cleaning and caring for the piercing and, of course, told me not to touch it. It's not like she didn't know who she was talking to. She handed me a large square Band-Aid. When she slid to the floor and bent over a book, I went into the kitchen and retrieved my coat, pulling some crumbled bills from the inside pocket.

I paid her silently and left.

Nylon
Karin Pomerantz

I like the way the light catches the edge of a sharp, serrated blade out of the corner of my eye. I like the way it sparkles like a diamond or something a girl is supposed to like. I like to watch it come closer, unable to move for fear of where it will land. I like putting my faith in your hands. I like being out of control and teased with the possibility of disaster. I like that.

I like being backed into a corner and seeing the look in the eye of my lover. The look of a starved beast. The look of desire and passion and wanting and anger. The look that only I can bring to your eyes. The one that says, "you're in for it tonight."

I like it when you get to your knees and run first your fingers, then the tip of your knife up and down the inside of my thigh. I like the way the sharp tip of the blade digs into the soft flesh around where my legs meet my ass. My eyes roll back as I feel the full length of the blade against me inching its way toward that place that knives should never go. That soft vulnerable place that my mother and your mother told us never to touch.

I especially like it when that shiny blade cut a small hole right through the nylon. Just large enough so that I could feel the air, but not so large that I could feel you. Just the little tip of your little finger trying to inch its way toward me being blocked by a layer of synthetic material. But you push your way in, don't you? You push your way past the nylon and into me. You're not surprised there's nothing under there. You know I never wear panties under my nylons.

One little finger sweeps past my clit. Not too much on me, but just enough to make me purr. "Yeah," you hear me say, and that is when you change your tune. You stop being so genteel and so kind. That's when you get to the part that I really want. That is when you give me what I like so much about you.

"Yeah?" you respond, and you hook that little innocent finger into the hole you made, and you pull. You pull down on that nylon between my legs, and we both feel it come away. The tearing sounds unlike cotton or any natural fiber. It tears hard, and the sound isn't sexy, just raw.

You push me back, don't you? From your position on your knees on the floor, you push me back into the counter. You watch me stumble on my heels and recompose myself before you can take full control. You watch me flounder, and a smile like the devil's comes over you. That's what you like, isn't it?

And slowly you stand. One foot, then the other, rising to your full height, puffing yourself up, trying to impress. Don't you know I'm already impressed? But you don't really care about that do you? You do have a supreme ego, and you use it as a shield to cover what we both know you are to me. Don't you?

My hands lay flat on the countertop behind me as I thrust my hips and my chest out just enough to catch your attention. You look me up and down. Like you've never seen me like this before. But you have, haven't you? Often enough to know exactly what I'm looking to you for and often enough to want to give it to me over and over again.

You, all arrogant, take a step closer. Just one. Just enough to let me know in which direction you're heading. I think for a moment to smile, but I know what response that would elicit, so I don't. I keep my thoughts in my head and keep silent and stone. You can't read me. You think you can sometimes, but you can't. I don't let you. Even after all this time. I won't let you into that place that you so much want to see. I won't go there, but you, in all your splendor and glory, you try as you might to get there. With your hands, with your face, with the shiny steel between your fingers.

One more step and you hover right in front of me. You know I like it when you tease me with your body, your mouth. You know I like that. Standing just inches from me but not extending a hand to touch me. Just a gaze. Almost a glare. And I close my eyes awaiting your arrival on my mouth, but you leave me there. Leave me waiting for you the way you know I like. The way you know that makes me crazy.

"Stay," you say as you turn and walk out of the room. "Don't move." I am left alone in silence and impending darkness. The light from the window is starting to fade, and it casts an eerie sort of a shadow on the vinyl flooring. You know I'll wait. You know I will do anything to elicit from you what I want. But you also know I don't have to.

You return shortly. But nothing seems to have changed. Not the look in your eye. Not the lump in your jeans. Not the steel in your hand. You left and returned the same. Only I have changed. In my mind I have been playing out the next hour or two or three, and all that has changed is my pussy. My cunt, my snatch that was barely wet moments ago, is now throbbing with the need for you.

"Come," you say. And I do. "Turn around," you say. And I do. "Bend over," you say. And I do. I bend at the waist and hold myself as steady as I can on my heels. With no support. You still have not laid a hand on me. There are no walls to hold me up, only my tired legs and my distorted sense of balance.

With my back to you I hear the click of your knife, the snap as it straightens into place, and my stomach jumps. Jumps from where it can be found on a daily basis to that place just below my heart where it goes when I'm inching toward ecstasy.

You're back on your knees behind me. I like it when you get on your knees for me. I never know what you're going to do when you're there. The nylon, still mostly whole, covers my legs. It is stubborn and does not want to be removed. You, blade in hand, press the sharp edge against my ass and run it down the back of my leg, tracing down the nylon as though you were tracing a seam. First one leg. Then the other. They snag, but they are stubborn, like me, and do not come off.

You take that steel blade that has not served you well this time, snap it closed, and thrust it into your pocket so that it can't disappoint you any longer. You reach up to the hole you made all that time ago between my legs, and you spread it even wider. First one hand, then two tearing through what covers me. It does not come off entirely, but you have what you want. The smell of sex hits us both like a semi; its ripe dampness like a blessing. It knocks you off your knees, balanced so precariously behind me. You weren't expecting something so pungent. You hadn't accounted for the way a pussy smells after it's been in nylon all day.

Your hand touches me ever so softly, brushes past the soft, well-trimmed hairs of my lips, and creates a whirl of sensation within me. I can't see you or what you are doing, but I can sense that your head is close to my ass, and I know what's coming next. Your tongue comes out and licks at the underside of my ass, just moistening me up enough to feel the chill in the winter air. I think to mention the potential result of cold air on my ass but am quickly distracted by your tongue, mouth, and teeth all playing softly with my ass, inner thighs, and clit. Your gentle nature does not last long, and soon the softness of your mouth on me turns to hard biting and nipping. I wince with the pleasure at the pain, my knees lock, and my thighs tighten. "Relax," you say. I don't. "I said *relax*," you say, "or I'll stop." I let myself go, just one small bit, but find that my balance is even more difficult to maintain now that my head is swooning with my scent and the feeling of your teeth.

You stand slowly, and as you do, drag your mouth up over my back biting lightly all along your path. When you get to your full height, I can feel your warm breath on the back of my neck. I can smell your cologne and the whisky and cigarettes on your breath. The smell that is only you. That stirs something inside me and has since the day I first saw you strutting your stuff in that dingy girl bar. You reach over my shoulder and take my face in your hand. You pull my cheek toward you and plant a kiss on it. A soft kiss made rough by your chapped lips. "You are such a pretty thing," you say "such a pretty thing."

You spin me around and for one brief moment look me in the eye and grin. Then your hand flies. A snap, and all I can feel is the imprint of your hand on my cheek. "Get on your knees, girl," you say, and I do. It doesn't take long before your hands move to unfasten the heavy silver buckle which closes your thick, black leather belt. You pull it from around your waist, grab it with both hands, and stretch it across the back of my neck. With one hand in the middle of my neck over the leather, you hold my head down; with the other you unbutton your faded jeans, reach inside, and pull out your cock. Your cock, always hard, hangs directly in front of my face, but you forbid me to touch it. You forbid me to take it in my mouth and suck. You make me wait. With your hand still on the back of my neck, and my face angled down, you make me wait.

"You want to suck me, don't you?" you ask. I know better than to answer. "I asked you a question, girl. Answer me." And with that, the hand that was releasing you comes under my chin, lifts my head, and stings my cheek, all before I can think to form an answer. "I said answer me."

"Yes, sir," I manage to mutter. Although the hard floor is beginning to hurt my delicate knees and my feet are starting to throb from having been packed into shoes all day, I take you in my mouth and suck. I take you all the way into my throat, the way I know you like. I know you like to watch me suck you off. First the head with my lips and tongue, I circle around you, feeling you feel me. Then I move slowly down you, nodding just slightly and opening my mouth wider to accommodate your size. Deliberately and agonizingly I move down your shaft until I have your entirety in my mouth. "That's it, girl," I hear you say, but your voice is barely audible over the sound of your cock beating against the back of my throat. Saliva starts to ooze from the corners of my mouth and down my chin. You keep your hand on the back of my neck.

You start to rock on your heels. Back and forth pushing yourself deeper into my mouth. Deeper and deeper until I gag a bit. Not too much because I know you won't be happy about that. And you push in farther. Faster into one hole when really it's the other that wants you. The one getting cold from the hard, vinyl floor.

You pull out, take my chin in your hand, and lift my head up. No words are exchanged, only a look from you that says something like "follow me," but something else like "careful, girl." You turn, and I follow. You know I'd follow you anywhere, but you also know I don't have to. You sit and pull me onto you. Not onto your lap really but onto your cock. My back to you. Your one hand maneuvers yourself under and into me, and the other reaches behind you. I know what you're doing, and you know I know.

I suck in air hard through my teeth as you enter me. From behind but not really. Through the hole you made in me, that part of you that just left my mouth became a part of me. My cunt opens for you. Wide. One of your arms wraps tightly around my belly to keep me pumping. There is no resting, no stopping. Keep the motion going. Out of the corner of my eye I can see it again, the glimmer and sparkle as the last remaining bit of sunlight hits your pointed steel.

Moving from my belly to my mouth, your hand repositions itself with rapidness and stealth. All I can taste is the sweat on the palm of your hand. To keep me silent. To keep me from uttering any sound when that knife of yours is raised to my neck.

I can feel the sharp edge dig into the soft side of my chin as I raise and lower myself onto you. Pumping and fucking harder and harder, I can taste the salt on your hands and the blood that soon may be oozing from my skin. I bite my lips to keep silent; I bite your hand to keep you there. I like to feel you under me, my weight and the weight of my sex burdening you. Your attitude summed up with a flick of your wrist and the click of your knife. I like it when you threaten me. I like it when you hurt me. I like it when you make it sting, but you also know I don't have to.

The Lesbian Blow Job (Rubberneck)

Gerry Gomez Pearlberg

mouth tips open like a baby bird's...not cuckoo but robin cardinal wren.

sword-swallowing silicon in gulpy syncopation a vertiginous throatladder climbing a kind of jazz in which the throat is full of notes notations mouth fuller with swing and salivary song.

now the eye-mind will be fixed in a tight gazing upward the mouth stuffed to contentment with a constellatory saber. thus comes the tranquilizing of lips and tongue through repetition of fervent suckling. thus comes succor. thus comes fervor. now geese shall fly in tight formation beneath and above the roof of mouth busy with thick intricacies.

this is the viewpoint of the one whose mouth tips open the mouth in which the trip is taken the visitor received.

the cocked one shall sense it sliding in the other's throat. the one slurping the cock shall sense it in the nub of her jeans.

both are fully cocked and both shall sense it in the mind and in the mind of the other. the induction coil of physiological ventriloquism will summon supreme pairings while physical motion will sustain rubidinous friction until nothing interrupts slurped and slurper   slurper and slurpee sliding moistly the passage of cavernous suction.

behind and before the mount
and harness comes Clitoris.
a very rasp or mulberry grotto.
it will steal its little wiles.

the clit astride the cock must be pressured into, ushered into pleasure. the goldfish must be obliquely stroked and swallowed. the goldfinch must be obliquely stung and strangled.

not strangled but singled. not singled but simple. not simple but suppled. not suppled but sojourned.

a sojourn is sucking perpetuated. history on its knees. sometimes history is sucking. it sucks. sometimes history is celibate. it celebrates. sometimes history juts out. unjustifiable. history is always a sojourn. never simple. never ever single.

now the harness loosens and tightens in the face of advanced sucking. in light of onward and upward. a blow job is phrasing. a blow job is timing. point and pierce and measure.

now she will gallop. now she will hold the hair. she will palm the back and the back of the throat. she will run her hand along the strong arm. she will try not to pull the hair too hard yet she will be braced. she will grasp the hair like reigns and the scalp will tingle and grow shrill. shrill with the force of pulling which is a very pleasureful pressure. she will hold on by the skin of her teeth. she will bite her lip. she will be held by the skin of her tit. held hard by the hard prick of her tit. her mouth will spawn a vortex. her mouth spurt a dust devil. salivary elixir. fizzing will then succeed in all quarters. in all quadrants fizzling shall replace numbness and numbness shall replace sensation and sensation shall replace boredom the equal and opposite universe will gallop through and through both bodies.

a stifling, continuous density avalanching by which all quarters and quadrants shall apex.

a rinsing commences.
cock may then be (or not be) suspended.
hair returns to its willful socket.

Asshole
Gerry Gomez Pearlberg

A forlorn nocturne wrongly accused yet somewhat sinister. A thing a place a sensation a circumstance. Some are assholes some or all of the time. Some are asshounds. Some kiss and wish for ass grasp or grab ass smooch or smack ass rub or pat ass reverentially whack ass worship disparage ignore ass, or simply pass on ass. Some know and love ass. Add or subtract ass. Some have written and read books on ass. One good one has written the ultimate guide to ass. Another has written haiku to welcome the book on ass. Life is a stretch. A hole to sketch. Or test. For some not the best of holes but for others the very best of holes and for still others the only hole that will do: the sole & soul hole. For some the worst of holes. In better times, the best of holes. A bursting thirst of stolen holes. Most fragile, elegant, self-sufficient, neglected of holes.

Anterior halos.

For T.

from *Shy Girl*
Elizabeth Stark

Alta cut the engine in the driveway of Shy's parents' empty house. She ushered Shy up the porch stairs, trying not to look across the drying lawn to her own mother's house.

"Do you have the key?" Alta said. Shy pulled it out of her purse absently.

Alta felt relieved to be inside that miserable house, and not just to be out of the throbbing heat. She looked at her watch. It was already almost five.

Shy sighed deeply. Her black party dress hung limp in the heat. "Okay, Alta, show me what you've found. I'm not saying I think it means anything, but if you want to show me, go ahead." She dropped her hand down, the one closest to Alta. Alta took it in her own. Shy led her up the stairs, and Alta remembered how much she'd trusted her once, how Shy used to show her secret outdoor places and teach her little things about life. Part of Shy's magic had been her age, that she was older than Alta yet she treated Alta as her peer.

Shy hesitated at the top of the stairs. "It's in there," Alta said, pointing to Mr. Mallon's office. But Shy opened her mother's door. The room was immaculate, as if Mrs. Mallon had known she was leaving and might never be back.

Shy crossed the room, one arm circling her belly. The dresser was heavy wood painted white. On top, in a frame of silver birds, Shy's young face smiled, exuberant, shadows falling across those smooth cheeks, bright eyes. Alta had only one picture of Shy. She hadn't looked at it since she'd left Mrs. Mallon's over five years before, but she knew exactly where it was, in a small box in the back of her closet with some school photographs and a picture of her father at the bar, holding a rag in his hand as if it were some kind of trophy. Shy at almost-fifteen, long, skinny white socks pulled up to her knees, her stiff school-skirt pleated around her hips. Shy laughing right at the camera. Alta had taken the picture in the Mallons' front yard, and if you know what to look for—and no one but Alta ever did—you could find out from Shy's eyes just how she felt about the photographer.

There was another photograph on the dresser, of Shy at about eighteen or nineteen, just before she'd left home for good. Shy half smiled from underneath her bangs, her eyes wide. It was a studio shot, one of those packaged deals from Macy's with the fake marbled background. Shy peered more closely without picking up the frame or touching the glass. She seemed to be studying the picture for some clue.

"I stopped cutting my bangs when I left," she almost whispered, looking not at Alta, but at the photograph.

Alta picked it up, as much to break the spell of the room as to look more closely. The bangs and the expression of youthful shock vivid on Shy's face were the only signs it was not a picture of her now.

"I wanted something of the change I'd been through to show on my body." She waited a moment, as if she expected Alta to say something. Alta thought about her work, why she pierced people's bodies. It was not about anger or aggression or any of the adolescent spins the mainstream media put on it. It was about letting something show on your body, having the courage to claim skin, flesh and life as your own, and shape it. Alta lived in a community that valued scars. She had no piercings herself—didn't want any more holes in her body—but she'd found other ways to own her body, to wear the clothes that she wanted even though they were sectioned off in the stores under signs she didn't fit, to walk as she pleased and to look damn good when she'd always been told growing up that she wasn't attractive.

Shy opened the top drawer. The sweetness of hidden sachets seeped up from neat layers of white silks. Shy unearthed one and held it to Alta's face. Alta breathed in the gentle comfort of Mrs. Mallon.

"To me," Shy said softly, "it smells exactly like fear." Alta remembered Old Spice and mothballs, disinfectant and the strong smell of urine. Could scent be the strongest part of childhood? Or only the most lasting? Shy pulled something out of the folds of cloth. Her eyes brightened and she held up a small, silver key. "Ah ha, Alta," she said, suddenly sarcastic. "Forget your paper trail. I found the key."

"To what?" Alta tried to ignore her tone.

"No idea." Shy shrugged. "Come on. You wanted to play detective." This time she reached for Alta's hand, but the gesture was devoid of sensuality, caught up in the hunt. Alta felt that old uncertainty about what mattered to Shy, what was important and what was a game.

She let herself be pulled along as Shy searched the house: Mr. Mallon's office with the twin bed; the kitchen which Shy had cleaned so thoroughly it was lifeless and still again, "just like my mother kept it"; even the bathroom, its medicine cabinet thick with bottles of pills, and unlockable. As silly as it seemed, the key had an old-fashioned air of promise. It must belong to something. But there were no locked doors on the cabinets, no boxes fastened and full of promise. Where Shy found a lock—on an old leather case with a broken zipper, in the open drawer of her father's desk—she pushed the key against an unwelcoming keyhole. They even searched Shy's old room, with its rumpled bed from two nights before. At last they returned to her mother's room, and Shy put the key on the dresser by the pictures.

"Sherlock," she said to Alta, "I'm afraid we've come to a dead end." She pushed her dark hair back and rested her face in her hands, fingertips pressed against her eyes. She looked up again, the sarcasm gone. "God, I hate this."

"Shy..." Alta felt out of place standing in the middle of that room.

"Do you realize I'm about to have a child of my own, and I'm still waiting for some sign from my mother, some clue, something...." Shy picked up the key and fingered it. "I don't know why we didn't talk, Alta. Why should I have thought to ask her? Ask what? If she had some kind of secret, why wouldn't she have told me? What could have been worse than not knowing?" Her voice tightened across her anger and frustration. "Nothing fits. Nothing works." With her thumb, she flicked the little key into the air. It dropped into the stacks of cushions and disappeared.

Quickly Shy went to the bed and ran her hand under the pillows. For a moment she searched frantically, as if she'd lost it, and then it was in her palm, Alta saw her fingers wrap around it, though from her face Alta could tell it was no comfort at all.

"Why is it important to show up for someone's death?" Shy asked angrily, sitting down on the bed. Alta went and sat beside her.

"You have to show up some time," Alta said. Shy curled up around her own jutting belly and put her head in Alta's lap. Alta ran her fingers through Shy's hair. It was thick and fine, spread across Alta's thighs. Alta leaned back into a mass of pillows. Shy lay, soft and still, against Alta's legs.

"I saw your mother yesterday."

Alta stopped moving her hands along Shy's scalp. "I'm surprised she didn't put you in a home for unwed mothers."

"You should be grateful you have a normal mother."

"She should be grateful she has a homo daughter."

"Are you happy now?"

"Now that you're here?"

"In your life...I don't know."

"I'm pretty happy," Alta said. "San Francisco's a good place for me...to be myself."

"It seems like there's no place you wouldn't be yourself."

"You don't understand what it's like."

Shy rolled over on her back and looked up at Alta. "I don't even know why I asked that. What does 'happy' mean, anyway?"

"Getting pretty philosophical there, Shy."

Shy looked from this angle as she used to when they'd watched television together, and without either of them acknowledging it, Alta'd slip her hand under her shirt, brush slowly across her midriff, move inch by inch toward her breasts.

"You've been really generous to me, Alta."

Alta shrugged uncomfortably. Shy picked up a small cushion embroidered with the words "Home Sweet Home" in tiny green and pink stitching..

"I never went to Europe. That's one thing I regret."

"You could still go one day."

"You think?"

"Get one of those baby packs...."

"What do you want to see, Alta?"

"That's a funny question."

"I mean of the world."

"Ah, the world. I want to see it change, the world." Alta took a few strands of Shy's hair, so much softer and thicker than her mother's, and braided them. "I want your baby to grow up and whatever kind of person it is, I want that to be okay. And not just okay." When Alta dropped the end of the braid it fell apart.

"You're kind of sweet under all that toughness."

"Sweet?" Alta growled mockingly.

"Like a kitten," Shy said, pronouncing each 't.'

"Hey," Alta pulled a fluffy pillow from behind her and threatened to put it down on Shy's face. "I'm a ferocious lion."

Shy laughed, plucking a feather from the pillow and tickling Alta's throat.

"Do you know why I'm not married?" she asked. Alta could literally feel her heart thudding. She'd loved Shy all these years; surely *her* feelings for Alta had affected her life. Shy hadn't, after all, married.

"No." Alta shook her head.

Shy pushed her hair back and held Alta's gaze. "I guess you've always known what you wanted. I've done lots of things I wasn't sure of. And I wasn't sure I wanted to marry Erik." She turned and lay on her back. "It seemed separate from the baby, even though he was there. It just seemed like maybe he was the accident. Erik." She laughed, a touch dramatically. "He's so funny. I mean, he's really serious. He works too much and he doesn't understand me, but he loves me anyway."

"But you don't...?"

"I don't need to marry him. I wanted the baby, and maybe I don't care what people think anymore. Maybe that's not what's important."

"Shy?" Alta took one of Shy's hands and tangled her fingers in it. Shy stayed there, holding on.

"Yeah?"

"I'm glad you know what you want." Alta could feel the deep hum of each breath fluttering to the bottom of her lungs. Alta leaned over Shy. Shy's face moved towards her, and a moment too soon, Shy closed her eyes. Her lips were soft, and Alta felt Shy's tongue reach for hers. Shy was kissing her back, and that shattered her and put her together again in one instant.

Shy smelled like vanilla, and she tasted faintly of cloves. Alta tasted these things—from her pores, and in the corners of her eyes and the creases of her elbows, her neck—even before she unbuttoned the long row down the front of Shy's dress and rolled her stockings gently off her. Alta lay her back on that heap of blankets and spread her legs, losing her face and dark hair behind the taut heap of her belly.

Alta grazed her teeth along its hard arch and understood, in the back of her mind, the impulse toward cannibalism, the desire to break flesh and taste blood. She teased Shy with a finger down that dark line from her belly button to her swollen lips, the hair matted and musky, trailing up to her ass. She slid her hands under Shy's back, down her spine to the flesh of her cheeks and the beginning of the valley between them. Every once in a while Alta would look up from the depth of her, her short nails digging into Shy slightly as she ran her eyes up Shy's fecund body. And all the time Alta kept thinking, this is Shy, this is Shy.

Alta blew on her clit and a moan stuck in Shy's throat, dry and half silent. Alta opened her eyes. The shadowy room had grown darker as daylight faded. Shy's hand was pressed against her own mouth. In that moment, Alta felt further from Shy than she had since she'd arrived. Shy seemed to be hiding behind her hand and the dusk. Alta jumped up and hit the light switch. The ache of light spread dark circles in front of her vision, but she stayed looking down at Shy until they cleared. Shy kept her eyes shut tight, her head turned away and her hands now grabbing the blanket as if holding back the other side of that moan. Alta reached down with one hand and turned Shy's chin so when Shy opened her eyes she would look into Alta's. With her other hand she continued to touch her. When Shy did open her eyes, Alta saw every bit of shame she'd feared she'd see. Tears crested at the edges of Shy's lower lids, and she looked away from Alta. Alta didn't stop the rhythmic motion of her hand, only let go of Shy's chin and cupped her full, brown-nippled breast and held her gaze. Everything about Shy was cool.

"Oh Shy," Alta shook her head. Sent heat down her arm. When Shy came she grabbed Alta's hand and stuffed the palm against her mouth. And Alta wanted to hold Shy, finally to stop running and lie down with everything she'd feared and wanted for so long. She picked up one of Shy's tears on the tip of her finger.

The phone rang. "Don't get it," Alta said.

"I have to," Shy said, turning away. "It's Erik." She slid to the edge of the bed and slowly launched herself from it, pushing her weight up with her arms. "Wait for me."

Alta looked down at the tear on her forefinger. Shy's teeth had made marks in the skin of Alta's hand, and that was the first message she ever left with Alta that Alta knew she would believe completely, even when Shy was gone.

She could hear Shy downstairs, her voice rocking into the empty house. The laces on Alta's boots had loosened, and now she retied them. She knew one thing: she was done waiting for Shy. She went down to the dining room.

"Shy?"

Shy looked up and her body tensed. She held one finger up. "I'm not happy," she said into the phone. "This is really hard. I can't sit around crying all the time, though. . . What did you do today?" She twisted the phone cord around her hand, just as she did when they were younger.

"Shy," Alta said again, more firmly.

"Erik? Hold on a sec, okay? Okay?" She put her hand over the mouthpiece. "I'm not going to be long, but he likes to talk to me in the evenings."

"I'm leaving. I have to work in the morning."

Now Alta had her attention, for the moment. Shy cleared her throat and spoke into the phone. "Erik? I just need to say good-bye to someone. Can I call you back in a minute?"

"Don't worry about it, Shy." Alta's words came out bitter and hard. Just once, she wanted to be the priority of someone who really knew her, and not just until that person came. Shy didn't say anything. The phone was in her hand, and some guy on the other end, some guy who'd impregnated her, who thought she loved him, probably, and maybe she did, this guy was listening to Alta want one more thing she couldn't have. Alta turned and walked down the stairs and out into the night. It was still velvety warm, though not as suffocatingly hot as in the daytime. She rolled her bike up Shy's driveway and then turned to walk it past her mother's house to the end of the block. She looked ahead down the dark street, at the rundown Lincolns and American trucks parked smugly along the curbs, all the different houses faded into uniform silhouettes. The quiet chilled her, even in the heat; whatever could hide in that stillness seemed scarier than the rowdy dangers of the city.

She had almost passed her old house, pushing the heavy bike along in the middle of the street. She felt as if she were fleeing Babylon. Then she thought she heard a noise, and she glanced back. Her mother's face peered from the front window, lit by a candle or small lamp below. Alta froze.

After a moment she became aware of her heart squeezed and knocking, and of the salty smell of sex around her. Alta straddled her bike, kicking the engine alive. The noise sputtered and then shot through the quiet night. Alta sped around the corner, her hands shaking, and headed for the bridge.

A Perfect Forecast
Peggy Munson

She became the meteorologist of my body.

For four days, she monitored me the way a hack tornado tracker stakes out a trailer court, poised for the catastrophic beauty of implosion. She felt my forehead to see if it was feverish, brought me cool drinks, stroked wind over my skin, and didn't talk but breathed currents, the way trees mutter when it's breezy. She waited for my pivotal moments, when the barometric pressure drops and air pockets start to yearn.

I awoke to find her sitting in my bay window, those Italian eyes of hers so dark you could press them into olive oil, and when I asked her what she was doing she said to me, "Watching the weather change." It was New Year's Eve, and she was scheduled for a night flight. I had just about reached my threshold of intimacy. Another day and I might start to become too attached, so she was going to let me have my bullshit independence and leave politely. But I knew she might ask if she could stay another day, and I knew I would probably say yes. When she asked.

When we had sex last night, she traced twelve-bar blues from my body like a rustic instrument, bent notes from me that I didn't know I had. It reminded me of the time I watched spellbound as a local harmonica virtuoso played for his pizza. This guy took a piece of tin with square holes and made it wail and scream and cry with just the power of his mouth. He was a master, and his eyes went almost white when he played, all snow blind and ethereal, as if he knew every inroad to heaven and the blues. I tell you, he knew how to *suck and blow*. And I'm not talking about the teenage party game where two people try to pass a credit card between their lips, even though that's how bad harmonica players play and bad kissers kiss. He played a summer storm that rips across the plains and washes the smell of your last lover's pussy off the mouth board of your instrument as you hitchhike farther into nowhere. That's just how she played me.

But she was a drummer, a purveyor of rhythm, and sometimes she snaked up to my ear like a castanet and sometimes she reached the deep hollow bass tones inside of me. I knew exactly why she chose to play percussion, too, not because she was another butch boy who liked to bang on things but because drums are made out of stretched skin. She liked to make taut skin give. In fact, that's how it started, as she lightly stroked my skin and pressed her lips against the pulse on my neck. She kissed me so intensely I felt like I was all steel girders and scaffolding and she was falling right through me. So when she asked me if she could stay just one more night I said *yes*. Then we ordered some food and settled onto the couch; I was contemplating rhythms.

"You know, I've never seen a lap dance," I said coyly, knowing about her weakness for the classics. "Not even in the movies."

"Never?" She looked at me quizzically, and I stared back with wide eyes trying to appear innocent. "Once, a woman lap danced for me while I was sitting at my drum set," she said. The edge of her lips curled up a little. "Yeah, that was nice."

But once she began telling me how the tramp straddled her and started grinding, the doorbell rang and a shy boy was holding our Thai food. She wouldn't take the crisp new twenty I tried to thrust at her for the sake of financial equity so I tucked it into the waistline of my pants and joked that it was tip money from erotic dancing. I liked the way it felt there, how it made me feel slutty and generic like every other woman with a president in her pants on this last day of The Year of Monica Lewinsky. I felt the sharp edge of it cutting into my skin as I ate the spicy food. I kept looking at her and thinking of ways I could get her to retrieve the dollar with her mouth or teeth. But she was on to my game, and she leaned down and kissed my belly near the fold of my jeans and said, "I don't want your money."

She knew I wanted to buy my way out of every partnership and get out of town, and she wasn't going to let me off that easy. After dinner, we curled up on a futon with the food cartons strewn all over the floor, and as we talked I reached down and pushed the bill beneath the elastic of my underwear. We pressed our bodies close together so that I could feel her breath on me, and I finally said into her ear, "Please let me tell you how you can get the money."

"If I have to listen," she said begrudgingly.

I reached down again so she could watch what I was doing and spread the bill out between my legs, over my wiry pubic hair, and said, "If you can drench it, it's yours. But if you reach down to get it too soon, you lose it."

"Deal," she answered. "But first I have a present for you."

Then she unzipped her bag and pulled out this gorgeous dog collar. She had impeccable taste.

It looked like a garter snake. Fine black leather with a silver buckle, but corded around the outside to give it a certain elegance. She put it on my neck, and it was tight enough so I felt somewhat constricted but she stuck four fingers underneath and told me it wasn't too tight if she could do that. Then she grabbed me by the edge of it and pulled me hard against her and kissed me in that way that made me skydive right into her. I could already tell that Andrew Jackson was getting sluiced. I love it when strong women get rough with me. Plus, I knew that she was mad at me for making her work to stay an extra day, and she was frustrated because I wouldn't tell her how I felt about her. She would use her extra time with me to get answers or to get even, and I loved that. I was ready to be used.

Our lesson started out very Zen.

Focus on the breath, she seemed to say, wrapping her knuckles under my collar and twisting a little so I felt my windpipe narrowing. She observed the simple changes in the regions of my body because she was the weatherman. Watching the windsock billowing with the onset of a pressure front and smelling the crisp air of January and listening to the wind move through a woman's body. Once, I meditated with a famous Buddhist in a San Francisco church, and he told us afterwards to write down obsessive thoughts. I was having many now. Leather. Lemon grass. Laundered bills in the corrupt autocracy of my cunt. I was also thinking about lap dancing for her and grinding my wet cunt down on the currency between us and trying to make it dissolve. But I knew this was impossible, as impossible as clearing the mind completely. As far as I was concerned, there would always be currency between us.

But she, the materialist, wanted to convince me otherwise.

She pulled me around by the collar and spoke to me in a low voice. Said I was a *bad girl* because I had dirty thoughts. She could see them. My Zen mind was a translucent dust bowl constantly stirring up filth. My mind kept flashing to images of her slapping my cheeks and interrogating me. I moaned every time she yanked on me and when she finally held me down on the futon with the weight of her body and her thumb through the metal ring on my collar, I could barely breathe or speak. "Tell me what you're thinking," she ordered.

"I...I'm..." I couldn't articulate, so she yanked me harder and growled into my ear, "Tell me *now*." Then I sputtered some more like a pathetic little thing, and she made it hard for me to breathe and repeated, *"Now."*

My voice was weak with humility. "I'm thinking about you slapping me and asking me questions. And I'd like to kneel in front of you." I wanted to crumble.

Then I remembered my manners. "Please?" I added plaintively.

She pulled my body upright because my own faculties were useless, and she placed me square in front of her and then whipped her hand across my face.

"Why did you ask me here," she inquired, "If you don't know what you want?" She sounded vaguely hurt but she was also stern and held me tight so I couldn't flee.

"I don't know," I mumbled. But that wasn't good enough. She pulled the collar up so my chin was pointing high and looked me square in the eyes and slapped me again and said, "What are you afraid of?"

"Getting hurt," I answered quickly and turned away from her. Every time she slapped me it felt paradoxically tender, and I yearned for her to do it again. And yet, I also wanted to just get fucked hard so I could feel a lot without feeling too much and be slapped around just a little, not be in a psychological thriller where she was the inquisitor and I was the prisoner of conscience. And suddenly I wanted to cry because I *did* hurt, I hurt deep in my marrow, and she knew that and wanted to go there. To find caverns where there seemed to be only bone.

"Maybe you don't trust me?" She asked, pulling tight on the collar and controlling my breath to prove to me I did trust her.

"I'm afraid of hurting *you,*" I said, and that made her loosen a little bit. In my head, I was bargaining with her to keep her from stopping. I resisted the urge to beg her to just hit me and trap me and fuck me so that I wouldn't do anything to harm her, but instead she just said quietly, "So, that's it. You're going to hurt me?"

"No..." I scrambled for an exit. "I didn't mean that. I..."

The truth is, I have been known to use people and hurt them and try not to get too involved. I don't know how to do easy things, like loving and being loved. I don't know anything about climate and seasons. I make chaos and live in my conceptual ecosphere and keep the real world at bay. She just wanted to grasp my glass globe and break it and suffer our lost youth. But this was no panoramic epic, it was real life, and I could smell her building sweat. She hurled me sideways toward the wall and got up close to my ear and made me feel every word. "Aren't you going to let yourself love anyone? Don't you want to love?"

"*I don't know.*" I hated these kinds of questions. I was starting to whimper.

Her voice got tender for a second. "Don't you want to let yourself love? Aren't you ever going to love again?"

"It's. Too. Hard." I answered, and then she pushed my face away from her, like she was disgusted, then slapped my cheek gently and kissed me hard on the mouth. Yesterday, she had characterized me as a *diehard,* and it is true what the French say about orgasms being little deaths. When somebody makes you breathless, then lets you suck in cool air, you do feel the kind of enlightenment that makes you love a little bit.

Then she stroked her hand down my face and said hotly into my ear, "I love the way your cheeks look, all pink and blotchy." And when she slapped me again I just moaned and fell into her. She manipulated my limbs and slapped me around and held me. She seesawed me with her pulls on my collar. Pulling on the front gave me a quick chiropractic adjustment to my cervical vertebrae and allowed her to move me like a marionette. Pulling on the back cut off my breath a little and made me want to fight her, though I tried to stay limp. I kept thinking of that Neruda poem I read to her the night before:

> I like for you to be still; it is as though you were absent, and you hear me from far away and my voice does not touch you.

I knew she liked hollow spaces full of tension, and I would be absent for her, and I would wait. Wait patiently. Wait limply. And she would say without saying anything to me,

> You are like my soul, a butterfly of dream, and you are like the word Melancholy.

As if she really knew me.

She held my face down, reaching underneath my prone body to unbutton my fly and pull my pants roughly off of me so I could feel nothing but the damp twenty stuck to my cunt. It stayed there like the socialist flyer under my windshield wiper that made me crash my only car. There it was, commerce, the only thing left on my body. She reached down and wiped me with it, then spread the bill out over my mouth as if she was mummifying me in wealth. Then she broke right into me, plunged her thumb deep into my cunt and hitchhiked us into heaven. I rode her hard, too, rode her thumb and then the two fingers she slid slowly into my ass. *Hitchhiker standing out in the rain, dark and dangerous nomad,* I moaned so hard the twenty fell off my face and I tasted my own juices on my lips and the chaos left me poor and wet and lost but nothing mattered with her fingers moving into me. Nothing mattered in that perfect absence.

Dark and dangerous nomad with the gypsy olive eyes, she rode. She rode hard into me. But she wasn't going to let me come with her. Not yet.

First, she yanked me back by the collar, so I lifted my ass into the air for her automatically and gasped for breath. She reached over and grabbed something else. She snapped a lead to my collar and held me back with it so I knew I couldn't slide back down onto my belly. Then she slapped me with another leather thing, a paddle, hard on my ass. I moaned. And then she slammed on my ass, with the paddle and her hand (which I loved, the tenderness, the sting). She could communicate everything about her power over me without saying anything. Dogs do that in the pack. They have a signal for play fighting, and then they lunge for each other's ears. And that's just what she did then. Leaned down over me while holding tight to the lead and bit me so hard on the cartilage at the top of my ear that I just wailed. In that moment, if there had been anything between us, I would have drowned several presidents.

She beat my ass good. Tenderized me. She put the flat leather of the lead into my mouth and made me bite down on it and hold it there like a bit. Sometimes her hits hurt too much, and I wanted to yell *stop,* but I didn't yell anything because the next one came too fast and tingled my ass in just the right way. I wanted to show her how much I could take so she would know she could really take me. I was already moaning to myself, oh *baby.* But she was nobody's baby. She was more of a Daddy. A leather Daddy or a weather Daddy.

Or at least that's who she was when she leaned over and took the lead out of my mouth and said, "Now I want you to be a good girl for me."

"Anything you want," I said through heavy breathing.

"I want you to lap dance for me."

My therapist said that in every relationship people play parent and child. But I don't think he was talking about the feeling I had when I climbed over her lap. She was the perfect omniscient parent and the one I wanted to please more than anybody. But I was a novice in this art, so I would have to make up for lack of skill with eagerness. I straddled her and thrust my nipples up into the air. I remembered how martial artists center all their power in the waist and move gracefully, so that's what I tried to do. I danced from the *tantien,* centered all of my power in my belly and then moved it down to my cunt, grinding down onto her until she was moaning and exclaiming "*Such* a good girl. You're being such a good girl."

Her praise made me want to do an even better job so I held onto her muscular shoulders and her tight Taurus neck and rode that mechanical bull right into the starving-artist sunset. I wore down her resolve and watched her sweat. I rode her no handed, and I shimmied over her with her head squeezed between my breasts. I rocked into her with rhythms from undiscovered, preindustrial societies where people traded gold for water. And I think I almost made her cry.

Earlier we couldn't find either my camera tripod to take pictures together or my dildo harness, so we joked they must be together in a back closet somewhere, the tripod standing tall like a stick figure wearing a strap-on. And for a moment I knew we were both lamenting the absence of one of them. "My God," she said, "I wish I was that tripod."

But we were happy to have three dimensions and depth would help us later on, when I knew, I already knew, she would go deeper into me. And she would do it without her dick this time. As I pushed harder against her, a sound broke out into the air, an explosion, and we both jerked to attention.

I forgot what day it was and remembered how I'd just been reading about *rapture,* which is the word some Christians use for the impending apocalypse, and how sexy it sounded to me. And I wondered if we were being bombed, right there in the den of depravity, right in the middle of our *rapture.* Then I remembered it was time for the midnight fireworks.

We kissed until the explosions ended, falling into the new year.

Then she pulled off her shirt, and I breathed hard. I was dying to feel her skin on mine, and it was so exquisite when she rubbed her breasts down my torso and pulled my pubic hair in her teeth. I reached down instinctively to touch my clit and then the wind scraped leaves against the sidewalk. This year, I became Father Time and she was Baby New Year, and when my hand went down between my legs, she started sucking on my fingers, pacifierlike. Then I pressed the heel of my hand down against my clit and thrust out my thumb, and she moved her lips up and down over it like she was giving Little Jack Horner a twenty-dollar blow job. Most dykes stick their tongues into my cunt with no subtlety at all. And I would choose *fellatio* over *cunnilingus* any day. I thrust into her like that for awhile, letting her taste me every once in awhile and burrowing far into her mouth. She was back on her haunches and working hard to please me, and I liked to see that, to just lie back and watch her work.

She's such a boy, I thought to myself, and gave her pats on the head for encouragement. Generally, when women go down on me, I'm practically wearing a bumper sticker that says, "I'd Rather Be on the Brooklyn Bridge in Rush Hour Traffic." I'm honking my horn trying to get them to move while I crank up the radio in my head and wait to reach dry land. And I'm wondering how many suicides happened here, and I'm yawning so wide you could cram a whole bagel in my mouth and they wouldn't notice. But not this time. This time, I was upright and ready.

And so, she sucked me off good, then kissed me so sweetly on the silky petals of my cunt.

Yesterday, she took my picture next to this old angel statue in a graveyard. I liked it because the angel was so androgynous, with hints of breasts and a permanent shadow on the marble suggesting a dick. And, she and I, we both liked to be poised on the edge of nowhere in the calm before a storm, anticipating what might come next. So when she realized I had gotten the upper hand, had her sucking me off like a submissive little pussy, she got hard with me. She pulled her head away slowly and the moisture of me just evaporated from her lips. She was full of dry heat. Then she wiped the back of her hand across her mouth just to be sure she wasn't smelling too much of my desire. And she said me, sternly, "Get your back against the wall."

Because I was shocked for a moment, I didn't move fast enough, so she slapped me hard across the cheek and shoved me a little and said, "I said against the wall. *Now.*"

I barely had time to brace myself against the cold surface before she was fucking me. She had one hand looped around my collar to hold me still and in position, and she was sliding two fingers into me, then three. So wonderful, hard, and real. I rocked up against her hand. She formed her fingers into a dandelion pod and squeezed all five up into me, and when they curled up into a round shape within me, I was a child blowing the seeds off a stem. I could feel my cunt dilating as it swallowed up her hand. The entire hand. *Rock my country-side, Weatherman. Make it rain.*

You know those baby swings that dangle a child in an A-frame like some sort of yo-yo trick, rocking the tyke into a stupor? That's the motion we went for. And yeah, it hurts at first, like the primal beginning of anything. But then the hurt inverts, and you rock and try to capture that moment, the instant when pain inverts. That's the preciousness of a fist pushing hard into me, capturing the split second when pain inverts. But there's also the awesome power of the fist, what it means. Revolution within a single curled hand. Every union strike and every human rights front, all the rage and the beauty. See, the people who want justice are the ones who can really fuck. That truism is curled there, in the fist.

And it seemed like we had something to fight for; we were ready to enlist.

"Wow," she said. "I can feel you pulling me in."

I have this theory that everything in life is a filling station. You stop at points along your wayward, transient journey trying to fill up the great cosmic hole. There is the eternal orifice, and there is what it means to be full. But the tank doesn't stay full for more than two feet past the gas pump. There is never really fullness, only the filling station. So, first you try to get close and then you go for empty, because outside of the filling station is the thrill of acceleration, the reckless thrill. All of this happened right there, with her fist inside my body. The filling, the emptying, the accelerating ride.

So, I was dangling from a string rocking into her, doing the cat in the cradle, moaning my way into the last year of the millennium. And I wanted to be full; she wanted to fill me. The moment of satiation is so brief, but worth everything. I was cramming myself onto her the way you try to make jigsaw pieces fit, down onto her hand. And sometimes there is more to life than the narrow span of reluctance. My body gave to her, opened, expanded, and she went farther in. When I looked down, her hand had disappeared to the tan line of her watch. I could almost imagine the first time a boat sees the Statue of Liberty. She was the woman, and I was the hand and the torch, erected together at the end. And together, dirty and perfect and uniform, we became freedom. We made freedom a belief.

"You feel so good," I exclaimed.

I roped my hands around her neck and hung from her and, she just rocked farther and harder into me. I could see how much she wanted a perfect fit, for me to feel like Cinderella, and we came pretty close. I loved the way she made me feel, open and welcoming, so generous. Like I was giving her the greatest gift when she asked, "Will you come for me?"

But when she actually asked, something stopped inside of me. Even though I had almost come about ten times already, I couldn't do it now. Even though she begged me.

Two nights before, we pretended we were lying in a barn in a rainstorm, afraid of getting caught, with sounds crashing all around us and a scratchy wool blanket waking up our skin. I lit candles, and I pretended there was no electricity, except the lightning, and that we were harbored from the rain. I could coop up with her for days and wouldn't notice the time. And that's how I felt with her fist inside of me, so wonderfully remote. But I was happy we had electricity, because she slowly pulled out of me, and then she said, "I'll get the vibrator." Then the corners of her mouth turned up wryly.

Some women can come on bicycles, but I'm not always one of them. I don't know why. It's physiology, and my love of suspense. I like to make the connection last. I don't live for the movie credits and the view of the floor full of sticky trash.

One woman said she thought using vibrators was like having sex on a motorcycle. But that just turned me on. I can think of worse things than the smell of leather and wind and Janis Joplin on the radio fighting ambient sounds. I can think of worse things than passing cars and riding reckless and courting danger and bearing down. And I can certainly think of worse things than buzzing off while riding her hand.

"I want you to tell me when I can come," I said to her. "I want your permission."

She pinned me to the wall again and jammed her hand inside of me, so fast I gasped from pain and pleasure both, and then I just wanted her deeper because she felt so good. I buzzed my clit just a little because I knew it would help me open up more. I wanted to see her wrist disappear. I wanted to feel her deep within me. Her hand felt utterly exquisite. I wanted to weather her. I wanted her to fill me up.

I waited patiently, because by then I was dying to come, and I didn't know if she would ever let me. I pushed onto her. I swallowed light, holed up at sea, and all the while she moved so tenderly and hard inside of me. She held my riches and delivered me. And then she finally said, "Please come for me."

"Can I really?"

"Come for me now."

She broke me open like a fossil in a rock. She divided me into parts, like a magician. Then she put my pieces back. She glued everything in me that was broken. I screamed out her name. I screamed the perfect affirmation. And she wouldn't let me stop. She wouldn't relent. She made me expand so far and wide I could not then possibly make a New Year's resolution that would counteract this hedonism. But I kept coming. Kept coming. Until she wiped my slate clean.

We couldn't talk when it was over. We couldn't. We just held each other tight.

The day before, the weatherman made a perfect forecast. He actually said there was one hundred percent chance of rain. I didn't believe her when she told me. "That's impossible. It's so cocky. You can't be that sure of anything."

"Yeah," she said so calmly. "I think you can."

And she was right; it did rain that day.

She left early, before I woke up, and I found the twenty curled over my computer mouse like a mechanical hand. I was empty and hollow as an old gumball machine. I felt raw. Fumbling to the refrigerator and squinting in, I coughed as I forced down some orange juice. I lilted from the kitchen to my office. Sitting down at my desk, I smelled the bill to see if it had my scent on it, but last night had been erased from currency. The bill just smelled like new money. I put it in my wallet with the others that were much more used and germy. I could still feel her inside of me. But I had nothing to buy. It didn't matter. I felt so rich.

About the Authors

Toni Amato is a thirty-one-year-old butch who lives in Boston. She contributed to *Best Lesbian Erotica 1998* and *Best Lesbian Erotica 1999*. Recently accepted to Joan Nestle's transgender anthology, *Our Own Voices*, Amato worships the ground femmes walk on and firmly believes in writing for the love of a beautiful woman. She is completing her first novel despite these lovely distractions.

Wendy Becker is a Ph.D. student in California, where she studies lesbian representation. When she's not writing about lesbian desire, she's learning about it in her seminars or enjoying it in her bedroom. Being equally drawn to fiction and fact, she is also a columnist for a queer newspaper. Her short story "Backstage Boys" appears in *Hot and Bothered II: Short Short Fiction on Lesbian Desire*.

Robin Bernstein is an editor of *Bridges*, a journal of Jewish feminist culture and politics; author of *Terrible, Terrible!*, a children's book; and coeditor of *Generation Q*, a finalist for the 1997 Lambda Literary Award for nonfiction anthology. Her fiction appears in *Friday the Rabbi Wore Lace, Hot and Bothered 2, The Oy of Sex, Women on the Verge,* and *Best Lesbian Erotica 1997.* In 1999, Bernstein received an honorable mention in the Astraea Foundation's Emerging Lesbian Writers competition for fiction.

Gwendolyn Bikis is a white dyke living in Oakland, California, where she teaches literacy in adult schools. Excerpts of *Cleo's Back* have appeared in *The Persistent Desire, Close Calls, Hers 3, Does Your Mama Know?* and *Best Lesbian Erotica 1998.* Excerpts of her novel *Soldiers* have appeared in *Catalyst, Conditions, Sleeping with Dionysis,* and *Sister/Stranger.* She is the recipient of the John Hay Preston Erotic Writing Award. She is completing a third novel, *Cleave to Me.*

Helen Bradley is an Australian born cybergrrl, journalist, and writer who met the butch of her dreams in a lesbian chat room. She currently lives and writes in California. Her nonfiction is published internationally, and recently her erotic stories have appeared in *The Lesbian Erotic Cookbook, Cosmopolitan,* and *Hot and Bothered 2.*

Cara Bruce lives in San Francisco and is a senior editor at GettingIt.com and editor of the e-zine *Venus or Vixen?* (www.venusorvixen.com). Her short fiction can be found in *The Unmade Bed* and *The Oy of Sex.* She is currently at work editing a compilation of bizarre erotica entitled *Viscera.*

Danielle Carriveau was born in Phoenix, Arizona, in 1971. After ending a lifelong association with the Jehovah's Witnesses, she began falling in love with women and performing her poetry. She promptly moved away from the Southwest and her family to New England, where she finished her B.A. in English and her M.A. in Education at the University of Massachusetts/Amherst. She now teaches writing and drama to high-school students in western Massachusetts.

C.C. Carter earned her M.A. in Creative Writing from Queens College in New York and is an instructor of Contemporary Literature in Chicago. She has won many slam and open-mic poetry competitions and has performed her erotic spoken words at several womyn's festivals. She is a member of Chicago's Performance Ensemble "A Real Read." She has two chapbooks and is working on her first collection of poetry. C.C. is a columnist for *Blacklines Magazine*.

M R Daniel is an African American writer and spoken word artist. She has performed her work at clubs, galleries, and performance spaces throughout the San Francisco Bay Area.

Jill Dearman is the author of *Queer Astrology For Men* and *Queer Astrology For Women*. Her plays have been performed at PS 122, Dixon Place, The Westbeth, and other New York City venues. She is also a filmmaker whose short works have been screened at festivals and theaters across the U.S. Keep an eye out for more magically themed material by Ms. Dearman in the near future!

María Helena Dolan grew up in the tropics but has lived and loved and agitated in Atlanta since 1976. Passionate on a variety of topics, she's published quite a bit, and she advises everyone to watch out as she prepares to unleash her Lesbian Mother Vampire Esmerelda onto an unsuspecting world via her forthcoming novel.

Kate Dominic is a freelance writer from Southern California. Her erotica has been published in the anthologies *Herotica 6*, *Lip Service*, and *Wicked Words* as well as in *Penthouse Variations* and *Libido* magazines.

Dawn Dougherty is a writer, educator, and consultant living in Boston. She has long, red nails and digs butch dykes with very short hair. Her work has appeared in *Bay Windows*, *Paramour, Sojourner, Lesbian Short Fiction, Best Lesbian Erotica 1999*, and several other very cool Boston-based zines (*Philogyny, Turn Magazine*, and *Dyka'tude*). Her all-time favorite name for a venue she has appeared at is *Faster Pussycat, Write! Write!* Meow.

A bilingual butch-loving bibliophile, **Gitana Garofalo** is the author of short fiction, erotica, two novels, and numerous personal ads. Special thanks to the writer retreats at Hedgebrook and Centrum for their generous support. Thanks also to La Peligrosa, Angie, JW, Monabutz, Becky, Ruth, Liyu, Sasha, bear, and the original boy/Daddy.

Sandra Lee Golvin is a psychotherapist, writer, dyke spiritual activist, and lawyer. Her work has appeared in numerous anthologies including *Opposite Sex, Looking Queer, Hers, Best Lesbian Erotica 1996* and *Best Lesbian Erotica 1997*. A native Los Angelena who lives in Venice Beach, she is currently pursuing her doctorate in Clinical Psychology with a focus on the lesbian psyche as soul. "Becoming Stone" is for CC, in honor of dyke hero(ine) Joan Nestle.

Sacchi Green lives and runs a business in the five-college area of western Massachusetts, hardly the real world but seldom boring. In an alternate persona she has published short fiction in science fiction, fantasy, and mystery publications, including some for children, but writing erotica is by far the most fun. She is especially proud of having placed a story in *Best Lesbian Erotica 1999*.

Kathe Izzo is a poet working in many mediums: page, performance, installation, film, mothering, teaching, community. Her poetry, memoirs, and short fiction have been published in numerous journals and anthologies including the upcoming *The Outlaw Bible of American Poetry*. Currently she is the recipient of a Massachusetts Cultural Council award for her Shadow Writing Project, a collaborative writing program for youth at risk, through which she publishes *Flicker*, a journal of teen writing. She is in the process of completing her novel *Hummer*, the inside story of a fifteen-year-old girl, exploring art, numbness, survival, and gender.

Dorian Key is a nice perverted boy who loves other boys. She lives in the San Francisco Bay Area and her work has appeared in *Best Lesbian Erotica 1998, On Our Backs, Strategic Sex,* and *Wicked Women.*

River Light is a thirty-one-year-old actor, writer, video maker, and poly dyke switch living in Vancouver, British Columbia. She pens plays, essays, fiction, and prose because she has to, and her work has appeared here and there.

Peggy Munson is a Midwest-born queer poet, essayist, and fiction writer with published work in places like *Hers 3, On Our Backs, San Francisco Bay Guardian,* and various literary journals. She is the editor of the forthcoming book *Stricken: Voices from a Hidden Epidemic,* and focuses much of her energy on CFIDS politics and disability rights, strumming her guitars, and hanging out with her hypoallergenic dog (or sometimes other good boys). She has won fellowships at the

Ragdale Foundation and Hedgebrook and has a B.A. in Writing from Oberlin College.

Dia Naevé is a student in the M.F.A. program in Fiction Writing at Mills College in Oakland, CA. She lives nearby in a house on a dangerous freeway off-ramp with her partner, her two stepchildren, two dogs, and a cat. She alternates working on three novels, a book of short stories, and a book on lesbian step-parenting. She is also a fiction editor for *580 Split*, the Mills graduate literary magazine.

Jill Nagle (www.jillnagle.com) edited *Whores and Other Feminists* and associate-edited *Male Lust: Pleasure, Power, and Transformation*. Her work has appeared in anthologies *Looking Queer, PoMoSexuals, First Person Sexual, Bisexual Politics,* and *Closer to Home,* as well as in such periodicals as *American Book Review, On Our Backs, Moxie,* and *Girlfriends*. Forthcoming books include *Girl Fag* and a book on flirtation. She is currently working on a screenplay about Edgar Cayce's life and work.

Gerry Gomez Pearlberg's book of poems *Marianne Faithfull's Cigarette* was a 1998 Lambda Literary Award recipient and finalist for a Firecracker Book Award. She also edited the Firecracker Award–winning *Queer Dog*. Her poems are forth-coming in *The Outlaw Bible of American Poetry* and *The World in Us*. The poems that appear in this book are from her "Dyke Dialects/Lesbian Objects" series and were triggered by Gertrude Stein's word portraits.

Karin Pomerantz is a writer and self-publisher living and try-ing to breathe in the cultural mecca otherwise known as Boston; however, if she had her druthers, she'd be living in the country, tending bees, and drinking lots of lemonade. Her work appears in *Skin Deep: Real Life Lesbian Sex Stories* and on her website www.turnmagazine.com.

Jean Roberta was born in the United States, and moved to Canada in the 1960s. She lives on the Canadian prairie where she teaches English at the local university. She has been active in the feminist and lesbian and gay communities. She has published and performed poems, short stories, and articles in various venues. She and her sweetie of ten years have raised three children together.

Lauren Sanders is a novelist and journalist who lives in the East Village. Her writing has appeared in *Time Out New York*, *The American Book Review*, *Poets & Writers*, and numerous other publications. She is coeditor of the anthology *Too Darn Hot: Writing About Sex Since Kinsey*. Her novel *Kamikaze Lust* will be published in April 2000.

M. N. Schoeman was born and raised in South Africa, where she worked as an adult educator. She was actively involved in the struggle to entrench equal rights for gays and lesbians in the South African constitution and was a founding member of several activist organizations. As an adult educator, she presented workshops on racism, sexism, and homophobia. She currently lives in Nelspruit, where she works as a bookseller and writer.

Elizabeth Stark earned her B.A. from the University of California at Santa Cruz and an M.F.A. from Columbia University. Stark has taught creative writing and composition at Laney, Merrit, and Ohlone Colleges, UCSC, Seattle's Powerful Schools, and the Dutch Flat Writers' Retreat. She was a founding producer of the Harvey Milk Institute's Femme Gender Conference. She now lives in Manhattan and spends time in San Francisco. She is the author of the novel *Shy Girl.* She's at work on her second novel.

Jeannie Sullivan lives in California with her partner of six years. Her loves include writing and reading all types of lesbian fiction and erotica, watching and discussing movies, and sharing life with a close, intimate circle of friends. She has been writing for a number of years, and her work also appears in *Lip Service.* She is currently working on a lesbian novel.

Cecilia Tan is the author of *Black Feathers: Erotic Dreams* and the editor of numerous erotic science fiction and fantasy anthologies. Her short stories have appeared in *Herotica 3, Herotica 4,* and *Herotica 5, Best American Erotica 1996* and *Best American Erotica 1998, Best Lesbian Erotica 1997,* and many other anthologies and magazines.

Robin G. White has contributed to *Best Lesbian Erotica 1999, Hot and Bothered 2, No Guest List, Dyka'tude, ButiVoxx,* and many other publications. Her work is widely performed by her renaissance soul band, Sweet Black Molasses. She has authored two produced plays, *PantyLiners* and *Shadowlands.* She resides in Georgia. Thank you, God.

Alex Wilder is a proud Scorpio and thrilled to be contributing to *Best Lesbian Erotica 2000.* When not out playing with her fabulous girlfriend, you may find her acting in films, taking photographs, or writing her next masterpiece. She lives and works in the greatest city on Earth and thanks the universe for where she lives.

Terry Wolverton is the author of *Bailey's Beads,* a novel, and two collections of poetry, *Black Slip* and *Mystery Bruise.* She has edited twelve literary compilations, including three volumes each of *His* and *Hers*. She is the founder of Writers at Work, a Los Angeles based creative writing center at which she teaches fiction and poetry.

About the Editors

Tristan Taormino is series editor of *Best Lesbian Erotica,* for which she has collaborated with Heather Lewis, Jewelle Gomez, Jenifer Levin, and Chrystos. The 1997 collection was nominated for a Lambda Literary Award, and the 1999 edition was a Firecracker Alternative Book Award nominee. She is the author of *The Ultimate Guide to Anal Sex for Women,* which won the 1998 Firecracker Award. She is director, producer and star of the video, Tristan Taormino's *Ultimate Guide to Anal Sex for Women,* distributed by Evil Angel Video. She is Editor of *On Our Backs,* a columnist for *The Village Voice,* and sex advice columnist for *Taboo* magazine. She was Publisher and Editrix of the sex magazine *Pucker Up,* and is webmistress for www.puckerup.com. She has been featured in *Playboy, Penthouse, Entertainment Weekly, Details, New York Magazine, Out Magazine, Spin,* and on HBO's *Real Sex.* Her new book *Lesbian Sex Tips for Men* will be published by Cleis Press in 2000. She teaches sex workshops and lectures on sex nationwide.

Joan Nestle was born in New York City in 1940, a working class Jew raised by her mother who worked as a bookkeeper in the garment industry. She came out as lesbian in Greenwich Village in the 1950s, marched in Selma in 1965, joined the ranks of the feminist movement in 1971, and helped establish the Gay Academic Union in 1972. In 1973, Nestle co-founded the Lesbian Herstory Archives, which now fills a three-story building in Park Slope, Brooklyn. Joan Nestle is the author of *A Fragile Union: New and Selected Writings* and *A Restricted Country* and editor of *The Persistent Desire: A Femme-Butch Reader*. She is co-editor (with Naomi Holoch) of *Worlds Unspoken: An Anthology of International Lesbian Fiction* and the *Women on Women* lesbian fiction series. With John Preston, she co-edited *Sister and Brother: Lesbians and Gay Men Write About Their Lives Together.*